The sun shone brightly with promises of a beautiful day. Andi walked around the courthouse observing the handsome dome and intricate details in the carvings gracing the arches that were located around the building. Since her grandmother was occupied with the computer course, Andi had a little breathing room to explore on her own. She stopped beneath the hanging tree her grandmother had pointed out to her on their previous visit. A chill swept over her as she stared up at the massive branches. *Hanging would be a horrible way to die*, she thought as her hand went to her throat.

"It would make me think twice before I committed a crime."

Andi turned to the voice. A tall woman with reddish golden hair that glowed in the sunlight stood gazing at her. She had an enormous book bag over her shoulder and held a large stack of folders in her arms.

"The way you were standing there clutching your throat made me wonder if you were anticipating embarking on a crime spree." She tilted her head to one side and gave Andi a dazzling, teasing smile.

"Well, if I were planning to, I'd do it someplace other than Texas," Andi replied.

"Wise woman." She shifted the folders and extended her hand to Andi. "I'm Janice Reed."

Andi found her hand being clasped in a firm but gentle manner. "Andrea Kane."

Visit

Bella Books

at

BellaBooks.com

or call our toll-free number
1-800-729-4992

For Every Season

frankie j. jones

Bella
BOOKS

2005

Bella Books, Inc.
P.O. Box 10543
Tallahassee, FL 32302

Printed in the United States of America on acid-free paper
First Edition

Editor: Christi Cassidy
Cover designer: Sandy Knowles

ISBN 1-59493-010-4

For Martha
My love for every season.

Acknowledgments

As always, I'd like to thank my partner, Martha Cabrera, for being my first reader and for putting up with all of my midnight mumbling. Your encouragement and unshakable belief in me helps keep everything on track. Thanks for your help in choosing a title.

I'd also like to say thanks to Peggy J. Herring for being my second reader and for pointing out all my wild commas. To Peggy's devoted fans, I apologize for taking her away from her own writing.

I'd like to thank everyone at Bella Books for all the hard work they do. You guys are the greatest.

Finally, I'd like to thank my editor, Christi Cassidy, for the effort she has put into this manuscript. Your patience and attention are greatly appreciated.

About the Author

Frankie J. Jones is the author of *Rhythm Tide, Whispers in the Wind, Captive Heart, Room for Love, Midas Touch* and *Survival of Love*. She enjoys fishing, traveling, outdoor photography and rummaging through flea markets in search of whimsical salt and pepper shakers.

Authors love to hear from their readers. You may contact Frankie through Bella Books at fjjones@bellabooks.com, or directly at FrankieJJones@aol.com.

Chapter One

Andrea "Andi" Kane watched the bead of coffee teetering on the lip of the cup. She held her breath, knowing there was nothing she could do to stop it. Any moment now, some microscopic element would shift and the glistening drop would either glide peacefully back into the cup or plunge over the lip and implode upon the pristine linen tablecloth.

The bead of coffee lost its battle with gravity and slid down the side of the cup. Andi forced her attention from the small dark stain and focused on the morning paper that shrouded her lover of nine months.

Trish's morning routine could have been chiseled in stone. Her alarm clock rang at six. She was showered and dressed by seven, followed by thirty minutes with a cup of strong black coffee, a plain English muffin and the *Dallas Morning News*. God help the poor misguided soul who intruded on this ritual.

Staring at the newspaper, Andi tried to remember what it was that had drawn her to this woman. They'd met at a housewarming party given for one of Andi's coworkers. The coworker cornered Andi and tried to convince her to give up her apartment and buy a house, but Andi resisted.

Her transfer to Dallas had been engineered to achieve one goal, the furtherance of her career. Her heart was still in San Antonio and she intended to move back at the first opportunity.

As the woman continued to gush, Andi glanced around, trying to find a way to escape. A buzz of activity drew her attention toward the door. The crowd parted as a short, smartly dressed woman strode across the room shaking hands and bestowing hugs along the way. Everything about her, from the top of her flawlessly styled hair to the tips of her exotic snakeskin boots, exuded power and success. An anticipatory silence fell as the woman stopped and slowly scanned the crowd with radar precision, until her sights locked onto her prey.

Andi's mouth went dry as the woman's appraising gaze languidly caressed her from head to foot.

With a satisfied smile, Trish Patterson closed in on Andi and never left her side for the remainder of the evening.

They left the party together and spent the rest of the weekend at Andi's apartment making love and talking about Trish's job. She spoke longingly of her dreams to branch out and form her own international real estate firm.

In the dark of night, Trish told Andi about growing up in the projects in San Antonio. Her mother had run off with the man who lived on the corner, leaving fourteen-year-old Trish and her twelve-year-old brother burdened with an alcoholic father. To escape the poverty, Trish worked wherever she could find employment. After graduating from high school, she held three jobs and went to night school to procure her real estate license. After obtaining her license, she was shocked to discover the San Antonio market saturated with real estate agents. She refused to give up her dream and finally obtained a job with a small, struggling firm. For the next five years, she worked seventy-hour weeks to build her client base and to put her brother through college. In the process of achieving her goal of becoming top seller, she didn't fret over bending the rules slightly or stealing clients from other agents. With her impressive sales record supporting her, she applied for a position with World Wide Realty, one of the leading international real estate firms. Before long, she began to handle nothing but the high-dollar listings that drew in the hefty commissions.

Andi's heart had gone out to the courageous young woman who'd struggled so hard to provide for herself and her brother.

During the subsequent weeks, Trish called Andi at work several times each day. She would pick her up for lunch and surprise her with flowers. Three weeks after their meeting, Andi moved into Trish's house. The passion lasted less than two months.

Trish began getting home later each evening. The phone calls and flowers stopped. She no longer had time to go to lunch. In fact, she rarely even had time to talk, and now, months later, as Andi watched the coffee cup disappear behind the newspaper again, she was beginning to doubt her impulsive decision to get involved with Trish.

When the cup reappeared, another droplet began to roll down the side to join the spreading stain. Andi watched it crawl at an agonizingly slow pace toward the tablecloth. In a sudden act of rebellion, she reached for the cup to set it on a napkin. Before she could grab it, the cup disappeared once again behind the paper.

Andi gritted her teeth and picked up her own cup to take to the kitchen sink. As she turned, her knee banged against the unforgiving leg of the massive wrought iron and glass dining table. The house and practically everything in it belonged to Trish. Andi hated the cold, colossal table and would have preferred sitting at the small breakfast nook in the kitchen, but Trish insisted they eat all their meals at the dining table.

Whenever Trish was traveling to one of her numerous conferences, Andi would purchase a burger and fries after work and take it home. There she would defy all of Trish's rules. After spreading a large beach towel beneath her, she would crawl into the middle of the guest room bed and eat her meal while watching television.

Andi rubbed her aching knee in silence before slipping away to

3

the kitchen. After rinsing her cup and placing it in the dishwasher, she gazed out the large kitchen window at the new three-and-a-half-story six-thousand-square-foot monstrosity being constructed on the adjacent lot. Until six months ago, the space had been a wooded area. Andi had spent hours sitting in the backyard, watching and listening to the birds. Oftentimes, a family of rabbits would sneak out for the raw vegetable scraps she would place by the fence for them. She wondered what had become of the rabbits.

A loud rustle of paper and the scraping of a chair against the hardwood floor told Andi it was seven-thirty. Time to leave for work. *I may not have a lover*, she thought ruefully, *but I have the best alarm clock in the city.*

Without a word, Trish reached past her and rinsed her coffee cup before placing it in the dishwasher. She never put anything in the dishwasher without rinsing it first.

Andi often wondered how someone so obsessed about one thing could be completely oblivious to others. Her best friend and coworker, also the self-proclaimed office psychologist, Becka Lewis, insisted Trish was passive/aggressive. Andi believed it was something much less complicated. Trish was simply too self-centered to care about anyone else.

She remained by the sink while Trish went to her small home office and gathered her briefcase. Andi watched her reappear into the hallway. Trish's attention was already focused on the day before her. Dressed in a stylishly tailored lightweight wool navy jacket and skirt and matching pumps of soft Italian leather, Trish looked every bit as powerful as she was. While only five-foot-two, and barely weighing a hundred pounds, she compensated for her physical size by her presence. Her long blond hair and creamy skin never failed to turn heads.

"I have a showing at five. I'll be late getting home." Trish's voice pulled Andi from her musing. "Why don't you make that dish you do with the butterfly pork chops, but no mashed potatoes this time? I hate mashed potatoes after they've been reheated. A tossed salad and broccoli will be fine," Trish said as she made her way to the door.

Andi continued to stand by the sink for several seconds after the door closed, wondering when she had become a wife. True, it had been her idea that she should prepare dinner, since she usually got home first, but somewhere along the way, the task had changed from a matter of convenience to obligation. Trish's success at her job hinged on her dedication to working late hours during the week as well as numerous weekends. She had been among the company's top three Sellers of the Year for the last eight years, and in the number one position five of those eight.

Andi went to the bedroom to change her shoes. She worked as a technical director for the phone company, having started right out of college as a call center manager twelve years ago. At first, there had been a sense of pride in her work, a goal to attain. But during the last five years, numerous layoffs, budget cuts and out-sourcings had created a cloud of discontent and uneasiness. Just six months earlier, Andi had been forced to lay off one-third of her twelve-member team. The rumor mill was churning out whispers of yet another round of layoffs.

She grabbed her briefcase from beside the bed and headed down the hallway. The phone rang just as she was locking the door. She rushed back inside. She had given her home phone number to her managers with strict instructions to call if they were going to miss work for any unscheduled reason. With the layoffs and uncertainty of the future, morale was at an all-time low and absenteeism was up considerably. She tried to warn her team not to do anything that would draw negative attention to themselves, but even she was finding it more and more difficult to face each day.

She grabbed the phone. It was her grandmother. "What's wrong?" Her grandmother never called her during the week. Their phone calls were reserved for Sunday afternoons.

"Nothing. I want you to come home. I need your help."

"My help? Is Mom or Dad sick? Are you okay?"

"Stop. Nobody's sick. I have a problem that I need your help with. When can you come home?"

Andi set her briefcase down and took a deep breath. Her grandmother didn't approve of her living in Dallas. She felt Andi should move back to San Antonio and live with her. In truth, her grandmother lived with Andi's parents, having moved in about eight years earlier after Andi's grandfather, Thomas Mimms, died. But there was no doubt that Grandmother Mimms was the matriarch of the house.

"I'm on my way to work. Can't you tell me what this is about?"

"No. I want you to come home."

"I can't. I have to go to work. I'll be there Thanksgiving week. That's only three weeks away. Can't it wait until then?"

Silence filled the phone. This was a bad time for her to be taking vacation. She could travel down over the weekend in her new Honda Accord. She cringed at having to make the five-hour drive from Dallas to San Antonio only to turn around and make the long drive back the following day. Guilt wormed its way through her. She could fly home for the weekend. The airfare was minimal. Besides, it wasn't as though Trish would miss her. *She probably won't even realize I'm gone until she sits down to eat and there's nothing on the table.*

"Would Saturday be soon enough? That's the day after tomorrow."

"I know when Saturday is. I may be seventy-four, but I'm not senile."

"I'm sorry, I didn't mean to imply . . ."

"No. No. It's me. I'm being a crazy old woman. You come Friday night. I'll make your favorite, *chiles rellenos* and cilantro rice."

Andi started to protest but stopped. Since there were several flights between Dallas and San Antonio, getting one after work wouldn't be an issue. Being away from Trish for a few days might help alleviate the increasing sense of discontent she'd been feeling, not to mention the fact that her Irish/Mexican grandmother made the best *chiles rellenos* in the world. "I'll see what I can do. I'll call you tonight and let you know what time my flight arrives."

"I've already told your papa he's to pick you up at the airport."

Andi grinned. Her father, Andrew Kane, was a corporate tax lawyer. He had been a partner in the firm of Diaz, Cooke and Kane for nearly fifteen years, but he still treaded lightly around his mother-in-law. "All right. I'll call you tonight."

On the drive to work, Andi tried to determine what her grandmother needed that was so important she had to go home.

A jerk in a Jaguar shot across two lanes and cut in front of her, only to slam on his brakes a second later. Andi stomped her own brakes and silently fumed as the traffic slowed to a crawl. Her daily commute was fifty-five minutes each way. Before moving in with Trish, she had lived less than twenty minutes from work. She pushed down the bitterness and tried to remember the happier moments of their relationship, but too much had passed between them and resentment tarnished those memories.

Traffic came to a complete standstill, allowing Andi's thoughts to drift again. She wished she had the courage to simply end the façade and walk away from the relationship, but the mere thought of the ugly confrontation that was bound to occur made her shiver. She knew she was a first-class wuss, but she couldn't help herself. She hated conflict of any kind.

The car behind her blasted its horn, demanding she focus on driving.

Chapter Two

Andi pondered her relationship with Trish as she waited for the coffee to finish perking. Common sense told her the relationship was hopeless. The smart thing to do would be to acknowledge it had ended and move out.

"There you are," her friend Becka called as she practically ran into the break room. The tall, lanky brunette never simply walked anywhere. "Have you heard?" she asked as she washed her giant yellow Tweety Bird cup. Becka was one grade-level below Andi. Her official title was project manager, but her predominate job seemed to be office information gatherer.

Andi had never been able to discover how Becka came about her information, but she was rarely wrong. "I just got in. What's up?" Andi asked.

"Don't tell me the Ice Woman fluctuated from her morning schedule and you were late." Becka stared at her in amazement.

"No. I received a telephone summons to come home this weekend."

"Is everything okay?"

"I guess. My grandmother has something she wants done, and apparently I'm the person she has chosen."

"And you're just going to drop everything and go?"

Andi sipped her coffee and chuckled. "You make it sound like I have all these plans. But to answer your question, yes. I would probably still go even if I did have plans. My grandmother is a very independent woman. Whatever she needs done is important to her or she wouldn't have asked."

Becka grabbed a handful of paper towels and began drying her coffee cup. "That's amazing. You are so family-oriented. I wish I were."

Andi shrugged. "What's stopping you?"

"I don't know. My brother lives across town and I haven't seen him in weeks."

"Why not?"

Becka's forehead wrinkled in concentration. "I don't like his wife and he doesn't like my girlfriend." Becka poured coffee into her Tweety Bird cup.

Andi watched in astonishment as a large portion of the pot disappeared into the cup. "What about your parents?" Andi asked. "Wouldn't you go home if they asked you to?"

"They live in Austin. I visit them when I can. But I can't imagine dropping everything and running home because they said to."

Andi tried to steer Becka away from talking about family. Most people didn't understand her commitment to her family. It wasn't something she could explain, it was just there. "What were you going to tell me earlier?"

Becka's eyes grew big and she stepped closer to whisper, "Rumor has it, there's been a big powwow at corporate headquarters and more layoffs are going to be announced today."

Andi suppressed a groan. "Who did you hear that from?"

"I have my sources and I shall never reveal them," Becka replied in a stage whisper.

"What sections are they going to hit this time?"

"I don't know about sections, but I heard it was across the board for both management and occupational." Becka sipped her coffee.

Andi leaned against the counter and ran a hand over her face. "Blast it. When is it going to stop? I'm already understaffed. I can't authorize overtime. My people are taking work home. They simply can't absorb any more work."

Becka held up her hands. "You're preaching to the choir, honey. My budget has been cut so much, I buy my own office supplies."

"When are these announcements supposed to take place?"

"I heard it was today. So probably before three," Becka answered with a shrug.

"Maybe I'll leave at two. They can't let me go if they can't find me." Andi tried to laugh off the sense of depression that was threatening to overwhelm her.

"They wouldn't let you go. You know they're going to hit the lower levels first."

Andi shook her head. "I don't know anything anymore."

Mary Malone, secretary to the VP of Andi's division, came in. She saw Andi and hesitated. Mary was something of a legend within the company, having started as an operator when she was seventeen and, over the next forty-two years, working her way up to executive secretary for an area vice president. Mary's sturdy frame and ruddy face made Andi think of a painting she had seen as a child. The painting depicted a wagon train of strong-limbed determined pioneers crossing the Great Plains.

When Mary failed to make eye contact, a new wave of doubt hit Andi. Could *she* be laid off? "Hi, Mary."

Mary scurried to the coffee station and filled a cup with hot water. "Good morning, Andi, Becka." She dropped a tea bag into the cup. "Have a good day." Without waiting for them to respond, she rushed out.

Andi looked at Becka in alarm. "Was she avoiding you or me?"

Becka's shoulders drooped. "Damn. I think it was both of us. Do you think she knows who's getting axed?"

"She's Hanover's secretary." Andi's stomach began to burn. She poured the rest of her coffee down the drain. "I have to go. Call me if you hear anything."

Andi was at her desk working through lunch when she heard a small noise. She glanced up to find Mary standing in the doorway. Andi started to smile, until she saw the security guard and her immediate supervisor, Eric Sutter, standing behind Mary.

"I'm so sorry, Andi. I hate this," Eric said as he pulled a sheet of paper from the folder he was holding. His hand trembled as he extended the letter to Andi.

Andi stared at the crisp white paper for several seconds before she took it with a strange mixture of feelings.

Clearly embarrassed by the situation, Sutter ran a hand over his thinning hair and cleared his throat. "You've been an excellent manager, Andi, and I hate to lose you. It's just that the company is having to realign and with all the recent PUC rulings against us, we have to tighten our belt."

Andi wanted to slap him with the letter, but she knew he wasn't directly responsible for the layoffs. They came from much higher up and would continue until the Public Utility Commission stopped ruling against the rate increases and long-distance expansion the telecommunications giant was demanding.

"As you know," he continued, "because of the sensitive nature of your position, we can't allow you to remain in the building. You have fifteen minutes to pack your personal items. Not that I'm concerned that you would ever do anything unethical. It's company policy and all." He stopped, clearly flustered. When no one spoke, he turned away. "Mary will help you with your stuff. I wish you the best of luck," he mumbled before rushing out of the cubicle.

"What an ass," Mary mumbled as Sutter scurried away. "I'm

sorry, Andi. I swear I don't know what's going to become of this place. When they lay off people like you and . . ." Tears choked off the rest of the statement. The security guard stared at the floor and shuffled from foot to foot.

"Don't cry." Andi stood and gave Mary a small hug. "I know the drill, and I know it's not your fault." Andi had performed the same unpleasant task more than once herself.

"I don't know what they're doing," Mary said. "How many more of us can they let go?"

Something in her voice made Andi pause. "Did they let you go?"

Mary shook her head. "No. They're going to *allow* me to retire. They've given me a sixty-day letter." She gave a small snort. "Sixty days, my butt. They just want me to train my replacement. I saw the applications already. They're going to replace me with a contractor. Someone they won't have to offer benefits." She turned to the security guard. "Hand me one of those boxes out there, please."

He stepped out but quickly reappeared with two cardboard boxes.

"Let me help you," Mary told Andi. "I didn't know how many boxes to bring. If you need more than two, I can get them."

Andi shook her head. "Thanks, but it should all fit into one box. I don't have anything but those photos and the items there on the wall." Andi nodded toward the wall that held her numerous recognition awards and a sampling of her favorite photos that she had taken over the years.

Mary set the box on the desk and together they started packing.

"Are you going to be all right?" Andi asked as Mary carefully placed the last plaque in the box.

Mary squared her shoulders. "Oh, yes. My husband, Harvey, retired from the police department two years ago. He's been trying to get me to quit working. He thinks I need to relax more. My daughter wants me to retire also. Of course, I suspect she's more interested in a full-time baby-sitter, but I have a surprise in store for her. Harvey and I are going to sell the house and buy a travel trailer. We're going to travel." She glanced around the office. "Will you be all right?"

Andi took a deep breath and slowly exhaled. "Yeah, I guess. I hadn't really planned for this."

"They have to give you a severance package. If you have any questions, call me." She grabbed a pen and pad from Andi's desk. "This is my home number. If you have any problems, let me know."

Andi didn't try to explain that she hadn't been referring to financial planning. What she would do with herself was a bigger concern. She couldn't tolerate being idle. "You have been so sweet to me. I'll never forget you." She hugged Mary.

Tears sprang back into Mary's eyes. "I have to go. Sutter has another letter to deliver, and as you can see he's not handling it very well."

At the mention of another letter, Andi's breath caught. "Who else?"

"Total of eight from the department."

"Becka?"

Mary glanced at the floor before she met Andi's gaze. "Yes. She's our last stop."

Andi sensed the unpleasant chore was wearing on Mary. "Do you want me to go with you?" Andi offered.

A spark of hope flared in Mary's eyes but was quickly extinguished by the security guard. "I'm sorry, ma'am, but I have to escort you from the building now." Intellectually Andi understood the need to have ex-employees from certain positions escorted from the building, but emotionally she felt like a common criminal.

Mary patted her arm. "Don't worry. You're a wonderful worker. Something better will come along." She pointed to the box where one of Andi's photos lay on top. "Maybe it's time for you to pursue your photography. You take such beautiful photographs."

Andi glanced at the photo of the sun sinking below a grove of trees. It was a nice shot, but she couldn't imagine anyone ever paying money for it.

"You take care of yourself and don't forget to call me if you need anything," Mary prompted.

Andi picked up the box and without warning tears began to stream down her face. As the guard escorted her from the building, she tried to imagine what she would do with her life. She was thirty-four and unemployed. Trish would blame her and accuse her of being too meek.

Chapter Three

Andi stood outside the front entrance of the building waiting for Becka. The early November sun danced through the thinning leaves of the crepe myrtle trees lining the sidewalk. As she watched the dancing patterns of light, a large black and blue butterfly landed on a lush clump of pink and yellow lantana. Andi's breath caught at the simple beauty of the butterfly against the blossoms. She regretted not having her camera to capture the scene.

She'd received her first camera when she was fifteen. She had been going through a particularly rough stage in her life where nothing seemed right for her. While other girls her age were learning the art of acquiring boyfriends, the thought of spending hours playing with makeup left her in tears and boys were irritants to be avoided at all cost.

Her parents tried getting her involved in piano lessons, and then guitar lessons. When these both failed, they tried sports, but the discipline required for practice seemed to only make her more restless. Finally, her father, a self-taught amateur photographer, gave her a Pentax K-1000 camera for her birthday and then drove her to the San Antonio Zoo to shoot photos of the animals. He spent hours patiently explaining film speeds, f-stops and apertures. Most of his explanations went unheard as Andi, aided with only the camera's light meter needle, became engrossed in capturing images of the laughing children, and some of the animals. A few days later, when the processed film was picked up, it was obvious to her parents that she possessed a natural talent for photography. They tried to get her to enroll in photography classes, but Andi resisted. She didn't want anything to restrict her newly acquired hobby. It wasn't until she was in college that she finally took a few courses to fill the requirements of her electives. One of her proudest moments was when her father enlarged one of her shots of Big Bend National Park and hung it in his office.

After going to work for the phone company, she used her first incentive award check to buy herself a top-of-the-line professional grade Nikon F5, but she seemed to always find herself going back and picking up the old K1000. Never satisfied with her photos, she constantly worked at improving her technique. Over the years, she turned more and more toward nature photography, and now she shot little else.

The thought of her father reminded her that she would have to tell her parents she was no longer employed. She knew the layoff wasn't her fault, but she couldn't help but feel like a failure. Tears stung her eyes. She set the box containing her possessions down, fished a tissue from her purse and dried her eyes. Finding another job wouldn't be easy. The unemployment rate had risen sharply in Dallas over the last several years, and the rash of recent cutbacks by several large employers would only make matters worse.

As she leaned over to pick up the box, a familiar voice called out. "What's with the box?" Ron Turner trotted past Andi with his gym bag. They had worked together off and on for most of Andi's career. Ron was a certified health nut and spent his lunch hour exercising at the nearby YMCA.

"My phone company career."

Ron stopped sharply and came back with a frown on his face. "You don't mean . . ."

She nodded.

"Aw crap, Andi. I'm sorry. I heard the rumors, but I was hoping that was all it was." The muscles in his shoulders rippled as he ran a hand through his thick black hair. He had once confessed to Andi that going bald was his greatest fear in life. He constantly ran his hand through his hair as if checking to ensure it was still there.

"I just found out myself." She blinked away the tears stinging her eyes.

Ron shifted the gym bag to his other hand and glanced around nervously.

"Don't panic," Andi said and forced a smile. "I'm not going to break down in front of everyone."

He tried to shrug off her comment, but a look of relief washed over his face. "When did you find out?"

"Fifteen minutes before security escorted me from the building."

"I hate that. Why do they have to be such shits about it? I mean, it's bad enough they let you go, but to escort you out like you were some kind of criminal."

Andi moved the box to her hip. "You know why. Think of the damage I could have done."

"Yeah, but still."

A large group of workers poured out of the building laughing and arguing about where to go for lunch. Ron and Andi stood quietly as the group rushed off toward the parking lot.

"What are you going to do?" he asked. "You know you're entitled to a pretty hefty severance."

Andi took a deep breath and nodded. "I don't know what I'm going to do. Maybe I won't do anything for a while. I could use some time off." She remembered the call from her grandmother. Had it only been a matter of hours since she had talked to her? "I might go home and visit my family for a few days." Before she could continue, a pale and visibly shaken Becka stumbled out clutching a box similar to Andi's.

17

"Not you too!" Ron gasped, eyeing the box.

Becka nodded. "They're letting Mary Malone go," she mumbled.

"What're they thinking?" Ron smoothed his hair. "I'd better go back up and make sure I still have a job," he said.

Andi shook her head. "You're fine. Mary told me she had already spoken to everyone but Becka."

"You knew I was getting axed?" Becka cried. "Why didn't you warn me?"

"I found out five minutes before you did," Andi said. "The security guard wouldn't let me go talk to you."

Becka nodded.

"I think I'll just go back up," Ron said. "Keep in touch." Without waiting for a response, he rushed off.

They watched him disappear into the building they were no longer authorized to enter. They continued staring at the door for several seconds until Andi finally broke the silence. "I don't feel like going home. Do you want to grab some lunch? We can go anywhere you like since we don't have to rush back."

Becka glanced down at her. "This is no joking matter. Where am I going to find another employer who will hire you, too?"

Andi smiled. "Let's go to my place. I'll pick up some beer. We'll order pizza and cry in our beer together."

"No offense, but not your place. If the Ice Woman comes home early, she'll kick me out. I can't handle two rejections in one day. Come over to the house. My refrigerator is already full of beer. Besides, Stacy has a parent-teacher conference tonight and won't be home until late." Stacy was Becka's partner.

Andi hesitated. It was true: Trish didn't like Becka. Extreme opposites in personality, Becka and Trish had clashed almost immediately. "All right, but I can only have a couple and then I have to get home."

Becka rolled her eyes but for once kept her comments to herself.

Chapter Four

As they worked their way through several beers, Andi and Becka decided the layoffs were a blessing in disguise. Now they could both move on and find jobs where their talents would be appreciated.

Becka's lover, Stacy Wilhelm, a sturdy woman of German descent, arrived home a little after eight to find the two women sitting in the middle of the kitchen floor surrounded by golf clubs.

"What's going on?" With raised eyebrows, Stacy glanced from the numerous empty beer bottles on the kitchen counter to the two women on the floor.

"We're going to start playing golf," Becka cried in a voice that was both too loud and badly slurred.

Stacy taught fifth grade in one of the lower-income districts of Dallas. She set her enormous bag filled with student papers down by the doorway and smiled. "I see. What brought on this sudden burst of—" She hesitated. "Activity?"

"We got fired," Andi announced with a deep sigh.

"Fired! What did you do?" Stacy demanded.

"We weren't fired," Becka argued. "We were axed by the greedy money-mongers of corporate America who are more interested in bottom-line figures than they are in human beings." She waved a rust-speckled putter wildly around her head.

Stacy grabbed the club and grimaced as her hand made contact with the sticky glob of duct tape Becka had used in an attempt to repair the grip. "You were both laid off?" Stacy frowned as she pulled the sticky putter loose from her hand and placed it on the kitchen counter.

"Yeah," Andi began. "But it's okay. We're gonna become pro golfers and travel the LGP . . . LPGA circuit. I'm gonna be Becka's caddie and we'll split her winnings." She made a clumsy attempt to push a wisp of her short hair away from her face and left a trail of cobwebs.

Spying the webs in Andi's hair, Becka pointed and began to laugh with drunken hysteria. Soon they were both laughing wildly.

Stacy waited patiently until they calmed down. "I think you two need to sleep it off. I'll call Trish and let her know you're spending the night," Stacy told Andi.

Andi frowned and tried to stand. "Can't spend the night. I gotta go home and make pork chops." She managed to pull herself up just as Becka yelled, "No. I don't want pork chops. I want pizza. We forgot to order pizza."

She began to twist around on the floor trying to stand. "Stacy, where's the phone? I wanna order a pizza."

Andi staggered to the counter for her purse as Becka gave up trying to stand and started scooting across the kitchen floor on her butt.

Stacy grabbed for Becka's foot and Andi's arm. She managed to hang on to Andi, but Becka pulled away and laughed.

"You can't catch me," Becka chortled. Before Stacy could release Andi and get across the room, Becka had snagged the handset from the corner table.

20

"Becka, you're too drunk to order pizza. Now, give me the phone. If you're hungry, I'll fix you something to eat."

Stacy reached for the handset, but Becka ducked to the side and yelled, "Catch, Andi." She slid the cordless phone across the ceramic tile floor.

Andi reached down and grabbed the phone. The effort sent her tumbling over. Stacy was almost on her when she zipped the unfortunate handset back to Becka.

After a couple more passes, Stacy lost her sense of humor. "Stop it!" she shouted, glaring down at them with her hands on her hips.

They both stopped and stared at her. Andi was rather shocked by Stacy's outburst.

"Stop acting like children. Becka, please give me the phone." She held out her hand. For a moment, Andi was certain that Becka was going to begin the game over. Stacy must have anticipated the same thing. "Don't even think about it," she warned. "I'm tired. I have a foot-high stack of papers to grade and I'm in no mood for childish games. Give me the phone."

Becka looked at Andi and shrugged. "That's the teacher voice. I'm in trouble." She hung her head.

"I'd better go home," Andi mumbled as she began digging through her purse for her keys.

"You set that purse down. You're in no condition to drive," Stacy said.

Andi quickly complied.

"Now she's giving *you* the teacher voice," Becka said in a near whisper.

"Yeah," Andi agreed. "The teacher voice is bad news." They both hung their heads.

Stacy sighed. "I'm sorry I yelled." She turned to Andi. "Do you want me to drive you home? Or shall I call Trish and let her know you'll be spending the night here? Or she can come and get you."

Andi nibbled on the inside of her cheek and tried to clear her head. She and Becka had started ranting over the injustice of their layoff and she'd lost track of the number of drinks she'd consumed.

She couldn't show up at Trish's both drunk and unemployed. But she didn't want Trish coming here to pick her up. She vaguely remembered that Trish had said she would be showing a house and would be home late. If she could get home and crawl into bed before Trish came in, maybe Trish wouldn't notice she was drunk. "Could you call a cab for me?" she asked.

Stacy shook her head. "No, sugar. I'm not putting you in a cab in your condition. Either you spend the night here or I'll drive you home."

"It looks like you're busted," Stacy said as she pulled into the driveway.

Andi opened her eyes and groaned at the dim glow of light coming from the front downstairs window of the two-story gray brick architectural nightmare. Upon first seeing the house, Andi thought it was one of the ugliest houses she'd ever seen. She quickly discovered the entire neighborhood was an overpriced collection of newly constructed modern homes. The slightly varied colors of the bricks were the house's only claim to individuality.

"Do you want us to come in with you?" Becka offered. "You know the Ice Woman is going to be pissed at you for coming home drunk."

Andi shook her head. "No. I'll be fine." The words didn't sound convincing, even to Andi.

"Do you want me to wait? Just in case," Stacy offered.

Andi gave an embarrassed laugh and slowly crawled out of the car. "No. Stop being silly. It'll be fine. You two go on home. I'll come for my car tomorrow." Andi stood in the driveway and waved until Stacy and Becka were out of sight. Then with several deep breaths, she tried to will herself to sober up as she slowly made her way into the house.

Chapter Five

The first thing Andi noticed when she walked into the house was the sense of coldness. Had it always been this cool or was she catching a cold? She eased the door closed and tiptoed toward the bedroom. If Trish was working in her office, she might be able to sneak past and slip into bed without being caught. It was already after nine.

Andi pulled off her shoes. As she bent to retrieve them, the room tilted at a sickening angle. She grabbed the back of the sofa for support and clung to it until the room eased back into its natural position. Afraid she'd fall if she tried again, she used her foot to push the shoes beneath the sofa. She would get them tomorrow after Trish left.

She tiptoed across the lushly carpeted living room and into the hallway. A thin sliver of light crawled from beneath Trish's office door. Andi eased down the cavernous hallway and wondered why she'd never noticed how long it was. As she drew even to Trish's office door, she held her breath. She could hear the steady click of computer keys. Carefully, she placed one foot firmly on the floor before attempting to lift the other. One hand trailed along the wall, providing balance. The office doorway was behind her, and the bedroom door was less than eight feet away. A giddy sense of accomplishment raced through her. She had made it. She'd jump into the shower. A cold shower would help sober her up. Breathing a sigh of relief, she picked up her pace.

"Where are your shoes?"

Startled, Andi spun and in the process the world spun with her. She was falling, but could do nothing to stop herself. Trish started toward her. As Trish drew closer, Andi saw her confusion turn to anger.

"You're drunk," Trish accused.

"I am not. You scared me. I turned too fast and lost my balance." To her mortification, the words came out slurred. She tried to stand but the room kept spinning. Swallowing what little pride she had left, she used the wall to pull herself up.

"Where have you been?" Trish demanded.

"Becka and I had a couple of drinks." She tried to look as though she was casually leaning against the wall, rather than depending on it for support.

"I might have known. I guess you two have been driving around town in this condition."

"No. We were at Becka's. Stacy drove me home after she got home from school."

Trish glanced at her watch. "It's after nine. I don't remember school closing so late."

Andi hadn't realized it was so late, but somewhere in her alcohol-sodden brain it made sense. That explained why Trish was home.

"She must have had a meeting," Andi rationalized.

"Undoubtedly." Trish put her hands on her hips. "I rushed through my last showing so I could get home early. I thought we'd have a nice dinner and then spend the evening together."

A tiny bubble of laughter began to build in Andi's throat. "Bull," she whispered.

"What did you say?"

Tired of feeling like a wayward adolescent, Andi pushed herself upright. "I said *bull*. When was the last time you came home before eight? And you most certainly would never jeopardize one of your precious sales for something as mundane as rushing home to have dinner with me."

Anger flashed in Trish's eyes. She whirled back toward her office. "Go to bed. You can sleep in the guest room. I have no desire to sleep with a drunk."

The alcohol clouded Andi's judgment. She gave a bitter laugh. "You have no desire to sleep with anyone, drunk or sober."

Trish stopped sharply and turned back toward her. She glared for a long moment. "Maybe it's you I have no desire to sleep with. Did it ever occur to you that you're the reason I don't come home at night? That maybe I'd rather work fourteen-hour days than come home and listen to your petty whining?"

Air burst from Andi's lungs. As she struggled to breathe, the alcohol ignited into fiery agony in her empty stomach. It took several seconds for her to regain her voice. "Living with you isn't exactly a picnic, you know," she rasped. "You're so busy trying to grab the almighty dollar, you don't have time to enjoy what you've earned. For all the good this does you"—she waved her hand to include the rest of the house—"you may as well be back in the projects where you started." Even in her alcoholic daze, Andi realized she had gone too far. "I'm sorry," she said, reaching for Trish. "That was a low blow. I'm sorry."

Trish gulped in air and glared at her. "Get out of my house," she spat. "I don't want to see you again."

Stunned, Andi stared at her. Was this the catalyst that would tear them apart? Despite the fact that she had been waiting for an excuse to move on, she felt compelled to resist being ejected. "You can't kick me out. This is my home too." The argument came out weak and ineffective.

Trish took a step toward her with a smile that made Andi shiver. "So you think this is your home, do you? Show me something that has your name on it."

"I've contributed half of the mortgage payments while I've been here. You can't deny that. I have the canceled checks. That should at least entitle me to stay until I can find a place." Andi tried to sound more confident than she felt. "If I leave, I won't be back," she bluffed.

"Who asked you to come back?"

There it was. The words that had hung between them for so long had finally been spoken. They glared at each other.

"I'll pack my bags." Andi turned toward the bedroom and fumed in silent frustration. All of her luggage except for one small carry-on that she used when she visited her family was stored in the attic. Because of her intoxication, she would either have to ask Trish to get the rest of her luggage down or risk falling and breaking her neck. *Why did I drink so damn much?* She chided herself as she struggled to pull the bag from the top shelf of her closet. The bag finally slipped off and tumbled down in a crash. The bag struck her shoulder, forcing her to bite her lip to keep from crying out in pain. She grabbed the case and pulled it toward her.

"Don't take anything that you didn't come with," Trish warned.

The words slapped Andi between the shoulder blades. Twice in one day was too much. She whirled around, slammed the case against the floor and stomped toward Trish. "Why don't you go fuck yourself?"

Trish paled and grabbed the dresser for support.

Andi pushed the suitcase away from her. She wasn't going to stay in this house a minute longer. She would come back for her stuff tomorrow while Trish was at work. Without another word, she walked out. It wasn't until she slammed the front door behind her and stomped out to the driveway that she remembered that her car was still at Becka's. She started back inside to call Becka, but realized she didn't have her purse, which held her keys and cell phone. The cold from the sidewalk began to seep into her feet. She glanced down, stunned to see she was still barefooted. She had no choice but to ring the doorbell. She swallowed her humiliation and walked up the sidewalk to the house. Her hand was reaching for the bell when she heard the sound of the deadbolt being thrown. It was an interior lock that could only be locked or unlocked from the inside. Trish had deliberately locked her out.

Anger sent her storming down the sidewalk. She'd be damned before she'd beg to be allowed back into that house.

The night air wasn't particularly cold, but the sidewalk was another story. By the time Andi had hobbled the half-mile or so to the security hut at the front gate, her feet were freezing. She swallowed her pride and pointedly ignored the guard's curious glances as she asked to use the phone. She dialed Stacy and Becka's number. As she dialed, she remembered she had forgotten to make her reservations to fly to San Antonio that weekend, and to call her grandmother as she'd promised.

She blinked back tears as Becka's phone rang. How had life gotten out of control so quickly?

Chapter Six

When Andi awakened the following morning, her pounding head clouded her memory. She struggled to open her eyes and for a moment she couldn't remember where she was. Slowly the horrible night began to reassert itself into her memory. She moaned and covered her eyes. What was she going to do?

A small tap sounded at the bedroom door. She tried to speak, but her mouth felt stuffed with cotton.

A smiling Becka eased the door open and held up a cup of coffee. "I thought I heard you starting to rustle around in here. I imagine you might want some of this."

Andi peeked from beneath her hand. "Why do you look so blamed healthy, when I'm clearly dying?"

Becka came into the room and handed the cup to Andi. "I never get a hangover. I attribute it to clean living and lots of coffee."

Andi grimaced and eased herself into an upright position before taking the cup. She took a tentative sip and waited to see if her stomach was going to allow it to remain. When it didn't return, she tried another sip.

"How are you doing?" Becka asked.

Andi sighed. "Well, I no longer have a job, or a girlfriend. I stormed out of the house with nothing more than the clothes on my back."

"Yeah, Stacy told me."

Stacy had been alone when she picked up Andi. She'd left Becka sleeping it off.

"I'm so damn stupid. I left without my shoes. By now, Trish has probably thrown all of my clothes out onto the lawn."

Becka glanced at her watch. "No. The Ice Woman wouldn't do that. Just think what the neighbors would say." She got up and returned a moment later with a handful of clothes and a pair of tennis shoes. "These are Stacy's. You two are about the same size. The shoes may be a little big, so I brought you a couple of pairs of socks. Your feet can probably use the extra padding anyway. Sorry, but there's no time to shower."

"What are you doing?" Andi asked, frowning.

"We're going to go get your stuff."

Andi hesitated. Now that the alcoholic heroism had disappeared, slipping into Trish's house didn't seem like such a good idea. "I don't know. I think I should probably wait until she gets home and then talk to her."

Becka rolled her eyes. "Don't tell me you want to try and patch things up."

Andi shook her head vigorously and instantly regretted it. She grabbed her head. "No, but I don't want to piss her off any more than she already is. Tomorrow is Saturday. I'll call her and talk to her then."

Becka dashed into the bathroom and returned with a bottle of aspirin and a paper cup of water. "Here, take a couple of these and get dressed. I don't trust that woman. We're going to get your things and that's that. Just because she won't throw your clothes out onto the lawn doesn't mean she won't toss them into the garbage."

Andi hesitated and nodded slowly. Unfortunately, what Becka said was true. Trish wouldn't hesitate to toss her things into the trash. "I don't have a key," Andi reminded her.

"Yes, you do," Becka said and held up a key ring. "Remember when you gave me a key to water your plants?"

It took Andi a moment to recall. She had given the key to Becka a few weeks after she'd moved in with Trish. Andi had gone to San Antonio for a few days and Trish was off on one of her trips. Andi asked Becka to check on the place and to water the plants. After returning, she told Becka to hang on to the spare key in case there was ever an emergency while they were away. Over time, she'd forgotten about it.

"Come on," Becka prompted. "We need to get your stuff out of there before she comes home."

Less than an hour later, they were approaching the guard's hut. To Andi's relief, a different guy was on duty. She wondered if he knew about her humiliating eviction. She held her breath as he spotted her. She watched his eyes and saw the flicker of recognition. He smiled politely and waved them through.

"At least she didn't tell them to keep me out," Andi said as they drove past the meticulously landscaped lawns of people who'd been her neighbors for nine months. She realized she didn't know a single person by name. They parked Becka's car in the driveway and slowly made their way up the sidewalk.

"What are we going to do if she's changed the alarm code?" Becka asked.

Andi shook her head. "She would never do anything like that herself. She'd call the alarm company and pay a service call." She slipped the key into the lock.

"Are you sure she isn't here?" Becka asked, glancing around as if expecting Trish to jump out at any moment.

"I thought you were going to be my Rock of Gibraltar. Where's all that courage you had a few minutes ago?"

Becka shrugged. "Don't you know by now I'm full of hot air? If she catches us here, she'll probably press charges and I'll be locked away in a tiny cell with a dozen women with names like Shark and Bugger."

Andi chuckled in spite of her headache. "You're such a nut. What would I do without you?" She turned the key and pushed the door open. She quickly keyed in the security code. To her relief, the red light stopped blinking. "See," she said. "I told you she wouldn't change the code." She closed the door and dropped the key into her pocket. "Do you want something to drink?" She started walking toward the kitchen. "I have to get some water before I start this. I feel completely dehydrated. I don't know why I let you talk me into drinking . . ." She stopped suddenly as she walked into the kitchen and stared in disbelief. Several large garbage bags sat by the kitchen door.

"What's all that?" Becka asked from behind her.

Andi didn't want to believe it, but she knew what the bags contained. She carefully opened the first one and found it filled with clothes. Her clothes. "My cameras." She sped down the hallway and into the spare bedroom. Running across the room to the closet where she kept her camera equipment stored, she threw open the closet door. Her camera bags, photo storage boxes and an assortment of miscellaneous equipment were just as she had left them.

"Everything okay?" Becka asked.

Andi nodded. "Let's start with this stuff."

It took several trips to move the camera equipment and the bags from the kitchen to Becka's van. Before leaving, Andi took time to call her grandmother. There was no answer. She left a message apologizing for not calling the previous night. She left a vague message that something had come up and she wouldn't be able to come home. She promised to call as soon as she could. As she hung up, she realized what she needed to do. She wanted to go home to San Antonio.

Chapter Seven

After a tearful farewell with promises from both sides to visit and call, Andi waved good-bye to Becka and Stacy on Monday morning. She made a quick stop by a post office to turn in a change of address request before heading home to San Antonio.

Rather than the faster, more hectic I-35 course, she drove home via US 281. The route took her through several small towns and allowed her time to think about possibly aiming her life in a new direction. She had decided to wait until she was face to face with her parents before telling them about the layoff and the breakup. She never doubted they would be sympathetic and supportive, but she wasn't in a hurry to announce her latest setbacks. She kept telling herself there was nothing she could've done to prevent being laid off, and the breakup had been inevitable from the beginning, but that didn't stop the niggling sense of failure hovering at the edge of her consciousness. She wondered if she lacked a basic gene needed to push one to success. Her parents certainly possessed this mysterious gene.

Despite coming from lower-income families, both her parents managed to earn scholarships to Princeton and had gone on to pursue highly successful careers. She often wondered if their children's less than stellar careers disappointed them. Even if she had remained with the phone company, she doubted she would've progressed beyond a mid-level management position. Richard, her brother, seemed very content to remain a third-grade teacher for the rest of his career. Even though teaching was a highly admirable profession, from an economic standpoint it lacked the social prestige that accompanied a scholastic leadership position such as that of a principal or superintendent.

Driving through the beautiful Texas Hill Country, she stopped several times to capture a few snapshots. While walking among the fallen leaves, she tried to make a plan for her future. She suspected she wouldn't have trouble securing a position with one of the larger corporations in San Antonio. She held an M.B.A. and was a Certified Professional Project Manager, but the thought of going back into the corporate madhouse made her feel ill. She tried to think of a career that held some appeal to her. She was only thirty-four. A change in careers wouldn't be out of the question. Unlike her mother and brother, she had no desire to enter the educational field. Her father was a corporate tax lawyer, but simply balancing her checkbook was too tedious for Andi. The medical profession was out of the question, since she couldn't tolerate the sight of blood. She loved to read but doubted there were many career opportunities for professional "leisure readers." She hated yard work and couldn't keep a cactus alive, so landscaping and gardening careers were out. Her photography was the only thing she truly loved to do, but she wasn't sure her snapshots were spectacular enough to merit public demand. With a deep sigh, she gave up. Project management was what she knew. She would start submitting her résumé to the major corporations and see what happened.

Andi drove along Alexander Boulevard, revisiting the landmarks of her childhood. She passed the grade school where she had lost a tooth after Billy Brown accidentally hit her in the mouth with the kickball; Monroe Park where her parents had taken her and Richard to fly kites on warm, windy Sunday afternoons; and St. Francis Catholic Church where she had been baptized and received her first communion. Turning right onto Wildflower Drive, she drove along the quiet street beneath a canopy of oak trees that were more than seventy years old. She knew everyone who lived in this block of the graceful old neighborhood. She knew their children and in many cases their grandchildren.

There was the Wilsons' gray and white Victorian. She and Lindsey Wilson had set up a lemonade stand in the front yard when they were nine. They were trying to raise enough money to buy a pair of roller blades that neither of their parents thought they should have. Next to the Victorian was the stucco and tile hacienda-style home of Mr. and Mrs. Salazar. Unlike the bland, perfectly manicured sameness of Trish's neighborhood, every house on this block was unique, reflecting the character of its owner. Yet the houses complemented and somehow enhanced one another.

As she drove by the houses, memories reemerged and with each one Andi felt herself coming a little closer to home. A sense of comfort came with knowing who lived in each of the houses. It was something she had missed in Dallas.

She tried to remember why she'd moved to Dallas in the first place. *Oh yes, the promotion.* A new billing office opened in Dallas and she had applied for and gotten one of the positions.

A few moths later, she met Karen, who worked for the Ramada Inn chain. They were together three years before Karen transferred to Chicago. The hardships of a long-distance relationship quickly proved to be too much. Despite the demise of the relationship, they managed to maintain a close friendship. They still called each other occasionally.

After Karen, almost two years went by before she met Trish. She pushed the thoughts of Trish away. Finding her belongings stuffed into trash bags caused Andi more pain than the actual breakup. Her biggest regret was that she hadn't possessed the courage to remove herself from the unhealthy situation sooner.

If Becka hadn't insisted on going back for Andi's belongings immediately, everything she owned would have been trashed or given to Goodwill. Having moved from a furnished apartment in San Antonio to another one in Dallas had saved her from having to purchase furniture. Never a collector, she'd never felt a great need to possess things. Her personal effects consisted predominately of her camera equipment, clothes, a few books and her boxes of photos.

After rescuing these items from Trish's, Andi had spent the weekend with Becka and Stacy. She used the time to sort through her things, weeding out the items she no longer wanted. Afterward, all of her worldly possessions fit into her car.

By the time she pulled into the driveway of the sprawling native stone house of her childhood, the only thing certain in her life was her relief to be home.

Andi let herself in with the key she'd carried on various key chains since she was twelve. The comforting smell of cinnamon and cloves greeted her. She smiled for the first time in days. She was home and her mother was baking her delicious cinnamon rolls. Andi's stomach gave an anticipatory rumble, reminding her that she hadn't eaten since breakfast.

"Hello," she called. "I'm home."

"There you are," her mother said as she came from the hallway dressed in a creamy cashmere sweater and slacks. Her short black hair fell in gentle waves, and her makeup was flawless. Andi couldn't remember ever seeing her mom without makeup. The only difference in Leticia Kane's home wardrobe and work wardrobe was the slacks. She never wore slacks to work. "I was starting to get a little worried," she continued. "Your father mentioned you called last night and said you would be here around noon."

When Andi called the previous evening and spoke to her father, she hadn't told him about losing her job and her girlfriend. She hugged her mother tightly and breathed in the soft faint scent of lavender, a fragrance she would always associate with warmth and security.

At fifty-five, Dr. Leticia Kane was as vigorous and active as any twenty-five-year-old. She stayed trim by performing a rigorous thirty-minute workout daily. She never settled for second best. She was fifteen when she decided she wanted to go to college, but not just any college. She wanted Princeton. Knowing her parents would never be able to afford the tuition, she began applying for grants and scholarships. She aced the SATs and graduated valedictorian of her class. The grades earned her the coveted South Texas Scholastic Scholarship, a full scholarship to Princeton.

During her second year at Princeton, she met Andrew Kane, the son of a steelworker from Pennsylvania. Andrew was also in his second year at Princeton. They fell in love, and when Leticia became pregnant during her senior year, she refused to drop out. She and Andrew were married in San Antonio during Christmas break. After graduating from Princeton, the young couple moved to San Antonio. Leticia secured a job at a local junior college and two years later Richard was born. Somehow she managed to raise two kids, maintain a household and a full-time teaching career and continue her education until she earned a doctorate in educational administration, while Andrew battled his way through law school. After receiving her doctorate, Leticia accepted a position as an assistant professor at Trinity University. Her hard work and dedication to the students earned the respect of both the faculty and the student body. She was now a fully tenured professor with an impressive listing of published works.

"Where are Dad and Grandmother?" Andi asked, setting her purse on the end of the sofa.

"Your father is playing golf, and Mom went to the market with Mrs. Salazar. She's preparing *chiles rellenos* for you tonight and insisted on driving all the way downtown to the Farmer's Market to get the chiles."

Andi rubbed her hands in anticipation. Her grandmother was a fantastic cook.

"Can you stay a while or is this just a short visit?" Her mother sat in a dark burgundy wing chair across from her.

Andi hesitated. She intended to tell everyone about losing her job and the breakup with Trish after dinner. She saw her mother frown slightly as she waited for Andi's answer.

"Actually, I may be here for a couple of weeks, if that's all right."

"You know you're always welcome, Andrea." Leticia Kane was the only person who insisted on using Andi's real name. As a teenager, Andi had pleaded with her mother to call her by her nickname, but Leticia refused.

"I was laid off," Andi admitted.

Her mother shook her head and sighed. "I'm sorry. I swear I can't imagine what's going to happen with this economy. Everywhere you turn, workers are being laid off. I heard on the news just this morning that USAA is letting over four hundred workers go."

Andi groaned. The insurance giant was on her list of possible employment opportunities. One more door closed against her.

"Have you thought about what you're going to do?" her ever-practical mom asked.

"I thought I'd send out résumés to the larger corporations here first. I don't want to look in other cities until I absolutely must."

"Here?" her mother asked.

Andi realized she had inadvertently opened the door to the rest of her story. "Trish and I have decided to split up." Andi saw no need to reveal the entire sordid details of the breakup.

Her mother moved to sit beside her. "I'm sorry, honey. Are you all right?"

Andi nodded. "It was time for it to end." Her words surprised her, but she realized they were true.

"The career or the relationship?"

"Both, I guess. My relationship with Trish was never what it should have been." Andi dropped her head against the back of the sofa. "Maybe I'm being unrealistic. I want the perfect relationship like the one you and Dad have. Is that too much to ask?"

Her mother chuckled. "No relationship is perfect, Andrea. Your father and I have had our share of problems, but love and family support pulled us through."

Andi looked at her. "When did you and Dad ever have problems?"

Her mom picked at a minuscule piece of lint on her slacks. "You were always such an idealist. Things were rough for us when we were first married. You came along much quicker than either of us planned."

Andi smiled. Her mother had been three months pregnant with Andi on her wedding day.

"My parents had big dreams for me. They weren't happy to learn that their Princeton-educated daughter was about to become an unwed mother." Her mother hesitated. "Life can be hard. Mom always accused me of overprotecting you and Richard, but I knew you'd have to face the uglier side of life soon enough. I wanted to protect you as long as I could."

Andi leaned over and hugged her mother. "Thank you. I love you."

"I love you, too. Is there anything your father and I can do to help you financially?"

"No. I've managed to save enough that I'll be fine for a while. But thanks for the offer."

A timer dinged in the kitchen. Leticia stood, clearly happy to move on to more pleasant things. "That's the cinnamon rolls. Come into the kitchen. I'll fix a pot of coffee, and we can talk while we sample the rolls."

Chapter Eight

After dinner, her father helped Andi move her meager possessions into her old room. While he went to get the last box from
her car, Andi walked around the room gazing at relics of her past.
She stopped in front of an old bookcase filled with many of her
childhood treasures. On the bottom shelf was an outdated set of
encyclopedias that she'd spent hours combing through for numerous homework assignments. Above them were several novels with
spines boasting classic titles—required reading by her mother. The
next two shelves were double-stacked with well-worn mysteries
and Western paperbacks—Andi's preferred reading material.
Several framed photos, including the first photo she had ever
taken, sat on the top shelf. The photo was a shot of a young boy,
four or five years old, feeding the ducks at the zoo. She took the
photo down and gazed at it. The shot wasn't as sharply focused as
it should have been, and she could have opened the aperture a little
more, but she'd managed to capture the combined look of fear and
exhilaration the child experienced as his tiny hand reached out

with a strip of bread. She had just happened by and snapped the photo. Suddenly, she wished she knew who he was. A slight sense of shock ran through her when she realized she had taken the photo nineteen years ago. The boy would now be twenty-three or twenty-four. She returned the photo to the shelf as she spied another relic. Tucked away in the back corner was a small tarnished trophy, a memento of one of her attempts at sports.

She had been nine and her best friend Natalie convinced her to join a softball team. It was quickly obvious that Andi lacked the necessary hand-eye coordination, as did many of the other players. The team ended the season in last place. In an attempt to soothe the crushed young egos, the team's sponsor, Robert's Hardware, presented a tiny trophy to each of the team members.

"That's the last of it," her father called as he brought in the box and set it in the corner. He gazed around the room. "I could put some shelves up for you if you need more space," he offered.

During dinner, she had told her dad and grandmother about the layoff and breakup with Trish. Andi studied her father and smiled. Dressed in well-worn jeans and a canary yellow polo shirt emblazoned with a pocket patch for a 5K run for Juvenile Diabetes, Andrew Kane didn't exude the persona of the successful corporate tax lawyer. Andi was certain that had her father been born two hundred years earlier, he would have been an explorer, one of those men who continuously forged ahead into new territories. He was always curious about what lay around the next corner. Although slight in stature, he possessed a presence that people gravitated toward, and he had never met a stranger. No matter where he went, he was quick to strike up a conversation with whoever was around.

"Dad, I'll only be here a couple of weeks. Just until I can find a place of my own, but thanks for the offer."

He looked disappointed but kissed her cheek. "Let me know if you change your mind." He headed for the door, then stopped. "Are you all right?"

Andi smiled. "I'm fine, Dad. I just need a little time to get myself back on track."

He nodded and toyed with the doorknob. "I don't mean to pry, but you'll let us know if there's anything your mother and I can do to help? I know a few people who might be able to help you find a position. Or if you need help financially."

She walked over to hug him. "Dad, if there's anything I learned from you, it would be to always save for the proverbial rainy day. I have my six-month emergency fund set aside, just as you taught Richard and me to do. Plus I should be receiving a severance check in a couple of weeks. I'll be fine."

He returned her hug and chuckled. "Good. I'm glad you were listening. I'll see you at breakfast." He pulled the door closed behind him. She could hear him humming as he walked away.

Andi glanced around the room. Her suitcases and camera bags sat at the foot of her bed. She tried to remember which clothes were packed into which suitcase. She really didn't intend to live at home any longer than necessary and didn't want to bother unpacking items she wouldn't be using. A wave of exhaustion swept over her. She pulled out the desk chair and sat down. Glancing at her watch, she was surprise to see it was only a little after eight. If she were still living with Trish, she would only now be thinking about what to prepare for dinner.

But I'm not with Trish anymore. I'm living with my parents.

A knock sounded at the door. Before Andi could respond, her grandmother opened the door and poked her head in.

"I thought I'd come by and make sure you were doing okay. See if you needed anything," her grandmother said.

Andi glanced at the eight cardboard boxes stacked in the corner. It was a pitiful showing for a lifetime. Tears blurred her vision and spilled over when her grandmother placed a hand on her shoulder.

"What's wrong?"

"I feel like such a failure."

Her grandmother hugged her. "No. No. Don't cry. Why do you think that?"

Andi eased away and grabbed a tissue from the box sitting on the desk. "Look at me," she said, waving her arm to take in the room. "I'm thirty-four and what do I have to show for myself? Nothing. No job, no relationship, no home."

Her grandmother sat on the foot of the bed and clucked her tongue. "You poor little thing."

A stab of irritation pierced Andi. Her grandmother didn't understand. "Just look at me," Andi cried. "Everything I have is in this room."

Her grandmother sighed and patted the bed beside her.

Andi hesitated a second before moving over to sit next to her. She was already regretting her childish outburst. She knew her grandmother wouldn't let it go unchallenged.

"I have a little money saved. Do you need to borrow it?" her grandmother asked, running a hand over her lush silver hair that was braided and pulled into a thick coil at the back of her head.

Andi forced herself not to smile. She had let her self-pity get out of hand and her grandmother was going to point it out. Andi glanced at her and felt a sliver of embarrassment. Andi's life had been a picnic compared to her grandmother's. Sarah Alicia Gray Mimms was the eldest child of Sean Patrick Gray, a first-generation Irish cabinetmaker, and Angelina Cortez, the youngest daughter of a Mexican migrant worker. Sarah's father died when she was a young girl, leaving a wife and four small children with nothing but a tiny three-room house, two goats and a half-dozen chickens. Her mother took in washing and ironing and occasionally sold the surplus goat's milk and cheese to provide for her small family. The experience instilled a strong work ethic and sense of survival in Sarah and left little tolerance for whiners.

"No, Grandmother. I don't need to borrow money."

Her grandmother nodded. "So you have enough?"

Andi thought of her severance pay, her hefty stock portfolio, and her 401/k and savings accounts. Except for the severance pay, most of her assets weren't liquid, but she maintained an emergency fund that would get her through at least six months. "Yes, I have enough money."

"Good. Then tomorrow we'll go and buy you some clothes."

Andi smiled in spite of herself at her grandmother's transparent game. "I don't need clothes. I have plenty of clothes. I also have food, a roof over my head, a loving family and friends who care for me," she said before her grandmother could complete her spiel. Andi put her arm around her grandmother's shoulders and hugged her. "I don't mean to be ungrateful. But sometimes I feel like a failure."

Her grandmother made a hissing sound. "When did my favorite granddaughter become so self-pitying? You have everything. What more do you want?"

Andi ignored the fact that she was her grandmother's only granddaughter and replied without thinking, "I want a purpose to my life. I want to be first in someone's life. I want to meet a woman who will love me beyond all else. The way Grandfather loved you and Dad loves Mom." She stopped, embarrassed by her impulsive outburst. When her grandmother didn't respond Andi sighed. "I'm still being selfish, aren't I?"

Her grandmother took Andi's hand and patted it. "No, dear. Wanting love isn't selfish. I was very lucky to have your grandfather. My life before Thomas was like an old silent movie. You know, all the necessities were there, but it was missing something. When Thomas came along, he brought color and music into my world."

Andi took a deep breath and admitted a fear she had secretly harbored for years. "I don't think I'll ever meet someone like that."

"Nonsense. One day you'll look up and there she'll be, right in front of you. You just have to remain open to the possibility and trust your instincts."

"My instincts haven't proven to be very good. Just look at my track record so far."

Her grandmother tilted her head. "Karen was nice. She was a

sweet girl and I think she loved you. But you and she had different journeys in life. And Trish." She stopped and merely shrugged.

Andi looked away to hide her smile. Her family had met Trish once. In the beginning of the relationship, Andi would invite Trish to go to San Antonio with her when she went to visit her family, but Trish always found excuses not to go. Deciding that perhaps San Antonio held too many bad memories for Trish, Andi changed her tactics and invited her parents and grandmother to Dallas for a long weekend. It was a mistake she would never repeat.

During the three days Andi's family was in Dallas, Trish left for work earlier and came home later than normal, leaving Andi to make excuses for her absence. After that weekend, Andi stopped asking Trish to join her and went home alone whenever she wanted to visit her family.

"No more sad faces," her grandmother said. "I want to talk to you. I need your help."

Andi suddenly remembered the phone call she received from her grandmother on the morning she was laid off. "Of course I'll help. What do you need?"

Many years later, Andi would think back to those simple words and remember how they had started her on a journey that would change her life forever.

Chapter Nine

Andi followed her grandmother through the house. A hallway connected her grandmother's two large rooms and bath to the main house by a hallway. The suite of rooms faced away from the main house and provided a view of the beautifully landscaped backyard.

Andi started to sit on the couch.

"No, come on back with me," her grandmother beckoned.

Andi shrugged but did as she was told. Her grandmother's bedroom smelled of vanilla. She glanced around until she found the source—a large oval candle on the antique maple dresser. A Double Wedding Ring quilt in pale shades of blue and red covered the full-size brass bed that was set against the far wall. The quilt had belonged to Andi's great-great-grandmother Gray. It was the sole surviving item that had accompanied the young couple on their journey to America. Next to the bed was a maple bedside table bearing a clock and a small stack of books. Across from the bed, a cream-colored armchair sat in front of a television. A small bookcase and a large steamer trunk were on either side of the armchair.

"Come over here and pull that box down for me," her grandmother instructed as she pointed to the top shelf of the closet.

Andi glanced at the box. "Grandmother, I don't think I can reach it. Why don't we wait until morning and I'll get Dad's ladder from the tool shed?"

"No. Use the chair." She started pulling the armchair toward the closet.

Andi hurried to help. "You shouldn't be moving this chair. It's heavy." A hiss of disapproval stopped her from saying more.

"I've been moving my own furniture for more years than you can remember," her grandmother scolded.

"I could have gotten the ladder," Andi insisted, beginning to get irritated with her grandmother's stubbornness.

"Your mother can see the tool shed from her window."

Andi turned to face her grandmother. "What's going on? Why would you be worried about Mom seeing me with the ladder?"

"Because when Leticia learns that I've told you, she's going to be angry with me."

"Mom never gets angry." Andi couldn't remember ever seeing her mom truly angry. She might get annoyed or displeased, but she never lost her temper. "What are you going to tell me?"

A rare flash of irritation flared in her grandmother's eyes. "That's what I'm trying to show you. Are you going to get the box down or do I have to climb up there and get it myself?"

Andi blinked in surprise. "No, I'll get it." Puzzled, she moved the chair over and climbed up on it to retrieve the box.

"*Cuidado, mija*. If you fall, your mother will never forgive me." Although her grandmother spoke Spanish fluently, she rarely did so unless she was highly agitated. Andi would later realize that her grandmother's lapse into Spanish should have warned her of the severity of the moment.

The wooden box, slightly larger than a boot box, was dark with age. Andi had no idea what type of wood the box was constructed of, but it had a heavily varnished finish. There was a hasp and a small lock sealing the box.

"You must have some juicy secret in here," Andi teased as she wrestled with the box. It was heavier than she had anticipated.

"Careful," her grandmother warned as the weight of the box slipped from the shelf.

"What's in here?" Andi asked as she eased the heavy container down to rest on the back of the chair.

"Let me have it," her grandmother said.

"No. It's too heavy. Help me balance it and I'll take it as soon as I get out of the chair." After climbing out of the chair, Andi lifted the box.

"Set it here." Her grandmother patted the end of the bed.

Andi put the box down and glanced at her grandmother. Why was she being so mysterious? Her family had always maintained open lines of communication between them. At the age of nine or ten, Andi realized that only six months separated her date of birth and her parents' wedding date. When she asked her mom about it, her mother explained that she'd been three months pregnant, and that even though they were already discussing plans for marriage after graduating, the wedding took place almost a year sooner than was originally intended.

Eight years later, when Andi realized her feelings for her best friend Christina were developing into something much stronger than a conventional friendship, she turned to her parents for help. Her mother had been a little slower to accept Andi's lesbianism, but once it was obvious to Andi where her true desires lay, her mother accepted them also.

"What's this big secret you have for me?" Andi asked. "Am I adopted? Or better yet, Richard's adopted." Andi loved her brother, but as teenagers they had teased each other mercilessly about the other being adopted. Richard and his wife, Connie, lived in Houston, but they rarely made it to San Antonio. Connie owned a small dress boutique. With only one part-time employee to help, she wasn't able to get away from the shop very often.

Her grandmother looked at her and Andi saw the hesitation and concern showing in her dark eyes.

"Maybe this isn't a good idea." Her grandmother placed a hand on top of the box.

Andi covered her grandmother's hand with her own and was surprised by how frail it felt. She glanced down, noticing for the first time the delicate network of veins and sprinkling of age spots that marred the nearly translucent skin.

In her youth, Sarah Gray had been a stunning beauty. Her waist-length glossy black hair and robin's-egg blue eyes often caused people to turn and stare after her. Time passed and the hair turned silver, but her eyes were just as penetrating and bright as ever. With a jolt, Andi realized her grandmother was seventy-four. Could she be sick? On an intellectual level, she understood her grandmother was growing older, and death was a certainty that everyone faced, but her heart couldn't accept the thought of her grandmother dying. She peered closer. Her grandmother looked healthy.

"Grandmother, are you sick? Is something wrong?"

"No. Of course not." She continued to hesitate.

Andi's apprehension increased. "What is it?"

Her grandmother sighed and pointed to the chair Andi had used as a ladder. "Sit down and I'll tell you."

Andi sat down and braced herself as she watched her grandmother struggle with what she had to reveal.

Sarah finally sat on the side of her bed, but she never removed her hand from the box beside her. "I'm going to tell you a story. Part of it you already know, but there are things that your mother decided many years ago to remain silent about."

"Why?"

Her grandmother shook her head. "Please, let me tell the story first."

Andi reluctantly nodded. She was impatient to know what the mysterious box held.

"As you know, your great-great-grandparents Patrick and Rebecca Gray came to America in eighteen ninety-six and settled in Tennessee. They lived there for a while before moving on to Texas. Your great-grandfather Sean Gray, my father, was eight when his parents and two older brothers, Patrick Junior and Connor, moved to Texas. They bought a small house in HiHo, where my grandfather worked as a carpenter."

Andi nodded. Although she'd never been there, she knew HiHo was a small town approximately forty miles southeast of San Antonio.

Her grandmother continued. "Both Patrick Junior and Connor were killed during World War One. That's how my father came to own the house after my grandfather died. Papa met my mother, Angelina Cortez, when he was sixteen and they were married. He was a cabinetmaker. Me, then your aunts Lupe and Magdalena, and finally your Uncle Ray, were all born and raised in that little house."

Andi kept silent but felt uneasy. She'd heard these recollections numerous times. There were no secrets in this story. Was her grandmother getting senile? She studied her closely and saw nothing about her that suggested confusion, but her grandmother had pulled the mysterious box nearer and was clutching it to her side.

"In nineteen thirty-nine," her grandmother began, but stopped. "In nineteen thirty-nine . . ." Tears spilled down her cheeks.

Andi sprang from the chair and raced to her side. "What's wrong? Why are you crying?"

Her grandmother looked down at the box and slowly ran a hand over its smooth top. She turned her gaze to Andi with a startling intensity. "I want you to find out who did it," she said, her voice trembling.

"Who did what?"

"I want you to find out who killed George Zucker."

Confused, Andi shook her head. "Grandmother, I'm not following you. Who is George Zucker?"

"He's the man my father was convicted of murdering. He's the reason Papa died in prison."

Chapter Ten

Andi wasn't sure how long she stood gaping at her grand-mother. She tried putting the information into a form she could get a handle on, but it kept slipping away from her. Sean Patrick Gray, her great-grandfather, had gone to prison for killing a man and this was the first she'd ever heard of the incident.

The old wind-up clock ticked loudly from the bedside table. Andi found the snippets of thoughts bounding around in her head and keeping time with the clock. Why hadn't she heard this story before? Did Richard know? She struggled to recall everything she'd ever heard about her grandparents. With a sinking feeling, she realized she'd never been very interested in learning about her ancestors. She knew her grandmother had been young when her father died, but she never bothered asking how he had died. She knew her grandmother grew up in a small town and times were hard, but that was during the 1930s and '40s, when the entire nation had been having a difficult time.

Her grandmother was watching her, obviously waiting for her to speak, but words wouldn't form.

"Will you do this for me?" Sarah asked at last. "I want to clear Papa's name before I die."

"Grandmother, are you sure you aren't sick? Why are you talking about dying?" Andi's voice trembled.

Her grandmother shook her head. "Andi, you never could hear anything other than what affects you. I'm not dying." She shrugged. "That's not true, of course. We're all dying. We start dying the moment we're born. You know that."

Andi waved her hands in frustration. "I'm not discussing philosophy. Are you sick?"

"No, but I'm seventy-four. No one lives forever. I want to get this taken care of before I die."

Somewhat reassured about her grandmother's health, Andi breathed a shaky sigh and held up her hands. "What can I do? I don't know anything about investigating a murder. I wouldn't even know where to begin."

"What is there to know? All you have to do is ask questions."

Andi shook her head. "It's more complicated than that. If you're serious about this, you should hire a private investigator. Someone who's trained for this kind of work."

Her grandmother lifted the lid on the box and began digging through the items inside. She pulled out several handfuls of paper. "I've hired three. They all told me the same thing."

Although she was certain she already knew the answer, Andi felt compelled to ask. "What did they tell you?"

"They told me my father killed that man, but I know better. You're smart and were so good at digging out things for those papers you were always writing in school. I know you could find out the truth." Tears shone in her grandmother's eyes.

Andi sat on the bed beside her and put an arm around her grandmother's shoulders. "Writing a term paper is a lot different than investigating a murder. Besides, I have to start looking for a job and a house. I'm not going to have time to do this."

"I'll pay you whatever you were making before you were laid off."

Andi rubbed a hand over her face. "This isn't about money. I'm simply not qualified. I honestly wouldn't know where to begin."

In a rare show of defeat, her grandmother dropped the papers back into the box. Then without warning she grabbed the box and thrust it in Andi's lap as if it were no more than a paperback novel. "You take this box and read everything in it. Then, if you can look me in the eye and tell me you have absolutely no doubt that he was guilty, I won't bother you again. One day. That's all I'm asking for. If you believe he's guilty after you read these things, then I'll not ask you for help. I need your stamina and determination, Andi."

Andi stared at the box in her lap. It occurred to her that regardless she wasn't coming out of this a winner. Either she would break her grandmother's heart, or she would have to learn how to investigate a sixty-five-year-old murder. She made the mistake of meeting her grandmother's gaze. The look of cautious hope and pleading she found there was her undoing. "All right, but I'm warning you right now. If he was convicted of murder there must have been some compelling evidence."

"Go through the box and look at the things that are in there and then we'll talk. There's one more thing."

Andi held her breath. She wasn't ready for another surprise.

"You can't tell your parents that you're doing this."

"Why not?"

Her grandmother hesitated before responding. "HiHo was a small town and kids can be cruel. Your mother remembers how hard it was growing up where all this happened. George Zucker was a well-known man and we were . . ." She hesitated. "We were poor and couldn't afford to move away for many years. After your grandfather and I were married, we continued to live with my mother until she died. Eventually your grandfather got a job with the railroad and we were able to move to San Antonio, but by then your mother was already ten. Some of her memories aren't good ones. She would rather not be reminded of those times. And your father . . ." She shrugged. "He protects Leticia. He wouldn't be happy to know I'm stirring up old memories."

"I can't lie to them if they ask me."

Her grandmother threw up her hands. "Why would they ask you? If you keep quiet, they'll never know. It'll be our secret."

Before Andi could respond, her grandmother scooted off the bed and began urging her toward the door.

Chapter Eleven

Andi placed the wooden box on the foot of her bed. There were more pressing matters than a sixty-five-year-old murder. She searched through the stack of boxes until she found the one marked as containing her laptop. Setting it on the desk, she quickly plugged it in and connected it to the phone jack. She made a couple of last-minute updates to her résumé and prepared to e-mail it. With a mental list of places she wanted to submit it to, she logged on to her Internet carrier and waited until the home page came up. She received a notification that sixteen unread messages awaited her. A quick glance showed they were all spam. She deleted them and clicked on the Write button. As she did so, her screen went blank. She watched in frustration as her laptop began to reboot. She waited impatiently while the computer's components whirled and whined their way back on. She received a message informing her there was a driver problem. Not certain exactly what a driver was, she tried signing on again and was immediately booted off. Twice more the system kicked her off-line. Disgusted, she gave up and started digging through her things, looking for a diskette. She would copy her résumé onto it and use her father's computer to send it out.

Not finding a diskette, she headed down the hallway to her father's office. She loved his office, even though it was a little too dark and masculine for her tastes. The dark walnut paneling and deep burgundy leather of the furniture filled her with a sense of comfort. How many times had she and Richard sat on the lushly carpeted floor playing while their father worked at his old roll-top desk? The desk originally belonged to his grandfather, who had owned a lumber mill in Virginia. The desk went with her father when he received a scholarship to Princeton and later it came to San Antonio with him and his new bride. Her mother had tried to get him to replace the relic with a new, more modern desk, but he refused.

Her father was sitting in his recliner reading. He looked up as she entered.

"Can I borrow a diskette and use your PC? My laptop keeps crashing. I don't know if it's the machine or the Internet service," she said.

"You're welcome to use the computer, but I'm not sure I have a diskette. I never use them. If I have any they'd be in the bottom drawer on the right-hand side."

Andi opened the drawer and found a stash of pencils, pens and an assortment of other office supplies, but no diskette. She closed the drawer and sighed. "No. You don't have any. I'll wait and try again later."

"Sorry I couldn't help."

"That's all right." She started to walk away, then stopped. "Did you ever study criminal law?"

The question surprised her. Statements had a way of rushing from her mouth before she realized it.

He looked at her and nodded. "Sure. I had to take classes, but I've never practiced criminal law."

She suspected she wasn't going to be able to just walk on out without some explanation for the question but tried it anyway. "Okay, thanks."

"Andi."

She stopped, trying desperately to think of something to say that would explain away the question.

"Are you interested in criminal law?" he asked.

Seeing the glint of hope in his eyes, she cursed her impulsive question. Like most parents, he had once held hopes that one of his children would follow in his professional footsteps. "No. I was just curious. You know . . . um . . . why you decided to go with corporate law rather than criminal."

He smiled. "Because I'm a pushover for a sad story. I'd never be able to look at cases objectively. I'd get too involved."

"You aren't a pushover." She kissed his cheek. "You're the gentlest, sweetest person I've ever known."

"See? My point exactly. Criminal lawyers can't be sweet and gentle. They have to be ruthless and cold-hearted."

Andi rolled her eyes. "Good night, Dad."

"Good night, honey."

Andi gave herself a good mental kick as she walked back to her room. She had been on the verge of asking her father how she could go about investigating a murder. *That's why no one should ever tell me a secret*, she thought. *I always forget and tell.*

When she returned to her room she walked over to the wooden box and stood staring at it. The fact that her great-grandfather killed a man didn't disturb her as much as knowing that her grandmother was still suffering from the act. How would she tell her grandmother that she would probably agree with the court's decision that he was guilty?

Why am I so quick to assume he was guilty? she wondered. *Innocent men went to prison. It happened. Could it have happened to him?* Without really meaning to, she reached into the box and pulled out the top sheets of paper. It was a final report from James Timmerman, a private investigator out of Corpus Christi.

Andi read the short summary.

After a thorough investigation, the following report is submitted for your records.

The accused, Sean Patrick Gray, 33, formerly of 519 W. Goliad Avenue, HiHo, Texas, was seen by Mrs. Eleanor Gleason (now deceased) entering Zucker's Grocery in this same town on the evening of May 4, 1939, at approximately 5:30 p.m. Seconds later, a shot rang out. Sheriff John Butler and Deputy Amos Duffy (both deceased), who were dining at a nearby restaurant, raced into the store and found Gray standing by the counter with a bag of money in his hands. The victim, Zucker, was slumped across the counter dead. An autopsy later proved that he died as the result of a bullet to the heart from a .45 caliber handgun. The store was searched thoroughly, but the murder weapon was never found, leading authorities to speculate Gray had an accomplice who escaped through the back door of the store, taking the weapon with him.

Sheriff Butler conducted a full investigation, but neither the accomplice nor the weapon was ever located.

Records show that Mr. Gray made a statement to the effect that he stopped by Zucker's on his way home to pick up a bottle of aspirin for his friend Ignacio Acosta who had broken his leg the previous day. Mr. Acosta verified his story. Mr. Gray claims the shot was fired as he entered the store. The counter was not visible from the doorway because of a large display of bolts of cloth. Mr. Gray stated he called out Zucker's name and heard what sounded like two people running away, but by the time he reached a position where he could see the counter, Mr. Zucker was already lying across the counter. Gray ran to the counter and saw the blood. He claimed the bag of money was lying open on the counter by Zucker's hand with some of the money spilling out. Mr. Gray claimed he had no memory of picking up the bag.

Since it was well known that Mr. Gray was having financial problems, the conclusion was quickly drawn that he had been in the process of robbing Zucker when something went wrong and Zucker was shot. After being arrested, Mr. Gray became belligerent and refused to cooperate further.

Mr. Gray had no record of past involvement with the police.

This case was unusual due to the considerable passage of time since the incident, and the fact that all known witnesses are now deceased.

I am sorry to say that our investigators were unable to locate any new evidence to indicate that George Zucker was murdered by anyone other than the accused, Sean Patrick Gray.

Attached to the report was an invoice. The amount made Andi's blood boil. Her grandmother had paid dearly for a wild goose chase. *One of her own making*, she reminded herself.

After rereading the final paragraph, she groaned and set the file aside. How could her grandmother think he was innocent? He had been caught with the bag of money in his hand.

A small hint of doubt gnawed at her subconscious. What had happened to the weapon? There must have been someone else with him. If so, then the partner must have been the one to pull the trigger. It made sense. Her great-grandfather's accomplice pulled the trigger, heard the sheriff and the deputy running into the store, and then fled through the back door. Why hadn't Sean Gray fled with him?

She reached into the box and removed another folder. This one was marked A&L Investigative Services. She glanced inside. There were several sheaves of paper. Andi set it aside and emptied the box of its contents. She found the third private investigator's folder, along with a much larger accordion file, a small cardboard box and four old newspaper clippings. She glanced into the accordion folder and found a large stack of old receipts and miscellaneous papers. None of them seemed connected to the murder. The smaller cardboard box held a cheaply made pocket watch, its once gold-colored finish now tarnished with age. Andi held the watch, trying to feel some leftover vestige of the man who had once owned it, but the watch held tightly to any secrets it possessed. Putting everything else to the side, she began to sort through the newspaper clippings. Someone had written a date on each article.

Andi quickly sorted them into date order and began to read the first one. It was short and to the point.

May 5, 1939 — George Zucker was shot and killed yesterday evening in his store. Money appears to be the motivation for this evil deed.

Sheriff Butler quickly apprehended one of the killers, an Irishman named Sean Gray. An unemployed cabinetmaker and sometimes handyman, Gray and his Mexican wife live in a small house located in the rougher, more unpleasant section of town most commonly referred to as Little Bean Town.

The second perpetrator fled the scene, taking the weapon with him and quite literally leaving his cohort holding the bag. The fact that the money was left behind, along with his partner, should quickly tell the reader what sort of low mentality was involved with this heinous act.

Sheriff Butler assured this reporter that the fugitive will be captured with haste, and justice will be swift in prosecuting both men, so as not to be too much of a drain on this fair community's already struggling coffers.

Mr. Zucker, an active member of the HiHo Lutheran Church, leaves behind a wife and two young children. He was the son of the late Ansel and Hazel Zucker, who opened a small hardware shop in this fair city in 1894. Through hard, honest work, George Zucker expanded his father's enterprise and added groceries and dry goods to his inventory when he purchased the old Henry Crawford building on First Street.

Mr. Zucker was a well-loved member of this community. His cheerful disposition and industrious spirit will be sorely missed. This office will print a special tribute tomorrow, saluting Mr. Zucker and his contributions to our beloved community.

Andi felt her face grow warm. The article made her feel dirty. She had never read anything so blatantly biased. She forced herself to read the article again and a tiny spark of anger began somewhere deep inside her.

The second article was no better than the first.

May 12, 1939 — Sheriff Butler is still on the lookout for the unknown accomplice of Sean Gray, who murdered George Zucker in cold blood on Wednesday of last week. As can be expected there was some rumbling down around Little Bean Town, but since the culprit was caught red-handed, there is little to be disputed. Anyone having information regarding this crime should contact the sheriff's office immediately.

Sheriff Butler told this reporter that Gray will be held in the HiHo city jail until his trial begins.

Numb with disbelief, she picked up the third article.

July 21, 1939 — After a speedy trial the Irishman known as Sean Gray was convicted to life in prison for the murder of George Zucker. Judge Wheeler informed Gray that he was lucky to have been caught with the money instead of the smoking gun, to wit, the electric chair would have been his fate for certain. Gray refused to reveal the name of his accomplice, continuing to mutter in his heavily accented English that he is innocent. He will be delivered to the authorities of Huntsville where he will undoubtedly enjoy a long and well cared for life, courtesy of the honest taxpaying citizens of this benevolent state.

The fourth article was much shorter and much simpler.

February 14, 1941 — Sean Gray, age thirty-five, died last week of pneumonia. Gray was serving a life sentence at the state prison in Huntsville, Texas, after brutally murdering Mr. George Zucker.

Gray is survived by his Mexican wife and four children, the youngest of which was born after Gray's incarceration. Services will be held at the Irish Catholic Church on Durango Street. Burial will be at the Catholic cemetery on the edge of town.

Something wet dripped onto Andi's arm. She was surprised to find tears streaming down her face. She threw the offensive articles back into the empty box. How could anyone be so heartless? Had her grandmother read these articles as a child? What must it have been like to live during that time? Had the family been ridiculed for the deeds of the father? Had the majority of the citizens in HiHo been as hateful as the reporter? Suddenly Andi understood why her grandmother didn't want Andi's mother to know she was doing this. Her mother had been born in HiHo.

The articles left her feeling contaminated. She could almost feel the hate seeping from the box. The musty scent from the box and papers permeated the room. She hopped up and raised the window by her bed. The cool November night air swept into the room, washing away the stale stench of the newspaper clippings. She stood before the window and gazed across the large expanse of lawn. By leaning slightly forward, she could see the flickering television from her grandmother's rooms.

Her cell phone rang, jarring her from her musing. It was Becka.

"We were just making sure you made it home safely," Becka said.

For a brief moment, Andi felt disoriented. Had it only been that morning that she'd left Dallas? She shook her head to clear the cobwebs away. "You're starting to sound like my mother," Andi teased. "But I'm glad you called."

"See? Admit it. You're already missing my witty conversation and valuable advice."

Andi chuckled. "Valuable advice, huh? Well, listen to this and tell me what you think. My grandmother wants me to solve a sixty-five-year-old murder case. Do you think I should take it on?"

Becka gasped. "Wow. Who was killed? Where? How? Why?"

Andi rolled her eyes. "I should tell her to call you. If I knew the answer to all those questions, I wouldn't need to investigate. I don't actually need to anyway. The case was solved seconds after it occurred."

"Whoa. You're losing me. I thought you said she wanted you to investigate, but if it was solved . . . I'm lost, girlfriend."

"Let me start at the beginning." Andi quickly filled her in on everything her grandmother told her. To Becka's credit, she managed to restrain herself with only a few whistles and gasps until Andi mentioned the box. It was too much.

"So what was in the box?" Becka insisted.

Andi found herself reluctant to bring up the newspaper articles, embarrassed by their ugliness. "The reports from the three private investigators she hired, a couple of other boxes that I've not looked at yet and . . ." She hesitated. "Some newspaper clippings."

"Clippings about the murder?"

"Yeah."

Silence hung between them. Finally, Becka broke it. "Well, give it up. What did they say?"

"They're kind of ugly. Yellow journalism at its best with a touch of racism and classism thrown in." She gave a brief synopsis of the articles and a quick overview of the one private investigator's report that she'd read.

"Yuck," Becka said. "HiHo doesn't sound like a place I'd want to live."

"It was nineteen thirty-nine. I doubt the sentiment would've been much different anywhere else." Andi gazed out her window.

"Do you think he was guilty?"

Andi sighed. "It looks pretty bad for him. I mean, they caught him with the money in his hands."

"Yeah, but why didn't he run? If someone else was with him, wouldn't they have run out together?"

"Who knows? Maybe he got scared and froze."

"Maybe, or maybe it happened just like he said it did and some murderer has been walking around free."

"It was sixty-five years ago. I doubt he would still be walking around."

"Hey, you never know," Becka protested. "How are you going to go about finding out who did it?"

Andi rolled her eyes. "Who said I was?"

"Come on, you can't just let it go. You know that. I'll bet you a hundred dollars he didn't do it."

"What makes you so sure?" Andi demanded.

"I'm not sure. I'm trying to give you some incentive to help your grandmother. I like her and I want you to help her."

"You don't even know my grandmother."

"Sure I do. I mean, I've never actually met her, but over the years you've talked about her so much I feel like I know her."

"Becka, you're something else."

"Yeah, I know. So what are you going to do?"

"I don't know. Nothing probably. I don't even know where to begin."

"Start by calling those private investigators. Maybe they can give you some idea on where to go next," Becka suggested.

"If there was anywhere else to look, they would have done so." Andi didn't want to discuss her family skeletons any further. "What have you been doing all day? Have you submitted your résumé anywhere?"

Becka chuckled. "Actually, that's the second reason why I called. You're never going to believe what I'm going to do."

"Try me."

"First of all, Stacy arranged for a substitute to fill in for her and we're going to Hawaii for two weeks."

"Two weeks! Oh, you lucky devil." Andi groaned. "I'm so jealous. Two weeks of sandy beaches and sunshine."

"Don't forget the mai tais."

"When are you leaving?"

"A week from Thursday."

"How did you get everything arranged so fast?"

"We bought into this timeshare a few years back and we've never seemed to have the time to really take advantage of it. After you left, I was sitting here feeling sorry for myself and I started playing around on the computer. I was looking at a travel Web site and I remembered the timeshare, so I go in to check it out and boom! There's a week opening at a resort in Maui and a consecutive week for one on the Big Island, so I called Stacy during her free period and bang, we decided right then and there to go." Becka began to laugh. "Now are you ready for the best part of the trip?"

"You're taking me with you," Andi exclaimed.

"No, that's not it."

"Oh. Then why do I care?"

"We're traveling on my frequent flyer miles from all those wretched trips the phone company sent me on."

"You're joking."

"Nope. The entire flight is costing me almost zilch."

"I hate you," Andi growled. "You're disgusting."

Becka giggled. "There's more."

"I don't want to hear it."

Becka ignored her and continued, "After we get back, I'm going back to school to get my teaching certificate."

Andi gasped. "You're not serious."

"Yeah. I sure am. I'm going to try to teach those little rug rats. Can you believe that?"

"I believe you'd better find another name for them. Most parents probably won't take too kindly to a teacher who refers to her students as rug rats."

"Well, yeah. I'll think of something else, but until then they're rug rats."

Andi laughed. Becka would be a wonderful teacher. For all her bluster and cynicism, she was a wonderfully sweet individual. "You'll do great. I'm so happy for you both. Of course, I'd be much happier if I were going to Hawaii with you."

They talked for several more minutes before Andi said goodbye and went to bed.

Chapter Twelve

By eight a.m. Tuesday morning, Andi had managed to remain online long enough to e-mail her résumé to several different companies. After sending them, she found herself in a quandary. She didn't like being idle and wanted to find a job, but anticipating the impending interviews and then starting over in a new position made her feel ill. She found herself alternately humming and then cursing the phone company for laying her off.

Her mother and grandmother were at the kitchen table reading the paper when Andi went in to get a cup of coffee.

"I put a breakfast casserole in the oven to keep warm," her mother said as Andi poured herself some coffee.

"You're going to spoil me." Andi took the casserole out of the oven as her mother dropped bread into the toaster.

"What are your plans for today?" her mother asked.

"I need to find a realtor and start looking for a house."

"A house. Andrea, you don't have a job. How are you going to buy a house?"

"I've managed to save quite a bit and I should be receiving my severance check soon."

"It must have been pretty hefty, if you can afford a house," her mother probed. When Andi didn't reply, she continued, "You know you're welcome to stay here."

"Thanks, Mom, but I want to get settled."

Her mother nodded. "You might want to call Linda Ramos. She's helped a couple of people in my department. Her card is in the Rolodex on my desk."

"Thanks."

"Are you looking anywhere in particular for a job?" her mother asked.

"Not really. I want to stay in San Antonio. I know I can eventually find work here. It may take a little while, but I've set aside enough to get me through the next few months. That's why I'm going to go ahead and look for a house. I didn't like living in Dallas and I certainly don't want to live in Houston. I e-mailed my résumé to several of the larger corporations here, looking for another project management position. If I don't get any leads, I'll start looking into the smaller companies." The toast popped up and Andi glanced up to finding her grandmother gazing at her. She felt bad about the disappointment in her eyes, knowing she was the cause of it. Andi jumped up to get the toast, but her mother was already handing it to her.

What can I do? Andi asked herself as she attempted to eat the sausage and egg casserole. *It's not as if I have any experience investigating murders.* The food kept lodging in her throat. She snuck a quick glance at her grandmother as the older woman took her cup to the sink. It would be horrible to have to watch your father go off to prison and then for him to die there. *What if he had been innocent?* Andi supposed it was only natural that a child would presume her father's innocence no matter what. She couldn't imagine being able to believe her own father would be capable of taking another person's life.

"What about you, Mom?" Leticia asked. "What do you have planned?"

66

"I'll probably go over to the senior center. There's a new mini-course on computer usage starting tomorrow. Edna and I were thinking about taking it, but we have to go register."

Andi looked up in surprise. "You're taking computer courses?"

Leticia turned to Andi. "Your grandmother has gotten to be quite the computer guru."

Andi put her fork down and glanced at her grandmother. "I should have called you last night when mine was acting up."

"If you like, I can have Hector—he's the instructor—look at it. He replaced Edna's hard drive for her," Sarah offered without looking at Andi.

Andi felt like a jerk. "Grandmother, I was thinking that if you have time soon, you might like to go for a drive with me. I was thinking about driving down to HiHo."

Her mother's head shot up and Andi realized her mistake. She shouldn't have mentioned the town.

"What interest do you have in HiHo?" her mother asked suspiciously.

"I asked her to drive me down there," Sarah said as she walked back to the table and patted Andi's shoulder. "I wanted to look around. See if the old house is still standing, and with the holidays coming up, I want to take some flowers out to the cemetery. Let me know when you're ready to leave, *mija*. I'll go call Edna and ask her to sign me up."

Andi turned her attention to the casserole. She could feel her mother eyeing her. After a long silence, her mom took her cup to the sink.

"I'll see you tonight then," she said as she walked away from Andi. She was almost to the door when she stopped and turned back. Andi could see the concern on her face. "I hate when she goes down there. She gets so depressed. You'll watch out for her, won't you?"

Andi had the eerie feeling that her mother knew exactly why they were going to HiHo. She swallowed and said, "I won't let anything happen to her."

Her mom nodded and seemed on the verge of saying more but

turned instead and picked up her purse and briefcase. Moments later, Andi heard the sound of her mom's car pulling out of the garage. She let out a long sigh and dumped the remainder of her breakfast down the garbage disposal. She quickly washed the handful of dirty dishes.

"So have you decided to help me?"

Andi turned to find her grandmother with her purse, ready to go. She smiled and nodded. "Yes, I guess I have, but you have to promise not to get angry with me if we find out he was guilty."

Her grandmother flinched slightly but pulled herself erect. "There's not many things in this life that I'm absolutely one-hundred percent positive of, but I know Papa didn't murder George Zucker."

Andi studied her. "How can you be so sure?"

"Because he told me he didn't and he never lied to me."

Andi wasn't sure how to respond, so she said nothing.

"When will you be ready to leave?" her grandmother asked.

Andi dried her hands. "Let me call the realtor and then we'll go."

Linda Ramos was out of her office, so Andi left a brief message and a phone number. She grabbed a light jacket. Glancing in the mirror, she gave her short black hair one last swipe with a brush. The commitment had been made. Now it was time to go to work. "I just wish I knew where to start," she whispered.

Chapter Thirteen

The town of HiHo was founded in 1852 when two brothers, Hiram and Horace Mendel, purchased a large tract of land. After building a saloon, a general store and a hotel, they promptly dubbed the new community HiHo. Located on the upper coastal plain of South Texas, the gently rolling terrain of loamy soils with clay subsoil supported lush grasses as well as blackjack, post oak, live oak, mesquite and cacti. This fertile farmland, ideal for peanuts, corn, wheat, sorghum, oats, hay, peaches, watermelons and pecans, drew more and more people to HiHo. With the influx of settlers, the need for goods and services increased. The growing demand for goods drew more merchants and new stores sprang up. Cattle flourished on the abundant grasslands. In 1859, HiHo became the county seat.

With the new honor bestowed upon the town, many of the newcomers argued to change the name of the bustling community to something more dignified. But as HiHo prospered, so had its founders, Hiram and Horace Mendel. They were determined that the name would remain unchanged and they used their influence and money to ensure it did. Hiram contracted the well-known architect Alfred Gooding to build a courthouse that would be so spectacular the citizens would forget about the town's unusual name. He and Horace donated fifteen acres of prime property for the location of the new courthouse. Their generosity also virtually guaranteed that the courthouse would become the center of town; this in turn led to the increase in value of the land around it, which of course they owned.

The Civil War and a protracted drought that lasted from 1862 until 1865 delayed the construction of the new building. The magnificent three-storied red Texas granite structure wouldn't be completed until 1869. The four sides of the building contained triple-arched entryways that led to galleries, where rows of sparkling floor-to-ceiling windows suffused the vast rooms with light. The crowning glory was the copper dome, topped by a twelve-foot-high statue of Justice. The new copper dome caught the sunlight, reflecting it for miles as a constant reminder that the busy community of HiHo resided at the end of that spectacular glow. During the ensuing years, oxidation slowly turned the brilliant natural reddish-brown of the copper to a darker brown-black and eventually to a noble green patina.

In 1886, a resurgence in beef prices and a spur of the San Antonio and Aransas Pass Railway brought HiHo's last large economic boom, which continued until the Depression brought about the death of the beef market. Financial setbacks forced the closure of the railroad line, and the iron tracks were torn out during World War II and used in the war effort.

Over the decades, the Mendel name slowly faded into HiHo's history. The last male heir died in Korea and the last remnants of the Mendel women died or moved away in search of more promising prospects.

⊷⊶

Andi drove slower than normal along the narrow, poorly maintained two-lane highway leading from IH-37 to HiHo. Still visible for miles, the tall courthouse dome was her first glimpse of HiHo. Except for a brief stop to purchase flowers, her grandmother sat silently staring out the window during most of the trip from San Antonio. Not wanting to intrude on her thoughts, Andi kept her curiosity curbed. A large freshly painted sign depicting a football player in a green and yellow jersey informed them that they were now entering the home of the HiHo Hornets.

"Turn right at the light," her grandmother said as they drew near the center of town.

Andi drove the two short blocks to the light and suppressed a laugh as the light turned red as she approached. There wasn't a single car at the intersection. Although she could have turned, she chose to use the time to look around. The town seemed to be laid out in a wagon-wheel pattern. The streets converged on the courthouse as the spokes on a wagon wheel converge on the hub. Several of the stores appeared empty, with the windows hidden behind weathered sheets of plywood.

The courthouse sat to Andi's left. From street level, most of the grand old building was hidden by a copse of ancient live oak and pecan trees. Many of the massive oaks possessed low-hanging branches that stretched lazily over the deep cushion of St. Augustine grass. Andi suspected that many of the limbs measured more than sixteen inches in diameter. Across the street from the courthouse, an old movie theater hunkered beneath a blanket of grime and graffiti, its once flashy marquee now scarred with time and indifference. The sightless windows of the old ticket booth left Andi with a sense of sadness and a desire to gently wash them and restore some measure of dignity to the old landmark.

"Your grandfather took me to the Rialto to see *The Farmer's Daughter* with Loretta Young. Afterward, we walked over to the square. There used to be a gazebo. He proposed to me beneath the old Treaty Tree."

"Treaty Tree?"

71

"It was a great big old oak. It died several years ago. Abuelita Cortez used to tell us that Geronimo once signed a peace treaty beneath that tree. I always intended to go to the library and research it, but I never did. It's probably just an old story."

Andi shrugged. "Maybe, but there's the Treaty Oak in Austin and I've read two or three articles about trees in other counties that bear the same claim. Who knows? With all the treaties that were signed, it could be true."

The Treaty Oak in Austin was the last survivor of the Council Oaks, fourteen trees that had served as a meeting place and temple for the Tonkowas and Comanches. Legend stated that Stephen F. Austin signed a boundary treaty in the 1800s with the local Indians.

In 1989, the majestic old oak had fallen victim to a vicious act of vandalism when it was deliberately poisoned and nearly destroyed. The citizens of Austin, with the support of calls and letters from people around the world, worked endless hours to save the old vanguard. Today less than half the tree remained, but it was beginning to show signs of recovery.

Andi had been a freshman in college when the vandalism occurred, but she could still remember her feelings of frustration and anger when she'd heard the news.

"Pull over here and stop," her grandmother directed.

Andi pulled into one of the nose-in parking slots in front of a boarded-up building. "What are we doing?"

Her grandmother nodded toward the store. "This was George Zucker's store. This is where he died."

Andi's gaze shot back to the dilapidated building. Upon closer inspection, she could barely see the faded script announcing this to be the home of ZUCKER'S MERCANTILE. Andi glanced at her grandmother and saw tears glinting in the old woman's eyes. She reached over and took her hand. "Do you want to get out?"

Her grandmother shook her head. "Let's go on over to the old house."

Andi backed the car out.

"Take a left at the stop sign, and a right onto First Street," her grandmother said.

Andi followed her grandmother's directions and found herself on a street of small but well maintained, homes.

Her grandmother leaned forward and peered through the windshield. "It's the blue one on the corner."

Andi let the car coast the last few yards. A double row of pansies marched along the sidewalk that ran parallel to the street. From the sidewalk, a small graveled walkway led to a porch running the width of the house. An old wooden rocker, gray from years of sun and weather, sat alongside the doorway. "Looks like someone is living here," Andi offered.

"That's good. A house needs a family just as a human does. Have you ever noticed, Andi, how quickly an empty house deteriorates?"

Andi nodded and hoped her grandmother wasn't going to want to knock on the door and ask to look around. She found herself wondering what it would be like to drive up to her parents' home and find someone else living there. The house on Wildflower Drive was the only childhood home Andi could remember. In truth, it was the only real home she had ever known. Her various apartments and Trish's house certainly never held the same sense of peace and love that her parents' house did. The thought of someone else living there disturbed her.

"Let's go on to the cemetery," her grandmother suggested.

With a sense of guilty relief that she wasn't going to have to ask a stranger for permission to enter their home, Andi followed her grandmother's directions toward the edge of town.

As they turned onto a gravel road, her grandmother pointed toward a large pecan tree. "The old Holstetter place used to be there. They had the best well in the county. When I was a kid, about once or twice a year, Papa would grab his fishing pole, Mama would pack a big picnic lunch, and we'd walk over to the San Antonio River. It's only about three miles over in that direction." She pointed to the west of where they were headed. "We

73

would stop at the Holstetters' place for a drink of water. It was the sweetest, coldest water I've ever had." She shook her head. "The entire town was upset when it caved in."

"Why did it cave in?" Andi asked.

Her grandmother frowned. "You know, I don't remember. It caved in about the same time as . . . as when Papa's problems started and I'm not sure I ever knew what happened. I know Mr. Holstetter tried to dig it out, but it caved in again and he let it go. By then, everyone was switching over to the new city water that was being piped straight into the house."

"I'm so spoiled," Andi said. "I take running water for granted. I can't imagine what it would be like to have to tote water for everything you do."

"We didn't waste as much, and we got a lot more exercise, that's for sure. But I have to admit, when we finally got indoor plumbing, I quickly learned to appreciate the convenience of not having to scurry to an outhouse in February." Her grandmother chuckled.

Andi maneuvered the car around a long curve. The closed cemetery gate loomed before them.

Chapter Fourteen

The wide, towering cemetery gates were unlocked. Andi swung them open before easing the car through. As she went back to close the gates, she heard the wind whisper through the cedar trees. It was a strangely comforting sound. *A person could choose a worse place to be buried*, she thought as she made her way back to the car.

The enormous cemetery consisted of four sections. The front section was post-1975 grave sites, and the back was pre-1975. Both areas were further divided into the Catholic and non-Catholic sides.

Andi followed the directions her grandmother gave and drove them to the midway point of the older graves. As her grandmother walked among the tombstones, Andi retrieved the flower arrangements from the back seat and followed silently. The final resting places of Sean Patrick Gray and Angelina Cortez Gray were nestled beneath the protective limbs of an ancient crepe myrtle tree.

A cement bench sat alongside the grave and a modest tombstone sat at the head of each.

Andi stepped forward, placed the arrangements on the graves and waited in silence. She was bursting to ask a dozen questions but held back out of respect.

"Did I ever tell you that one of your Cortez ancestors was an officer in the Mexican Army long before Texas was ever a part of the United States? He received a land grant of one hundred and twenty-five acres in this area. His family maintained a ranch there until after the Texas Revolution. After Texas won her independence from Mexico, many of the original landowners found themselves having to prove ownership of the land they had lived on for many years. He went to court to try to reclaim it, but the courthouse containing the land records mysteriously burned during the trial and the records went with it. Settlers started pouring in and snatching up land anywhere they could find it. Many of the Mexicans holding large land grants weren't able to prove ownership and lost their property." She eased over and gently brushed leaves from the tombstone.

"Wait a minute." Andi raced back to her car and retrieved an old blanket that she kept in her trunk. Running back, she spread the blanket over the bench. "Sit here and talk to me. I'll do that for you."

Sarah slowly straightened her back. "I'm perfectly capable of cleaning away a few leaves."

"I'm sorry. I never meant to imply you weren't." Andi knelt down beside her grandmother and began to help. "I was hoping that you might feel like telling me what you remembered about the murder."

They worked in silence for several minutes before Sarah began to talk.

"I was ten. My sisters Lupe and Magdalena were eight and five. Mama was five months pregnant with Ray. Mama was preparing supper. We didn't have plumbing in the house. Our water came from a well located at the front corner of the yard. Mama sent me to get a bucket of water, and just as I was drawing the bucket up from the well, Sheriff Butler's car pulled into the yard. Mama must have heard the car, because when I looked up she was already at the door. He told her Papa had been arrested for murder. She kept shaking her head." Sarah slowly stood. Andi reached out her hand to steady her. Together they moved to the bench and sat.

When it became obvious she wasn't going to continue, Andi gently prodded, "Why are you so absolutely sure he's innocent? I know he told you he didn't kill Mr. Zucker, but wouldn't you expect him to say that to spare a ten-year-old child?"

"Do you think your father could kill anyone?" Sarah asked.

Andi's first instinct was to say no, but she took a deep breath. "Under normal circumstances, no. But we both know that a person can be driven to almost anything."

"We were poor. Cabinetmaking wasn't the most lucrative profession, but Papa had started taking jobs as a handyman. He was getting more work. He and Mama were talking about either enlarging the house or adding indoor plumbing. We weren't rich, but we weren't going hungry. Besides, he had known George Zucker for years."

"What was he like?"

"Zucker?"

Andi nodded.

Her grandmother chuckled. "He was a penny-pinching miser who would count the grounds in a pound of coffee just to make sure you didn't get any extra."

Andi looked at her and blinked.

Seeing her surprise, her grandmother laughed. "Okay, so I may have slightly over-exaggerated. He didn't literally count the grounds, but I swear he would have if he could've found a way to do so."

"Could he have done something to make your father angry?"

"Sure. Papa had a fast temper, but it disappeared as quickly as it appeared."

Andi braced her hands against the bench and poked at a pebble with the toe of her shoe. Nothing she was hearing helped convince her of his innocence.

Her grandmother patted her hand. "I'm sorry to be so much trouble, *mija*. If I could do this myself, I would. I should've done this years ago. I know I've added another burden on you."

Andi shook her head. "It's not a burden, really. I'm afraid I'm going to hurt you," she admitted.

"That's because you still believe he's guilty."

The statement was true, and Andi couldn't reply.

Her grandmother gave a deep sigh. "All right. I know how you like to analyze everything. I'll tell you my reasoning on why he couldn't have killed George Zucker and you can play the devil's advocate. My father hated guns. Both of his brothers were killed during the First World War. He knew what guns did to families. He wouldn't even hunt. He didn't own a gun, and as far as I know, he'd never even handled one."

"There was someone else with him and he had the gun," Andi countered.

"His best friend, Ignacio Acosta, was at home in bed with a broken leg. He was the reason Papa was at Zucker's. Iggy—Papa always called him Iggy—was in pain and Papa walked over to get him some aspirins."

"He met someone on the way to the store," Andi said, grasping at straws.

Her grandmother huffed. "If we're going to do this you have to be logical. What sense does that make? He's walking down the street and runs into another pal and suddenly they decide to rob Zucker?"

Andi nodded. "You're right. That was reaching. But couldn't they have been planning this before and used Mr. Acosta's broken leg as an alibi?"

"How could they have planned for Iggy's broken leg? You don't honestly think he broke it to provide someone an alibi." She seemed to be studying her parents' tombstones. "For what purpose? We weren't hungry or sick."

"Your mother was expecting another child. That had to be of some concern to them."

"Things were different then. A child wasn't as big a financial burden then as they are now. When I was a child, clothes were passed down until they wore out. There were no daycare costs or play schools. My gosh, now a child has to have a social security number practically from birth." She shook her head. "Yes, another child would've caused them a small amount of concern, but not enough to kill someone for."

"Maybe they never intended to kill him. Perhaps they only intended to rob the store."

"No. It was a small town. Zucker would have recognized anyone from town."

"They could have worn masks or disguises."

Sarah shook her head vigorously.

Andi realized it was a dead end, no matter what she said; her grandmother wasn't going to change her mind. "Let's look at this another way," Andi offered. "If your father didn't kill George Zucker, who did?"

"That's what I want you to find out," Sarah said with a groan.

Andi tried to place herself in the shoes of the killer. "If Zucker would have recognized everyone in town, it makes sense that anyone planning to rob the store would know they were going to have to kill him. That's premeditated murder, and I think you'd have to be pretty desperate to attempt it, especially at that time of day, when anyone could walk into the store at any given moment." Andi thought better when she moved. She stood and began pacing around the tiny perimeter of the bench. "According to the newspaper articles in the box you gave me, Sheriff Butler and a deputy were nearby when they heard the shot. They raced into the store and found your father holding a bag of money. There was no mention of anyone seen racing from the store, but there was a back door leading into an alley. Why would anyone go into a store, rob it, stand by and watch the owner being shot, and then continue to stand there, knowing people would hear the shot and come running?"

"If Papa froze from shock or fear, as some said he did, why didn't the other person with him grab the money before he ran?" Sarah asked.

"It could be they really didn't mean to kill him and they both freaked out."

"Where were the masks? Did the other person grab Papa's mask and take it with him? Whoever robbed him would have used a mask, because they knew Zucker would recognize them. Unless they went in with the intention of killing him."

"You said he was a penny-pincher. Maybe he cheated people on their accounts—"

"No," Sarah interrupted. "George Zucker was an honest man. He was cheap, but I don't think he ever cheated anyone. He gave you exactly what you paid for."

Andi frowned. Her grandmother had been a child and probably remembered things from a child's point of view.

"I know I was young," she replied as though reading Andi's thoughts, "but you ask anyone who knew him and they'll tell you he was an honest man."

"Anyone still living would have been a child then also," Andi reminded her.

"Not necessarily. Iggy's still living."

Andi stopped suddenly and turned back to her grandmother. "Your father's best friend? The guy he went to the store for is still living?"

Sarah nodded. "At least he was last December. I get a Christmas card from him every year."

"How old is he?"

Sarah thought for a moment. "He was younger than Papa, but he's probably in his nineties."

The wind began to blow harder. It snatched at their clothing and hair. Andi swept her hair from her eyes. She saw her grand-mother shiver. "If you're ready, let's drive back into town. I could use a cup of coffee," Andi said. As they made their way back to the car Andi's thoughts turned to Ignacio Acosta. *How much would he remember after all these years?* Talking to him would probably prove useless. If he had known anything relevant, he would have spoken up during the trial. As she closed her grandmother's door, she watched a small dust devil begin to form. It gathered fallen leaves and discarded flowers as it whipped randomly across the cemetery.

Chapter Fifteen

Andi parked her car in front of the Blue Moon Café. The temperature seemed to be dropping, or maybe it was just the wind cutting through her thin jacket. The café, located to the west side of the courthouse, had a large neon blue moon painted over the doorway. The smell of fresh coffee and frying hamburgers greeted them at the doorway. Andi glanced at her watch and was shocked to see it was almost eleven.

"Sit wherever you like," a voice called from the kitchen.

A few of the booths along the wall were occupied, so Andi chose a table near the front window. It would allow a clear view of the courthouse and surrounding area. They were barely seated when a tall, thin woman with a flaming red beehive emerged from the kitchen. She carried a full pot of coffee and menus.

"Would you ladies care for a cup of hot coffee?" she asked as she approached and offered them menus.

Andi and Sarah murmured their gratitude for the coffee but declined the menus.

"Don't recall seeing you ladies before. Ya'll new around here?" the waitress asked.

"I grew up in HiHo but moved away several years ago," Sarah said. "My granddaughter drove me down to look around."

The waitress nodded and rested one hand on her hip. "Well, you'll probably find things have changed. My husband and I moved here about fifteen years ago after he retired from the Air Force, and a lot has changed since we've been here. Do you still have family around?"

Sarah shook her head. "Not anymore."

"Well, my name's Noreen. Ya'll just give a holler if you need anything. I'll be in the kitchen."

After Noreen disappeared into the kitchen, Sarah turned to gaze out the window. "Do you see that big oak tree there in the far corner?"

Andi turned to look where her grandmother had pointed. "The one with the steel cables supporting the limbs?"

"Yes. That was the hanging tree. They used it up until nineteen twenty-three when the state switched over to the electric chair."

Shocked, Andi stared out at the gracious old tree, horrified that it could have been the scene of such brutality. "Why didn't your father receive the death penalty?" Andi asked. "I thought it was automatic in murder cases."

Sarah sipped her coffee and nodded her approval of its rich flavor. "Since they never found the weapon, there wasn't enough evidence to convict him of premeditated murder. He was convicted of being an accomplice to murder during the commission of a robbery."

Andi tried to recall the information from the newspaper article she'd read. She was certain it indicated that he had been sentenced to life in prison for murder. "Didn't the newspaper article—"

"Piss on that newspaper," Sarah spat.

Andi blinked in surprise. That was as close as she'd ever come to hearing her grandmother curse.

"R. L. Weiss owned the newspaper then. He used it to spout his vile hatred of everything that wasn't just like him." Sarah took another sip of coffee.

"The articles were pretty nasty." Andi gazed at her grandmother. "What was it like living here then?"

She saw a glimmer of tears before Sarah turned her attention back out the window. "It was hard, but most of it fell on Mama's shoulders. She was five months pregnant and already had three kids to feed. There weren't many jobs for women then. She got a job doing the laundry and ironing for the hotel that was out on the highway, and she sold whatever goat's milk and cheese we didn't use. When I was twelve, I got a job at the same hotel. I helped clean the rooms on weekends and during the summer."

Andi watched helplessly as her grandmother struggled with the past.

"The time during the trial and the first few weeks afterwards were the worst. People would stare and point at us, and the kids at school called us names. I tried to ignore them because I knew Papa was innocent. Time went by and people began to forget, but it seemed like something was always happening to remind everyone." Sarah brushed a hand over her eyes.

Andi reached across the table and patted her grandmother's arm. "I'm sorry I've upset you."

Sarah shook her head. "After Papa died, I thought that would be the last of it, but I soon learned that in a small town nothing is ever truly forgotten. There was always someone willing to drag it all back to the surface." She paused. "After I graduated from high school, I went to work at the grain elevator. I worked in the office, typing up invoices and such. I worked there until your grandfather, Thomas, and I were married in nineteen forty-eight. We moved into a little one-bedroom house over on Third Street, but Mama started having health problems. Lupe was married and living in San Antonio, and Magdalena was living with her while she

84

attended business school. Thomas and I moved back to the old house so I could take care of Mama and help with Ray. He was only nine then."

Noreen emerged from the kitchen and made another round with the coffeepot. She refilled their cups and disappeared back into the kitchen.

"We were living there when your mother was born. It would be four years before your Uncle Timothy was born, followed two years later by Michael, and three years after that Angie. During those years, we added indoor plumbing to the old house and after Timothy was born, we built on another room. Ray eventually moved to San Antonio and found a job working as a carpenter. Then Mama had a stroke that paralyzed her left side. About the same time, a group of locals decided to start a historical society. They published a weekly article in the paper and one of them was about Mr. Zucker's murder. There's nothing as exciting in a small town as a murder, especially if the victim is well known. I was so busy with trying to take care of Mama, I didn't have time to worry much about it." She sipped her coffee and gazed out the window as a pickup loaded with hay drove by.

Andi's gaze returned to the hanging tree.

Sarah sighed softly and continued with her story. "I should have paid more attention to what was going on. Leticia was ten or eleven and in the same grade as George Zucker's great-grandson, Jason Braun. He began to make Leti's life miserable, taunting her about her grandfather being a murderer and how he had died in prison. She never said anything to us about it. I'm not even sure how long it went on. The first I knew about it was when she came home from school one day with blood all over her. I was scared to death." Sarah chuckled softly. "Your mother had finally gotten her fill of Jason Braun and busted his nose."

Andi gasped. "Mom was in a fight? I can't imagine. She's always so . . . so . . . proper." She stirred her coffee and tried to picture a young Leticia in a fistfight.

"Thomas was working as a clerk at the feed store. When he

85

came home that afternoon and heard what was going on, he went to see Jason's father. They had words. Thomas later told me it wasn't too hard to figure out where Jason heard the awful things he had been saying to Leti. The next morning when Thomas went to work he was fired. Jason's father was a nephew to the owner of the feed store. Losing his job hurt, but we had managed to put a little away, and we got by. Thomas went to San Antonio and submitted an application for a position with the railroad. Mama died a week later. Just when I was sure our world would never right itself, Thomas got the job with the railroad. A few weeks later, we sold Papa's old house and moved to San Antonio."

"Sounds horrible," Andi said. "But I still can't imagine Mom in a fistfight."

Sarah looked at her. "I'm not sure she ever really got over Jason's taunting. Afterward, she always seemed a little withdrawn and became almost obsessive in her appearance. She drove herself to always be better at everything she did. She was never happy with just good grades in school. She had to have the best grades. If someone else received a higher test score or grade, she would stay up most of the night studying. I used to wake up at two or three in the morning and find her studying."

"I guess it was that drive that earned her a scholarship to Princeton," Andi said.

Sarah nodded. "Once she made up her mind to go to Princeton, there was no talking her out of it. I tried to explain to her that there was no way we could afford to send her, but she just shrugged and told me she would take care of it." Sarah rubbed her fingers across the back of her hand. "And she did. Whatever she set her mind to, she did. So I wasn't really surprised that after you and Richard were born she came to me one day and forbade me from ever saying anything to either of you about Papa being in prison."

Andi nodded. She now understood a lot more about her mother and her constant struggle to better herself. She had spent her life trying to erase Jason Braun's ugly teasing.

86

Chapter Sixteen

By the time they arrived back in San Antonio, Andi had decided on a starting point. After parting from her grandmother, she went to her room, pulled the box Sarah had given her from beneath the bed and booted up her laptop. She dug through the papers until she found the report from James Timmerman, the third private investigator her grandmother hired. His report had been more detailed than the other two. She called the phone number shown on the report and was surprised when he answered the phone himself. After introducing herself, Andi gave him a brief background on the case until he recalled the job.

"Yes, I remember the case on Sean Gray, but anything about it is confidential. I can't discuss the case with you without Mrs. Mimms' permission."

"I understand, but I have your report here." Andi quickly read him enough of the report to convince him that she was telling the truth.

"Well, since you have my report, I don't suppose there would be any reason why I couldn't answer your questions. What can I do for you, Ms. Kane?"

"My grandmother, Mrs. Mimms, wants me to look into this matter further and I was hoping you might be able to give me some suggestions on where to go from here," Andi admitted. She reasoned that James Timmerman had charged her grandmother a great deal of money and had given very little in return. She didn't feel she was imposing by asking him for a little advice.

He cleared his throat. "I'm sorry, but there's nowhere else to go. All the witnesses have died. As I recall, Mr. Gray was found standing by the body, holding a bag of money. There's no doubt in my mind that he was guilty. You must remember, your grandmother was a child when all this happened. It's only natural that she'd believe in her father's innocence. Most family members do. I've yet to meet a mother who believes her son or daughter is guilty of the crime for which they've been accused."

Andi hesitated. There had to be something else she could do. "Is there nothing else? I have to do something for her. I can't just blow this off. It's too important to her."

"Believe me, if there had been any other leads to follow I would have done so. I quit when I did because, as I said, there was no doubt in my mind of his guilt. I couldn't in good conscience continue taking your grandmother's money."

"What if they hadn't caught him with the money? If the store had been empty when the sheriff came in, what would you have pursued next?"

He paused. "Well, I suppose I would have tried to interview anyone still alive who had been living in HiHo during that time."

"If they had information wouldn't they have come forward during the trial?" Andi asked.

"Possibly, but oftentimes people don't realize they know something important. It's not until one action is linked with another that the connection becomes clear. Am I making sense?"

"Yes, I think so. How would you have gone about determining who was living there then?"

"I'd go to the *HiHo News*. Newspapers are a wonderful source of information, particularly in small towns. I'd check to see if there's a local historical society. Go to the library and talk to the librarian. They can sometimes point you to other sources. Talk to the district attorney. After all this time, he probably won't be able to tell you much, but you never know when you'll be handed the key that'll tear the case wide open."

"What should my major goal be? I mean other than proving him innocent."

"Find the gun," he said without hesitation. "That was the only snag in the entire case. But I warn you, after all these years, there's very little chance of that."

Remembering his advice, she tried one last question. "Mr. Timmerman, was there anything that you came across during your investigation that you didn't deem important enough to include in your report?"

He laughed. "You're a fast learner. Hold on a moment while I pull my notes out."

She waited. She could hear the sound of a drawer opening and closing, followed by the rustling of paper.

He came back on the line. "No. I don't see anything here that could help you. The only thing I found that wasn't in the report was the thing with the barber's son."

Andi's attention perked up. "What about the barber's son?"

"It turned out to be nothing. His name is Clyde Doleski and he was nine then. He claimed he was in the back of his grandfather's barbershop sweeping up. The barbershop was three doors down from the mercantile. Anyway, he claimed he heard a loud popping noise and saw a red-haired person running past the alleyway window shortly afterwards."

"Why is that nothing? There was speculation that the killer ran out the back door."

"Yes, but even now, a couple of the town elders I talked to who knew him agreed that Clyde Doleski was one of those boys who cried wolf too often. Besides, according to old city maps, a seven-foot-high board fence separated the mercantile from the café next door. It seems Mr. Zucker didn't appreciate the sight of the café's garbage cans. The fence that high would have been difficult to climb. Clyde Doleski was a child when the murder took place. I poked around a little to see if anything in his story might have merit but it didn't amount to anything. He was just a kid looking to get a little attention."

"Oh." Andi typed Clyde's name into her notes as she tried to think of something else that might help her. When nothing else came to mind, she thanked him for his assistance and hung up.

Andi was going over her notes when her cell phone rang. It was the realtor, Linda Ramos. Andi listened in disappointment as Linda explained she was preparing to leave for a conference and would be unavailable for the next two days. But after getting an idea of what Andi was looking for in her home, she promised to fax her some spec sheets that Andi could review.

"If you find anything of interest, you may want to drive by and take a look around the neighborhood," Linda said. "If you like what you see, give my office a call and tell the receptionist to set up a time to view the house. I'll call you when I get back Friday and we can talk more then."

Andi gave her father's fax number and thanked her. Before she could put the phone down, it rang again. The Caller ID display read Hogan Enterprises. Andi recognized the name of a mega-million-dollar cable company that had moved into South Texas and gobbled up many of the smaller businesses. She had sent her résumé to them.

She answered the phone and listened as an impersonal recorded voice informed her she had been scheduled for a preliminary interview for the following week. The mechanical voice instructed her to press one if she would be attending, two if she wished to be rescheduled or three if she no longer wished to be considered a candidate for employment.

Andi lowered the phone from her ear and placed her finger over the number one, but hesitated. What kind of company used a recording to schedule their interviews? *Is this the sort of company I want to work for?* she thought. Pushing away the nagging voice telling her that any job was better than no job, she quickly pressed three and disconnected. She sat staring at the phone for several minutes trying to understand her decision to remove her name from consideration. She finally gave up and gathered her camera equipment and several rolls of film. After leaving a note informing her mom she wouldn't be home for dinner, Andi headed downtown to spend the rest of the day and early evening capturing shots along the Riverwalk.

Chapter Seventeen

By midmorning on Wednesday, Andi was parking her car in the small lot beside the HiHo courthouse. The district attorney's office was located behind the courthouse on State Street. This part of town was in much better condition than the area on the opposite side of the courthouse. Here the buildings were occupied and well maintained.

The sun shone brightly with promises of a beautiful day. She walked around the courthouse observing the handsome dome and intricate details in the carvings gracing the arches that were located around the building. Since her grandmother was occupied with the computer course, Andi had a little breathing room to explore on her own. She stopped beneath the hanging tree her grandmother had pointed out to her on their previous visit. A chill swept over her as she stared up at the massive branches. *Hanging would be a horrible way to die*, she thought as her hand went to her throat.

"It would make me think twice before I committed a crime."

Andi turned to the voice. A tall woman with reddish golden hair that glowed in the sunlight stood gazing at her. She had an enormous book bag over her shoulder and held a large stack of folders in her arms.

"The way you were standing there clutching your throat made me wonder if you were anticipating embarking on a crime spree." She tilted her head to one side and gave Andi a dazzling, teasing smile.

"Well, if I were planning to, I'd do it someplace other than Texas," Andi replied.

"Wise woman." She shifted the folders and extended her hand to Andi. "I'm Janice Reed."

Andi found her hand being clasped in a firm but gentle manner. "Andrea Kane."

"Are you a new member of our little paradise or one of the hundreds who pass through on their way to the coast?" Janice asked.

"I'm sort of here on business. I was on my way to the district attorney's office."

Janice studied her for a moment. "If you're ready, I'll show you the way. I was headed there myself." They started walking. "I don't remember your name on my list of appointments this morning, so I'm assuming you weren't coming to see me."

When Andi glanced up, Janice seemed to be studying her.

"I'm the district attorney," she said.

"Oh, sorry. I didn't know your name and I don't have an appointment."

Janice nodded toward an office building. "In that case, you have as much time as it takes us to walk to that green-trimmed building, but afterward I have back-to-back meetings and court appearances, so you'd better talk fast."

Andi took a second to gather her thoughts and began. "My great-grandfather was convicted of murder in nineteen thirty-nine, and my grandmother is absolutely positive he's innocent. She's asked me to try and prove his innocence." Andi frowned. Her explanation hadn't sounded as forceful and positive as she had intended it to, and she felt silly.

"Was he convicted here in HiHo?" Janice asked.

"Yes. He was sentenced to life at Huntsville, but he died two years later."

Janice made a small noise of condolence and sighed. "Andrea . . ."

"Please, call me Andi. My mother is the only person who calls me Andrea."

"All right. Andi, I don't mean to sound harsh or to minimize your family's pain, but family members rarely believe their loved one is capable of committing a violent crime."

Andi kept quiet. James Timmerman, the private investigator, had told her the same thing.

"If your great-grandfather was found guilty, there was obviously some compelling evidence against him. Who was the murder victim?"

"George Zucker. He ran a mercantile."

Janice shook her head. "I'm sorry, I'm not much of a history buff. I'm vaguely familiar with the murder, but that's only because, thankfully, there haven't been that many in our area. I don't know any of the details."

"Could I get a copy of the trial transcripts and the police report?" Andi asked.

"Records that old would already be archived and stored in the old jailhouse. I don't have the manpower to send someone over there and dig around until they find them. To be perfectly honest, the files weren't stored in an organized manner. When the district attorney's office moved to this building seven years ago, there wasn't enough room to bring all the old case files. So they were packed away in boxes, loaded onto a truck and taken to the old jail. They've been sitting there untouched ever since. It could take hours to find your great-grandfather's records."

"Could I look for them?"

"No. I couldn't allow you to do that. Some of those files contain sensitive information. If the citizens of the county found out I was letting you dig around in there, they'd boot me out of office before the sun went down and, as hairy as it gets sometimes, I have to admit that I love this job." She looked at Andi and smiled.

They arrived at the door of the district attorney's office. Janice juggled the folders around. Andi quickly reached across her and opened the door. For the briefest moment, their gazes locked and held. "This is really important to my grandmother."

Janice nodded and pushed through the doorway. "Betty," she called out. "This is Andi Kane. Please make her an appointment to see me as soon as possible." Janice turned back to Andi. "If, and that's a big if, I get time, I'll poke around and see what I can find out about your great-grandfather. Give Betty all the information, especially names and dates. But I'm warning you ahead of time, if he was convicted, there's a ninety-nine-point-nine percent chance he was guilty." She started to walk away.

"If you're so sure, why would you even bother to look into it?" Andi asked.

Janice stopped and gave her another dazzling smile. "Because I have a hunch about you and I always play my hunches." Without waiting for Andi's response, she turned and disappeared down a hallway.

Andi's face grew warm as she stared after Janice. Had she been insinuating what Andi thought she had? She replayed the comment and shook her head. *Of course not. This is a small town. Even if Janice is gay, she certainly wouldn't advertise it so blatantly.*

"Ms. Kane."

Embarrassed, Andi realized the receptionist had been calling her name. With a last glance toward the hallway where Janice disappeared, Andi turned her attention to the receptionist. "If you could give me the information."

Andi quickly gave her the names and dates she could remember from the newspaper articles.

After writing Andi's information down, the receptionist turned to her computer. "How about Friday morning at eleven?"

Andi tried not to groan. It looked as though the road to HiHo was going to become extremely familiar to her. "There's no way I could see her later today?" she asked.

The receptionist glanced at her computer screen. "No, I'm sorry. She's booked solid today and tomorrow. And I really should warn you. If there's any kind of problems over at the jail or courthouse, she may have to cancel this appointment. We recently lost one of our assistant DAs, and as you can imagine, things can get rather hectic."

Andi couldn't imagine. She was about to issue a smart remark about the probability of a town so small being plagued by a crime spree. As she opened her mouth, it suddenly struck her that she was there to discuss a murder, and she had met Janice Reed standing beneath the hanging tree. She swallowed her witticism and waited for the appointment card the receptionist was writing out.

"I understand you have a historical society," Andi said.

"Oh, no. That dissolved several years ago. People are too busy now to worry about the past. It makes me sad to think that it'll all be lost and forgotten."

Andi nodded, but there were some things that were better forgotten.

"If you're interested in our local history, you should go see Rhonda Younger. She's our unofficial historian." She handed the appointment card to Andi.

"Where would I find her?" Andi slid the card into the hip pocket of her jeans. Since today was Wednesday and the appointment was for Friday, she wasn't likely to forget it.

"Over at the *HiHo News*. She's the editor. Let me tell you, she took this town by storm. First woman editor we ever had, but everyone agrees she's ten times better than what we had before. The paper is never late and it has honest-to-God news."

Andi smiled and glanced at the nameplate on the desk. "Betty, thank you for all your help and information. Maybe I'll drop by and talk to Rhonda."

"Well, you just tell her Betty sent you over. If you're lucky, she'll have a plate of those sand dollar cookies she makes. That woman makes the best cookies."

Andi thanked her and made a quick exit before Betty could find another tangent to take off on. It wasn't until she left the office that she realized she had no idea where the *HiHo News* was located. She walked to the corner and stood letting the warmth of the sun embrace her. She took a deep breath. The air seemed cleaner, crisper here, or maybe it was just her imagination. She suddenly realized there were very few cars driving around. Maybe the air was cleaner.

"Can I help you find something?"

Andi turned and discovered a tiny woman with dark curious eyes squinting up at her. A dog leash dangled, almost as an afterthought, in her small work-roughened hand. At the other end of the leash was the largest black poodle Andi had ever seen. An abundance of gray sparkled from its muzzle, and judging by its eyes, the poor dog was almost blind.

Andi remembered her manners and nodded. "Good morning. Yes. In fact, I'm looking for the office of the *HiHo News.*"

"I'm Maudie Anderson, but the paper won't be out until tomorrow. Paper always comes out on Thursday, and by now there won't be any copies of last week's paper left. They go like that." With the fingers of her free hand she produced a loud snap that made the dog's head fly up.

Andi laughed at the dog's reaction.

"Oh, sorry, Ellie." Maudie patted the dog's head. "She thought I was calling her for her treat. Strangest thing. I can call her and call her and she ignores me, but I snap my fingers and she comes running. Just like my late husband." Maudie burst into laughter.

Andi found herself laughing with her. "I'm not needing a paper," Andi explained. "I want to talk to the editor," she said as soon as Maudie settled down.

"What for?"

Andi blinked in surprise. "Uh. Well, um, I understand she's the local historian."

"Historian." Maudie blew a loud raspberry.

At a loss for what to say or do, Andi did nothing.

"How can someone that young be a historian?" Maudie began walking, and short of being rude, Andi had no choice but to follow. "Me and Ellie, we could be historians. We've been around so long we *are* the history. Right, girl?" She patted the dog's head again. "Why would you be needing a historian?" She peered up at Andi.

"I'm curious about the local history. HiHo is a beautiful town and I'd like to know more about it." Andi edged around the woman's question as she distractedly watched a large man wearing coveralls that announced he worked for City Public Service dash to the other side of the street.

"Well, ask me. I'll tell you whatever you need to know."

Andi hesitated.

"Well, speak up, girl, I can't tell you if you don't ask."

"All right. Do you know where Ignacio Acosta or Clyde Doleski live?"

Maudie's spindly arms flashed through the air. Luckily for Ellie, the leash had plenty of slack in it. "Do I look like a city directory? Ask me history questions."

Andi struggled to find a question that involved history. She didn't want to get into a discussion about her great-grandfather with Maudie Anderson. As she fumbled around for a question to ask, she saw a young woman approaching them suddenly turn and dart in the opposite direction.

"Jera May," Maudie shouted. "I know you saw me, girl. You get on over here."

The young woman seemed to cringe but did as ordered. As she slowly made her way toward them, Maudie began to shake her head.

"What's become of kids today? No respect. No respect, I'm telling you. I know her mama taught her better." As the young woman drew closer, Maudie directed her lecture to Jera May. "Why'd you turn around and run off like that when you saw me coming, girl? I should tell your mama."

"I'm sorry, Grandma, but I just remembered that I think I forgot to turn off the coffeepot. I was going to run back home to check on it."

Maudie gave a loud snort. "Now, let me see. In the last few weeks, you've forgotten the stove, the toaster plugged in, the door unlocked, the car lights on, and now the coffeepot. If I didn't know better, I'd think you were getting senile."

Andi shuffled uncomfortably and glanced around. On the corner, she saw her beacon of rescue, a large red and white sign announcing the building to be home of the *HiHo News*. When Maudie took a breath, Andi jumped in. "Maudie, thank you so much for showing me the way to the newspaper office. I hope I see you again before I leave." She patted Ellie's head and gave a quick sympathetic nod to the young woman before escaping across the street.

"You never did ask me a history question," Maudie yelled after her. "I can tell you more than that youngster."

Andi waved an acknowledgment but didn't slow down.

Chapter Eighteen

Safely inside the newspaper office, Andi peered through the window until she was sure Maudie wasn't following her. She turned and was greeted with a round of applause.

A sturdy woman dressed in a blue and gray checkered flannel shirt and jeans stood at the end of the counter. Her short blond hair was swept up away from her face. From where she was standing, she would've been able to witness Andi's less than gracious exit.

"I see you had a successful escape from the clutches of Ms. Maudie."

Andi smiled and nodded. "She's quite a character."

A long walnut counter connected to a matching railing that portioned off a small front entrance. Beyond the railing were three desks; each held a large computer screen. Shelves filled with various-size boxes ran along two of the walls. A partially closed door indicated another room at the rear of the building. From that room came a thin off-key voice struggling to sing along with a country song.

The woman behind the railing stepped around and opened the gate before extending her hand to Andi. "I'm Rhonda Younger. What can I do for you?"

Andi stepped forward to shake hands and introduced herself. The old wooden floor creaked beneath her feet. As the woman drew closer, the first thing Andi noticed about her was the deep laugh lines and several unhidden squint lines. She guessed the woman to be in her early to mid fifties. Her second observation was that the woman was probably a lesbian. "The receptionist"— Andi struggled to remember her name—"Betty from the district attorney's office told me you're the town's unofficial historian."

Rhonda chuckled. "I don't know if I qualify as a historian, but I'm a bit of history buff, and thanks to the previous owners' having the foresight to maintain a complete archive of the *HiHo News*, I have a pretty good source of reference material. What did you need?"

"It's kind of a long story. Do you have time?"

Rhonda pinched her lip. "If you don't mind talking while I work on some last-minute adjustments to this week's layout. I just received word that the wedding for the future Mr. and Mrs. Ronald Enge has been canceled. This week's issue is scheduled to run tonight, and I need to remove the congratulatory insert for the couple and find something to fill that spot."

It was Andi's turn to chuckle. "I'm starting to think that HiHo's serene appearance is a façade."

"Most definitely. You're now in a hotbed of political and sexual intrigue. HiHo is actually an acronym for High Hollywood. Come on back." Rhonda opened the gate wider and motioned Andi to follow.

The voice in the back hit a particularly flat note and Andi flinched.

"Don't mind Kenny. If he's singing I know he's working." Rhonda picked up a wooden desk chair and carried it back with her. She placed the chair next to an old battered walnut desk. "Have a seat." She went back to the open door. "Kenny, we have a customer, so I'm going to close the door. Yell if you need me."

The musical screeching halted long enough to return an affirmative reply. Rhonda closed the door before returning to the desk and sitting down.

On the desk was an enormous computer screen, a keyboard and a small pile of papers. Beside the screen was an eight-by-ten photo of Rhonda with her arm around another woman. If she saw Andi scrutinizing the photo, she gave no indication.

"I grew up in a household of seven kids so don't worry about distracting me," Rhonda said as she turned to her keyboard. "I can work on the paper, interview a political candidate, eat lunch and plan my weekend all at the same time." She winked playfully at Andi and started clicking away on the keyboard. "So what did you need to know?"

Andi found the clacking of the keys distracting. Rhonda might be able to multitask, but she preferred to handle one thing at a time.

Rhonda seemed to sense her hesitation but misinterpreted the cause. "It's okay. You won't distract me," she assured her.

Andi started slowly. She told Rhonda about her grandmother's call, discovering her great-grandfather had died a convicted murderer, and the old newspaper clippings. She mentioned talking to James Timmerman and learning about Ignacio Acosta and Clyde Doleski. When she reached the part about George Zucker's murder, Rhonda stopped typing and gave Andi her full attention. When Andi finished her story, Rhonda leaned back in the chair so far that Andi began to fear it would flip over.

"Wow," Rhonda said as she let the chair swing upright. "Your grandmother wants you to clear your great-grandfather's name by solving a murder case that's over sixty years old." She idly scratched her chin. "What are you going to do?"

Andi shrugged. "I thought I'd talk to Mr. Acosta and Mr.

Doleski. Maybe they'll remember something that'll give me a clue as to where to look."

Rhonda shook her head. "I hate to be negative, but you don't have a snowball's chance in hell of solving this after all these years."

A streak of stubbornness shot through Andi. She was about to protest when Rhonda took the starch out of her argument.

"Do you think he's innocent?"

Honesty made Andi want to say no, but loyalty to her grandmother won out. "My grandmother thinks he is and that's enough to make me pursue this."

Rhonda pinched her lip between her thumb and forefinger again. "What can I do to help?" She held out her hands in surrender. "Hey, history and a mystery, it doesn't get any better."

"I need to talk to those two men. I hoped I might be able to pick your brain about anyone else who might have been living here then and is still living today. And if you have any ideas on any other avenues I can explore, I'd certainly be interested in hearing them."

Rhonda grabbed a calculator and began punching in numbers. For a moment, Andi thought she had gone back to her multitasking. "You'll be looking for people over the age of seventy and who lived here in nineteen thirty-nine. I don't think we have to concern ourselves about anyone who was under the age of six when this happened. I can check the archives to see if there are other articles regarding the murder, but whoever saved the articles you have would've probably saved everything that was written." Rhonda pushed the calculator away and turned to Andi. "As for who lived here then, I'd have to do some digging. I moved here about fifteen years ago. I was living in Austin and working for the paper there when I heard through a friend of a friend that the paper here was about to close. I was ready for a chance to stretch my wings, so I called up the owner and the rest is history." She jumped up and returned with a thick hardbound book. "Here are the city directories for the nineteen thirties." Reaching into her desk, she retrieved a much smaller one. "This is the current city directory.

I'm sorry we don't have them on microfiche, but money is always an issue."

Andi groaned.

"It's not as bad as it looks. All you would need to do is compare the old directory to the current one." She placed the books on the desk in front of Andi. "That's the hard way. Now let's figure out an easier way." She sat back down and began spinning the pen again. "There's tax records and voting records, but if the person was underage then those are useless. Birth records won't help because you'd have to check each one to see if they were still alive and living here then." She spun the pen a few more times and stopped. "Before you waste several hours manually cross-referencing these" —she tapped the city directories—"you should start by talking to those two guys. They should know who's still living. If that doesn't work, come on back and I'll let you borrow the directories."

Rhonda grabbed a thin phone book and began flipping through it. "Here's the addresses for Iggy Acosta and Clyde Doleski." She jotted the numbers on a notepad before continuing. "I don't know too much about either of them. Iggy is something of a small-town hero. He joined the Army, fought in World War Two and Korea, and was decorated for bravery in both. He did his thirty years and moved back here with his family." She swung the chair back to face Andi. "Clyde Doleski I only know by sight. I seem to remember hearing that he went to New York or California as a young man and moved back here after he retired." She ripped the paper from the pad and began drawing a series of lines on the back of the paper. "Here's a crude map to help you find them." She held out the paper to Andi. "I don't feel like I was much help, but maybe you'll be able to find something of use."

"Thanks, you've been a big help." Andi reached out to shake her hand.

"If those don't pan out, you can always call Maudie."

Andi laughed. "I actually kind of liked her," she admitted.

Rhonda smiled. "Good, because you should. Maudie is a softie at heart. Actually, she probably couldn't help you. I don't think she moved to HiHo until the late fifties. I'll tell you a secret if you swear you'll never repeat it." She waited until Andi nodded. "Every December, Maudie slips an envelope under the shop's front door. Inside are five crisp twenty-dollar bills and a note instructing me to use the money to buy gifts for the children's home over in Dugan."

"Why doesn't she just give the money to the home?" Andi asked.

Rhonda looked down at her desk.

Andi didn't think she was going to answer the question at first, but Rhonda finally looked up. "Because she grew up there and doesn't trust the caretakers to use the money for the kids."

Andi nodded and folded the paper with the addresses and slipped it into her pocket. As they walked toward the front of the shop, Andi saw Maudie standing on the corner patting Ellie's head.

"What are you going to do first?" Rhonda asked.

Andi stared out the window at the old woman and her dog for several seconds before replying. "I'm hungry. I think I'll go see if Ms. Maudie and Ellie would like to join me for lunch."

Chapter Nineteen

After lunch with Maudie, Andi called Ignacio Acosta only to learn from his granddaughter that he had gone to Baytown and wouldn't be back until Saturday. She tried Clyde Doleski next, but no one answered. As the phone continued to ring, it became obvious there was no voice mail. With no further leads to follow and no one else to talk to, she drove back to San Antonio empty-handed.

It was almost four when she returned to her parents' house. The house was quiet. As she walked down the hallway to her room it struck her that she now considered this her parents' house. When had it stopped being her house? It would always be home to her, but there was a subtle difference in the way she felt here. Remembering that Linda Ramos had promised to fax the spec sheets for potential houses, Andi went back to her father's office. A stack of about eighteen spec sheets from Linda were on the fax machine. With a new wave of determination, she spent the next hour in her room going over the sheets. Some she ruled out imme-diately; these she pitched into the trash. She placed the listings she classified as "weak maybes" in one stack and the "strong maybes" in another.

At some point during this time, she was vaguely aware of the sound of her mother's car entering the garage. Her father would be home later and would park in the driveway. The arrangement worked well for them because he always came home later and left earlier.

She continued systemically wading through the options of each house. After going through the sheets several times, she narrowed her choices down to five. She would discuss these with her parents over dinner.

Andi heard her mother moving about the house. She would be starting dinner soon. Andi quickly typed in the new information on Ignacio Acosta and Clyde Doleski. Her worksheet was not pro-gressing as she had hoped. Disgusted, she turned the laptop off and went to help her mother with dinner.

"There you are," Leticia called as Andi walked into the kitchen.

"What can I do to help?"

"Actually, you and I are on our own tonight. Mom's going somewhere with Mrs. Salazar and Andrew has dinner plans with a client. What do you feel like?"

"I'm not very hungry," Andi admitted.

"Are you sick?"

Andi laughed. "No, Mom, I'm not sick. I just pigged out at lunch."

"Oh, where did you eat?"

"At the Blue Moon."

Leticia tilted her head in concentration. "The Blue Moon. I don't think I've ever heard of it."

Andi barely suppressed a groan. *Why do I always do that?* she screamed in silence. "It's a greasy spoon, you wouldn't like it."

Leticia shuddered. "You're right, never mind."

Knowing she had barely scraped by, Andi quickly changed the

subject. "Linda Ramos faxed me some spec sheet for houses and a few of them look pretty good. I thought that maybe you and Dad could look over them with me. It's been a while since I've lived in San Antonio and I'm sure things have changed some."

Leticia gave a small clap. It was an image from Andi's childhood. Anytime her mother got excited about something, she would give a small clap. "I can prepare us a salad and we can look over the listings. If you still have questions about an area, you can ask your father when he gets home."

After discussing the neighborhoods and prices with her mother, she discarded two more. Later that evening, after returning to her room, she consulted a city map to pinpoint the exact location of each home. She planned to drive by each of them before calling Linda Ramos back.

Before going to bed, she checked her e-mail. There were no responses to her résumés. As she crawled into bed, she felt a tiny trickle of dread. What if the interview she turned down was the only one she would receive? She thought about the cold, disembodied voice that had made the interview offer and her stomach unclenched. She made up her mind to hang tough and not to settle for just any job. *My next job will be fun and rewarding*, she promised herself as she drifted off to sleep.

The following morning, Andi left the house shortly before nine. After carefully reviewing the directions she had written out, she drove to the first house on the list. She decided to look at them in location order rather than in preference order. The first house was only about five miles from her parents'. It was a newer two-story modern that had absolutely no character on the outside but was loaded with amenities inside. A drive through the neighborhood revealed that it was made up of several young families.

Basketball hoops attached to metal poles seated in old tires filled with cement sat in many of the driveways. An occasional opened gate allowed her to peek into backyards filled with a variety of play sets and discarded toys. She was looking for something more peaceful. She marked the house off her list before heading to the second one.

This one looked promising. It was a beautiful older Victorian. The house was painted sky blue with dazzling white trim. Roses ran over an arbor beside the house. A major drawback quickly appeared in the number of FOR SALE or FOR RENT signs in the yards of several of the houses in the surrounding blocks. The neighborhood was in transition and she had no way of knowing which way it would go. With some regret, she marked the house off her list.

She rejected the third house immediately. It was located in the middle of a floodplain. Watermarks from the last flood were still visible around the base of the house.

Disappointed with the waste of time, Andi called Linda Ramos's office and left a message with what she hoped would be clearer instructions on what she was looking for. She wasn't going to rush through this. She intended to purchase the home she wanted. She always took the easy route and compromised, but this time she wanted to do it right.

As she drove home, she decided to take a detour and swing by the main library to see if she could find anything in the San Antonio newspaper archives about Sean Gray's trial.

With the help of a research assistant, Andi was able to locate two small articles about the trial; neither gave her any new information. As she was returning the last reel, she noticed that the library also carried copies of the *HiHo News*. She pulled the two reels for 1939. There were several smaller articles on the murder and the trial, but they failed to yield any new leads.

She was returning the last reel to its box when the research assistant who had helped her earlier walked by and noticed the name of the newspaper.

"We have paper copies for the last two years if you'd like to look through them," he told her.

Andi started to decline, but on a whim, she requested them. She started with the oldest issues and worked forward.

She found a July Fourth special edition that honored the men and women of HiHo who had served in the military. One was a grainy black and white photo of Ignacio Acosta surrounded by his large family. She squinted at the poorly reproduced image and tried to make out his features, but the photo was too grainy.

As she continued to flip through the paper she found an article that described Janice Reed's successful bid for a third consecutive term as district attorney. There was a large photo of Janice waving at the voters. The comprehensive article told how Janice's great-great-grandfather Clayton Mabry had settled in HiHo in 1859. After distinguishing himself in the Civil War, Clayton Mabry returned to his small claim in Texas, joined the Texas Rangers and eventually served as a county judge. The article went on to highlight the successful lives of Clayton's descendants. Andi was about to set the article aside when she noticed a paragraph that simply mentioned that Janice's parents had died in an automobile accident. Andi left the paper opened to Janice's photo and went to search through the microfiche that would cover the date of the accident.

It took her almost an hour to wade back through the microfiche reels and locate the article related to the horrible traffic accident that killed Roger Reed and his wife, the former Amelia Ann Mabry. The accident left their two-month-old daughter an orphan. A drunk driver had crossed the center line and hit the young couple head-on as they were returning from a Christmas party in San Antonio. The drunk driver walked away without a scratch. He received a three-year probated sentence for his carelessness.

Saddened by Janice's loss, Andi stared at the photo taken after Janice won reelection. Was there a touch of sadness in her large luminous eyes? she wondered.

"She's a looker, isn't she?"

Startled, Andi glanced up to find the research assistant peering over her shoulder. His intrusion caused a stab of irritation. She was about to remark when he continued. "Too bad she's gay. What a waste."

Andi stared at Janice's photo. "She's not gay," she said without conviction. She was remembering the comment Janice had made.

He sighed as if educating her was causing him great stress. "Go back and read the articles before the election. She admits it."

Andi must have looked as though she doubted his sanity because he flounced off in a huff. It took her several minutes to find the article, but it was true. Janice Reed had proclaimed her sexual orientation to the entire county, and apparently the majority of the citizens didn't care, because she had won the election with a resounding majority.

Andi picked up the paper with the photo and gazed at it closer. Janice Reed wasn't a classic beauty, but something about her hinted that she was a person who got what she wanted. Her eyes portrayed a sense of strong determination that was only slightly tempered by her faint teasing smile.

As Andi studied the photo, she found herself smiling and looking forward to their appointment the following day.

Chapter Twenty

Eager to get started, Andi arrived ten minutes early for her Friday-morning meeting with Janice Reed. She used the few extra minutes to rehearse her plea. She didn't want to sound like this was some frivolous way to pass time while she waited to be called for a job. *But isn't that what it is?* she wondered. *I wouldn't be doing this if I were still employed in my profession.*

At exactly eleven, the intercom on Betty's desk buzzed. "You can go on back now," Betty called from her desk. "Her office is the second door on the left."

Andi nodded and thanked her. As she walked down the corridor, she caught herself checking her hair and tucking in her blouse a little neater. To her horror, she realized she was primping. She had never primped for anyone in her life. As she knocked on the door, she tried to tell herself that she just wanted to make a good impression for her grandmother's sake. It had nothing to do with the fact that Janice Reed was attractive, or that Andi wouldn't mind getting to know her better.

Rather than calling out permission to enter, Janice opened the door herself. As the door swung open, Andi found herself immersed in a gentle cloud of fragrance. She tried to pinpoint the comforting smell, but it eluded her.

"You're still on the case, huh?" Janice asked without preamble.

Thrown off by the lack of greeting, and desperately trying to ignore the enticing scent that kept vying for her attention, Andi mumbled some inane greeting. Feeling like an imbecile, she tried to respond in an intelligent manner, but her brain froze. Suddenly, she was in the fourth grade again, standing in front of the class. She was supposed to be reciting a poem. One that she had been practicing for days and had recited beautifully for her parents the night before, but the minute she stepped to the front of the class-room, all of her careful preparations flew right out the window. As her discomfort escalated to sheer terror, she began to babble uncontrollably. She said whatever came to mind and was completely helpless to stop. The teacher finally sent her to the principal's office and her mother was called to come and pick her up. To this day, Andi wasn't completely sure what she'd said, but it took her several days to live down the humiliating experience in school, and she had ended the class with the only C of all her educational endeavors.

"Are you all right?" Janice was leaning toward her.

"Lavender," Andi blurted. "You smell like my mother." *Oh, my God.* Andi cringed. *Did I really say she smelled like my mother, aloud? Oh, this is so sick.* "I'm sorry. Of course you don't smell like my mother. Because I would never be attracted to someone who smells like my mother." Andi clasped a hand over her mouth to stop its blabbering.

Janice stepped back, clearly startled, but quickly regained her composure and smiled. "Well, I'm glad you're attracted to me, and since you're being so honest, I'll admit that I was attracted to you when I first saw you standing beneath the hanging tree."

Andi felt her face flood with embarrassment. She was on the verge of turning and fleeing when to her surprise Janice turned and walked back into her office.

Janice sat on the corner of her desk. "Would you like to forget any of this happened and start this meeting over from the beginning?"

Andi nodded and attempted to meet Janice's gaze. As she looked into the pale blue eyes, she felt a sense of comfort and peace descend over her. "Could we, please?"

Janice nodded, walked back to the door and closed it.

It wasn't until the door closed that Andi realized she was still standing in the hallway. She glanced quickly toward Betty's desk and was relieved to discover Betty wouldn't have been able to see them.

"You'll have to knock. I don't know you're out there," Janice called softly from the other side of the door.

Andi smiled. "Knock, knock."

"Who's there?"

"Ima."

"Ima who?"

"I'm a feeling like a fool out here."

Janice opened the door and smiled. "I like a person with a sense of humor. I don't see much humor in my profession." She stepped back and waved Andi into her office. "Please come in and have a seat. Would you like something to drink?"

Andi declined the drink and sat in one of the two matching upholstered chairs in front of Janice's rather plain government-issued metal desk.

The minute Janice was seated behind the desk she became all business. "Now, what can I do for you?"

"I really need to see the trial transcripts and the police records for Sean Gray," Andi reminded her.

Janice shook her head. "As I told you before, that's impossible. I don't have the manpower to search for those records."

Andi started to protest, but Janice held up a hand to stop her.

"I can't allow you in there, but if you can provide me with a compelling enough reason as to why you believe your grandfather—"

"Great-grandfather," Andi corrected.

"Sorry. Your great-grandfather was innocent, I'll reopen the case myself."

Andi's carefully prepared argument died in her throat. "You will?"

"Yes. Andi, it would be terribly disturbing to me to discover that someone has been unjustly punished. I'm not here to hurt innocent people. My job is to put the guilty behind bars."

Andi's moment of excitement quickly faded. "But how am I going to find a compelling reason if I can't view the police report or the trial transcripts?"

"What makes you so sure there's something in those records that will clear his name? Do you know of something in particular?"

Andi shook her head in defeat. She didn't want to admit that the records were no more than a drowning man grasping at a straw.

"Tell me what you discovered that convinced you of his innocence."

Andi focused her attention on the bookcase that filled the wall behind Janice's head. "I don't have anything physical. It's just that . . . that . . . he told my grandmother he was innocent." She waited for the laughter that was sure to escort her from Janice's office. Instead, she heard only a small sigh.

"How old was your grandmother when all this happened?"

"She was ten when he was convicted and twelve when he died." Andi wondered how many times she had answered these questions in the last five days.

"It must have been rough on her to lose her father so young."

Andi glanced up. Janice had lost both of her parents at a much younger age.

"Don't you think it's more likely that your great-grandfather lied to her? Thinking he was protecting her."

"I guess it's possible."

"Do you think he's innocent?" Janice asked.

Andi hesitated a fraction too long.

"I think it's wonderful that you're going to so much effort to help your grandmother."

A knock at the door interrupted them. "Yes," Janice called out.

Betty opened the door and poked her head in. "Judge Crammer's office just called. The jury is back."

Janice glanced at her watch and smiled. "Already. Maybe this is going to turn into a really good day." She looked at Andi. "I have to go. Hopefully, I'm about to nail a wife-beater." She looked back to Betty. "Tell them I'm on my way."

As soon as the door closed, Janice stood. "I'm sorry I couldn't help you. I know it's little consolation, but despite what a lot of the more sensational news reporters would like the world to think, it's rare that an innocent person is convicted."

"But it does happen," Andi protested, more for her grandmother's sake than her own.

"Yes, it does occasionally, and as I said, you give a compelling reason and I'll do my best to set things right." She grabbed a card from her desk and began writing on the back. "Here's my card. I've written my home and cell numbers on the back. If you find something, give me a call." She stopped and looked up, smiling. "Or you could just call me sometime." She handed the card to Andi. "Now, if you'll excuse me, I have to run."

And run she did. Seconds after Andi left her office, Janice Reed left the DA's office from a rear door. Andi watched her as she ran across the back parking lot to the courthouse.

Andi decided to stop by the *HiHo News* to see Rhonda. She had enjoyed their previous conversation. Maybe she would have some suggestions as to how Andi should proceed. As she walked the two blocks, she knew that no matter what happened, for her grandmother, losing her father could never be set right.

Chapter Twenty-one

"Hey, it's the private investigator," Rhonda called out as Andi stepped into the shop. "How's the investigation going?"

Andi grimaced. "I don't think I should quit my day job." She shrugged. "Well, if I had a day job, I wouldn't quit it anyway."

"Come on back. We were just about to send out for lunch."

Andi saw a young man with long brown hair and a gangly young girl standing around Rhonda's desk. "I didn't mean to interrupt. I was in town and thought I'd drop by to see you."

"You're not interrupting. This is our weekly celebratory lunch. Every Friday we celebrate the completion of yet another issue of the paper. Do you like pepperoni and mushrooms? That's our poison of the day."

Andi nodded and opened the gate on the walnut railing. "I've never met a pizza I didn't like," she teased.

"Good." Rhonda handed the young man some bills. He and the girl nodded as they walked past Andi and disappeared out the front door.

"They're a little short on manners, but they're both good workers," Rhonda said. "Kenny works miracles on that old press."

"The girl looks young," Andi said.

"She is. She works here during the afternoons as part of a school program. She gets extra credits for work experience and I get an additional pair of hands that I couldn't afford otherwise." She nodded to a chair. "Have a seat and tell me what you've managed to uncover. They'll be back soon."

Andi sat down. "I don't know anymore than I did. Mr. Acosta is out of town until sometime tomorrow and I couldn't reach Mr. Doleski. I did finally manage to talk to Janice Reed."

Rhonda leaned back in her chair and smiled. "What did you think of our fine DA?"

Andi blushed as she recalled her humiliating outburst. "I kind of made a of fool of myself."

Rhonda sat quietly.

Andi glanced at the photo that she had seen on her last visit, the one of Rhonda with her arm around the other woman.

Rhonda followed her gaze. "That's Carol, my partner. We've been together eighteen years."

"Congratulations."

"What happened with Janice?"

Andi told her about her awkward outburst.

"Ouch. What did she say?"

Andi swallowed her embarrassment and hesitantly repeated Janice's cavalier admission that she had been attracted to her when they first met.

Rhonda's chair popped forward. "Janice Reed actually admitted that she was attracted to you?" she asked, her eyes wide with astonishment.

Andi nodded.

Rhonda stared at her. "Wow," she whispered.

"What?" Andi asked.

Rhonda picked up her pen and began to spin it on the desk. She glanced back at Andi. "I probably shouldn't be telling you this, but since practically everyone in town already knows, I guess it doesn't matter. Janice had been an Assistant DA for several years when she decided to run for the DA's position about six years ago. Her opponent, the current DA then, began to play hardball. He started hinting there was something about Janice that he would reveal at an open forum. It seems Janice had come out to him when she began her career in his office. She told me that she wanted everything to be aboveboard with him. He was going to use that against her, but Janice beat him to the punch and made a public announcement that she was gay."

"Pretty smart move on her part," Andi said with a small nod of approval.

Rhonda set the pen down and leaned forward, putting her elbows on her knees. "I'm telling you, I really thought her career was over, but I underestimated the people in this county. Now, don't get me wrong. There was some major fallout, but she never gave in. She put her record out there and let it speak for itself. In the end, she lost a few voters, but she gained a lot more."

"How?" Andi asked.

"People decided her record of convictions was more important than what she did in private, and that since she was honest about her sexuality, she'd make an honest DA. This was something the town had been lacking before Janice, and I'd imagine her grandfather's reputation helped her some. The town loves that old man."

"Why is he so special?"

"He spent his whole life trying to make things better here in HiHo. He was instrumental in getting new programs introduced at the school. When the hospital threatened to close its doors and move on to greener pastures, he convinced them to stay. The state tried to put one of those low-security prisons at the edge of town, and the old man hopped in his car and was sitting on the governor's doorstep when he arrived the following morning."

"It sounds like he's pretty powerful."

Rhonda shook her head. "Not in the normal sense. He never seemed to be loaded down with money or an army of high-level friends. Although his family has been here for almost as long as the town." Rhonda rubbed a finger along her chin. "It's almost as if he was driven to improve things."

"You keep saying *was*. Is he dead?"

"No. He had a stroke a couple of years ago, and he's paralyzed on one side. He's not doing well." She leaned back and waved a hand. "I drifted from my original story. When Janice came out, her partner Fran took off. She couldn't handle the public scrutiny. That was almost six years ago and Janice has been alone since then. So it's no small matter that Janice admitted she was attracted to you."

"I'm sure she was only being nice and trying to alleviate my embarrassment."

Rhonda chuckled. "Janice is a sweet person, but she would never have said something she didn't mean. She's way too above-board to do that. If she tells you something, you can bet on it."

Flustered, Andi looked away, but not before the soft glow warmed her cheeks.

"Did you invite her to dinner?" Rhonda asked with a teasing smile.

"No."

Rhonda leaned forward again and peered at Andi closely. "My gaydar and my investigative nose haven't malfunctioned on me, have they? I mean, you *are* gay and single, aren't you?"

Andi rolled her eyes. "Yes, I'm gay and single. But I don't know Janice well enough to invite her to dinner."

"How are you going to get to know her, if you don't invite her out?"

Uncomfortable, Andi shifted in her chair. "What if I don't want to know her better?"

Rhonda leaned back and nodded. "Well, there's that. If you don't like her."

"I didn't say I didn't like her," Andi protested.

"So, you do like her?"

Andi sighed in exasperation. "Has anyone ever told you that you can be irritating?"

"Carol tells me every day, but you must remember I'm a newspaper woman." She clasped her hands over her heart. "It's my job to dig deep to extract the tiny vulnerable kernel of truth from amidst the murky slime of lies and deceit."

Andi giggled. "I think you're more inclined to be full of bull."

Rhonda's hands fell into her lap. "Well, yes, I've been told that also. But I'll defend my current position. If Janice Reed said she was attracted to you, she meant it."

"How did you guess I was single?" Andi asked, changing the subject.

Rhonda studied her. "That one was a little tougher. I guess it's that thin hint of discontentment that hovers around you. Not exactly sad, but not exactly happy either." When Andi didn't respond, Rhonda jumped back in. "Tell me about Andi Kane. What's her story?"

Andi gave her a brief rundown on her life and ended with her breakup with Trish and the loss of her job.

"Bummer," Rhonda replied when Andi had finished. "Losing your girlfriend and your job on the same day would be a pisser."

"I miss the job more than the girlfriend, and to be honest, I don't miss the job that much."

"Ouch." Rhonda waved her hands as if to ward Andi off.

"I'm sorry," Andi said. "I guess that sounded pretty cold."

"I lived with someone like Trish for two years. Thankfully, I met Carol soon after I broke up with this woman, and she renewed my faith in women. So I understand how frightening it can be taking that first step back into dating."

"I'm not taking that step yet," Andi assured her.

"Everyone has to move at their own pace, but don't be surprised if your phone rings and it's Janice. She can be pretty relentless once she sets her mind."

"Well, I wish she would get her mind set on letting me search through those archives for my great-grandfather's files."

"I'm sure she would if she could, but you have to remember there's probably a lot of sensitive information stored with those files. You can't expect her to get excited about a case that was closed sixty-five years ago."

Andi was about to argue the point when the front door opened, and the room filled with the aroma of fresh pizza.

Chapter Twenty-two

Rejuvenated by the pizza and conversation with Rhonda, Andi left the newspaper office and headed back to her car. She dialed Clyde Doleski's number and was rewarded with a prompt answer.

She gave her name and explained that she would like to talk to him about the murder of George Zucker.

He was silent for a long moment but finally gave her directions to his house, located on the edge of town. Less than ten minutes later, Andi was knocking on the door of his small cottage-style home. She heard the soft hum of a motor just before the door opened. Mr. Doleski sat in a motorized wheelchair. He began to back the chair up the small hallway.

"Come on in," he called. "I'll have to get this thing out of the way before you can get in."

She waited until he had the chair backed away from the door before entering.

"Mr. Doleski, I'm Andrea Kane."

"I figured as much. I don't get many visitors these days." He continued to back the chair up until he was in the living room. "Have a seat." He motioned toward a large recliner that looked capable of swallowing Andi.

She perched on the edge and tried not to stare at the man in the wheelchair. She was certain he was several inches over six feet. The stroke had rendered his left arm useless. He had the shirtsleeve of his left arm pinned firmly to his shirtfront. His hand extended from the sleeve twisted and deformed.

"What's your interest in George Zucker?"

"My great-grandfather was Sean Gray."

His right hand plucked at the thin fringe of gray hair that sprouted around his head. "Sean Gray's great-granddaughter," he muttered.

"Do you remember him?"

The old man grimaced. "Ms. Kane, there haven't been many days of my life that I've not thought of Sean Gray. It's my fault he went to prison."

The wind rushed from Andi's lungs. "You killed George Zucker?"

Startled, his head shot up. "No. I didn't kill him, but because of my propensity to exaggerate, no one believed me when I told them who did kill him."

"You know who killed him?" Andi asked in a near whisper.

He nodded. "I was in the back of my granddad's barbershop and there was a loud bang. It was hard to tell, but I was pretty sure it was a gunshot. I ran out front to the shop, but Granddad scolded me and sent me back to the storeroom to finish sweeping. I'd just gotten back when I saw the top of his head as he ran past the window. I knew right then and there who it was."

Andi's excitement died. "You only saw the top of his head?"

"That's all I needed to see."

Andi ran a hand over her face. It felt hot and flushed. She wondered vaguely if she was coming down with something. "Mr. Doleski, if you only saw the top of his head, how can you be sure who you saw?"

"Like I told you, my granddad was the barber and I had been sweeping up hair in his shop since I was six. Only one person in the entire town had hair that red: Gary Wayne Mabry."

A chord sounded deep within Andi. She was certain she had heard the name recently but couldn't pinpoint where. "If you knew who it was, why didn't anyone listen to you?"

He looked down and tried to pull the pinned-up sleeve farther down over his deformed hand. "I used to make up these wild tales. I'd do stupid stuff. Like, one time at recess, I rubbed mulberry juice on my shirt and then ripped the sleeve off and tore off the buttons and waited until after the teacher rang the bell. I gave everyone time to get settled before I staggered in and told them a bear attacked me. Another time, I dropped my hat and books out by the old sinkhole, knowing some of the other kids would see them when they came along. Sure enough, MaryLou Jensen, who lived just down the road, went screaming home, telling her mama I'd fallen in the sinkhole. I hid in the woods while half the men in town turned out to try and dredge my body out of there. I guess the clincher was a few weeks before Mr. Zucker was killed, I ran to the sheriff's office and told him the bank was being robbed by a gang of armed men." He took a deep breath. "Poor old Sheriff Butler grabbed his double-barrel shotgun and almost gave himself a heart attack racing over to the bank. When the sheriff busted through the door with the bright sun shining behind him, he screamed, 'Throw your hands up.' The banker, Mr. Wyle, thought it was a holdup and fainted. The Widow Taney, who was practically blind, blame near broke Sheriff Butler's arm when she cracked him a good one with her cane." He shook his head. "That wasn't my first stunt, but it was the worst. My dad took me to the woodshed that night and gave me a whipping that I remember to this day, and a few weeks later I was shipped off to a military academy." He shook his head and stared out the window. "That was my last practical joke, but unfortunately it was already too late. No one would believe me when I said I saw Gary Wayne run past the window."

Andi nodded without comment, uncertain how much of his story she believed.

125

"I was nine years old," he continued. "My parents kept me at the academy until I graduated. Afterward I packed my bags and headed for California. I lived there until I retired, but I always remembered HiHo. Those years I spent helping my granddad in his barbershop were among the happiest years of my life. I never forgot them."

Trying to corral her thoughts, Andi sat quietly. Was he telling the truth or was he still a prankster? How could he be so sure who had run past the window if all he saw was the top of the person's head? Surely there was more than one person in town with red hair, and besides, how could he be certain that it was even someone from town? A part of her wanted to grab on to his explanation. She felt certain Janice Reed wouldn't consider his story worthwhile. She realized he was waiting for her to speak, but she wasn't sure what to say. "Were you a barber in California?" she asked to give herself time to think.

"No. When I first got there, I worked on the San Francisco docks and went to night school. After I got my degree, I moved to Los Angeles and got a job with MGM. I eventually worked as a screenwriter."

Andi glanced up at him. "A screenwriter?"

He nodded. "I never did anything really big, but I made a good living at it."

Andi felt her doubt of him begin to grow. If he had been so successful in Hollywood, why was he living in this tiny house in HiHo?

"You don't believe I saw the murder, do you?" He tugged at the pinned sleeve again.

"Mr. Doleski, I don't know what to believe. I'm sure you believed you knew who ran past the window, but surely someone would have taken you seriously, considering they suspected that the shooter ran out the back door." She suddenly remembered her grandmother telling her about the fence in the alley. "What about the fence? Wasn't there a fence in the alleyway?"

He snorted. "Yes, there was a fence, but the boards next to the wall were loose. I used to sneak through there all the time. The

126

building between the barbershop and Mr. Zucker's housed a restaurant. They would leave the door to the kitchen open when it got too hot. I'd wait until the cook was busy then sneak in and grab a piece of cake, pie, or cookies sometimes. Then I'd hotfoot it through the fence and back to the barbershop."

"But how would a grown man slip through?" Andi questioned.

"Gary Wayne was only sixteen, and he was a scrawny kid." He continued to watch her. "You still don't believe me. I've thought about this for sixty-some-odd years, and I know what I saw."

"Surely there was more than one person in town with red hair. It could have been a stranger from out of town," Andi reasoned.

He shook his head. "No. I've never seen anyone with hair as bright as Gary Wayne's, and it had to be someone small to squeeze through that fence."

"Maybe the shooter didn't go through the hole in the fence. Maybe he climbed over the fence."

Again, he shook his head. "If the person had been tall enough to jump up and pull themselves over the fence, I would've been able to see their face and not just the top of his head. The person who ran past that window was short, and Gary Wayne is still short."

Andi's body grew deathly still. "Are you saying this man is still alive?" she asked quietly.

"Yes. He lives about a mile outside of town. Out on the Old Holstetter Road. Well, it's not called Holstetter Road anymore. It's now County Road two-twenty-one."

Holstetter. Her grandmother had told her something about the Holstetters' place. She tried to think of something else to ask him, but she was already thinking about how she would present this information to Janice Reed. She thanked him for his help and stood. "If I think of anything else, would you mind if I called you?" she asked.

"I'd be more than happy to help," he assured her.

As she headed down the hall, he slowly followed her in his wheelchair.

"Ms. Kane," he called.

127

She turned. "Please, call me Andi."

He nodded. "Okay, Andi. I want you to know how sorry I am that I couldn't do anything to stop what happened. It has always bothered me. I guess I've always felt like it was my fault that Mr. Gray went to prison." Tears blurred his eyes.

"Mr. Doleski, you were only a child. The only person to blame is the one who pulled the trigger." On impulse, Andi walked back and gave him a quick hug. "Thank you again for talking to me."

She hurried to her car and headed toward the district attorney's office. As she drove back to the center of town, she tried to block the voice that was asking whether she was going so she could deliver her newly discovered information, or if she was more interested in seeing Janice Reed.

Chapter Twenty-three

Andi waited over an hour before she was able to see Janice Reed. Betty encouraged her to make an appointment for the following week, but Andi didn't want to delay.

When Janice came in and saw Andi waiting, she smiled. "Don't tell me you've already found something that will make me reopen the case."

Andi stood. "I may have."

Janice looked surprised and gazed at her for a moment. "All right. Give me a second." She handed Betty a large stack of papers. "Call Gillian and Judd and tell them I'll be a little late." She turned back to Andi. "Come on back and let's see what you've found."

As soon as they were in her office, Janice grabbed a notepad and a pen and set them in front of her. "I'm all ears. Tell me what you found."

"I spoke to a man named Clyde Doleski. Do you know him?"

Janice nodded. "I know of him. He's the guy in the wheelchair, right? I've seen him around town."

"Yes. He was nine when George Zucker was killed. His grandfather owned the barbershop that was a couple of doors down from the mercantile. Clyde Doleski says he saw the top of the man's head as he ran down the alley right after the shooting."

"Why didn't he tell someone then?"

"He did, but they didn't believe him. Apparently he was something of a practical joker and no one took him seriously."

Janice lightly tapped her fingers on the arm of her chair. "And you believe he's telling the truth?"

Andi turned her hands over and shrugged. "He sounds sincere, and what he says makes sense. There was a seven-foot-high fence in the alleyway, but he said the boards next to the wall were loose and there was room for a small person to squeeze through. Whoever shot George Zucker had to go out the back door, otherwise the sheriff or deputy would have seen them."

"You said the authorities never located the weapon, correct?"

Andi nodded.

"It's too bad he couldn't recognize the man's head."

"But he did."

Janice leaned forward. "How could he have identified a person when all he saw was the top of their head?"

"Mr. Doleski said the person who ran beneath the window was a sixteen-year-old boy he knew, who had really bright red hair. He was scrawny enough to slip through the fence and the height of the window indicated he was short. He knew the boy from around town, and he said the man is still living."

Janice retrieved the pen and pulled the pad toward her. "I'm not sure he could have identified a person by merely seeing the top of his head." Andi started to protest, and Janice held up her hand. "Give me this mystery man's name and I'll look into it. I'll see if he has a record. I'm not promising anything. As I told you before, after sixty-five years the best we can hope for is that the killer will confess. I suspect that if he's gotten away with it this long, you can bet your bottom dollar he isn't going to suddenly confess. But you never know. Sometimes the guilt gets to be too much and they're afraid of dying without confessing. So who was he?"

"His name is Gary Wayne Mabry."

A strangled gasp escaped Janice as she came out of her chair. "Lady, if this is your idea of a joke, you are sadly mistaken. Now, exactly what are you trying to do?"

Confused, Andi stared into Janice's ashen face. Why had she reacted so strongly to the name?

"What are you doing?" Janice demanded again.

"Nothing. I'm trying to clear my great-grandfather's name."

"By slandering a man who has single-handedly done more for this community than the rest of us combined will ever be able to do. A man who has devoted his entire life to helping others. A man who—" She stopped suddenly and turned away. "Ms. Kane, I think it would be best if you left now."

Andi stood. "Do you know Gary Wayne Mabry?"

Janice turned back, her face frozen in anger. "Yes." Her voice shook. "He's my grandfather. Now get the hell out of my office." Without waiting for Andi to respond, Janice turned her back.

Stunned, Andi stepped out into the hallway. She had barely cleared the doorway when the door slammed behind her. She slowly made her way back to the front office. Betty stared at her but thankfully kept silent. Andi was getting into her car when she remembered why Mabry's name sounded familiar. The article in the San Antonio paper detailing the death of Janice's parents had mentioned her mother's name, Amelia Ann Mabry. Andi grabbed her head and groaned. Why was everything always so damn complicated?

She sat in her car trying to unravel the mess that she had fallen into. Was Clyde Doleski mistaken? It was the most logical explanation. He had only been nine. How much would he have observed? Could he be getting revenge for some petty childhood slight? She needed to talk to someone. She grabbed her cell and dialed Becka's number. She listened in frustration as the call failed to go through. Twice more she tried and both times failed. She threw the phone on the seat. "So much for technology," she grumbled.

As she sat staring out the window, it occurred to her that she should probably go talk to Gary Wayne Mabry herself. Doing so would make Janice even angrier at her. Besides that, what if Clyde Doleski was right and Gary Wayne really was the killer? How was he going to react to her showing up and asking him questions? A shiver ran down her spine. Facing a killer wasn't something she was quite ready to tackle. She decided to leave talking to him as her absolute last possible option.

"As though I haven't already reached my last option," she grumbled.

Andi remained in the car for several minutes. When she couldn't convince herself to drive out and talk to Gary Wayne Mabry in person, she walked back to the newspaper office. She tried the knob and found it locked. She noticed the Closed sign. Disappointed, she turned away. She had only gone a few steps when she heard her name. Looking back, she saw Rhonda standing in the doorway waving at her.

Andi suddenly wished she had just driven home. Rhonda and Janice were friends. Rhonda would probably send her packing also.

"What's wrong?" Rhonda asked as Andi approached the door. "You look like you've just lost your last friend."

Andi stopped beside her and stared off down the street. "I just accused Janice's grandfather of murdering George Zucker."

"What!"

"I went to see Clyde Doleski and he's absolutely positive that it was Gary Wayne Mabry that he saw running past the window that day."

Rhonda groaned and rubbed her forehead. "Kenny and Shawna have already left for the day. Why don't you come on in and tell me exactly what happened."

They sat at Rhonda's desk and after Andi repeated Clyde Doleski's story, she leaned forward in her chair and asked, "What do you think?"

Rhonda began to spin her pen on her desk. Without replying, she turned to her computer and began typing.

Andi felt like screaming that now was not the time to be multi-tasking, but she held her tongue.

Rhonda continued to type in brief commands. "It's possible that Mr. Doleski is still being a practical joker," she began. "I don't see anything about him here. If he was a screenwriter, I should be able to eventually find something on him. Did he mention anything he worked on?"

"No. He did say he worked for MGM for a while, but that may have been before he became a screenwriter. I don't remember."

Rhonda turned away from the screen. "I can look into this further tonight or tomorrow. In the meantime, what're you going to do?"

Andi closed her eyes. "I'm too chicken to talk to Gary Wayne. I'm going home, e-mail my résumé to every corporation in San Antonio and take the first job I'm offered. I'm tired. I'm not qualified to do this. So far, the only thing I've accomplished is to piss everyone off."

Rhonda laughed. "Not talking to Gary Wayne is probably your smartest move. He has a lot of influence around here. You start pointing a finger toward him and you may find that no one will be eager to talk to you. I think you need some downtime. We're having a barbecue out at the house tomorrow. Why don't you come and have a little fun?"

"Won't Janice be there?" Andi asked.

Rhonda shrugged. "She may drop by for a while, but she said she's swamped and may not be able to show up at all. Either way, there will be a lot of people, and you won't have to talk to her if you don't want to."

"She may shoot me on sight."

"Janice? Never. She's an old softie."

"Somehow, I doubt that." She hesitated. "Do you know her grandfather?"

Rhonda nodded. "Everyone around here knows Gary Wayne Mabry. I won't make you feel worse by reiterating everything he's done for the community. He raised Janice after her parents died when she was a baby."

Andi nodded. "I saw the article in the San Antonio newspaper archives."

Rhonda gazed at her. "You knew about her parents?"

"Yes. I was looking for articles on my great-grandfather when I discovered they had archives of the *HiHo News*. I ran across the article while searching through those archives."

"Did the paper tell you it was Gary Wayne that took Janice in and raised her?"

"No." She felt like she was trampling on the feet of a saint and said as much.

"I don't think he would qualify for sainthood," Rhonda said. "Except in Janice's eyes. If you were to ask around town, you would find plenty of people who would describe him as a hard-nosed old fart. Like several generations of Mabrys before him, he started as a rancher. As the economy changed, so did he. He owned a thriving cattle business, later he became an oilman, he owned a uranium extraction company, and who knows what else. I also know he didn't have an easy life. He and his wife had four children, three girls and finally a boy. According to local gossips, Sonny was Gary Wayne's pride and joy, but he pushed the boy hard. Sonny joined the Army and was killed in Vietnam. Gary Wayne's wife blamed him for Sonny's death and divorced him. The only one of his daughters who continued to have any contact with him was Janice's mother."

"And she was killed in the car accident," Andi said.

"I've met Gary Wayne several times and he seems like a nice enough guy. I can't imagine him killing anyone. Of course, you read about friends and family members saying the same thing about serial killers."

"Is his hair red?"

Rhonda laughed. "It might have been when he still had hair. He has been bald since I've known him."

Andi rubbed a hand over her face. "I'm making such a mess of everything."

Rhonda stood and patted her shoulder. "Go home and get a good night's sleep. Come to the barbecue tomorrow and I'll show you one of the great wonders of the world."

Andi rolled her eyes. "Now there's a tired old line."

Rhonda laughed a deep rich sound. "Did you know that HiHo is the unofficial Gay Mecca of Texas?"

It was Andi's turn to laugh.

"I'm serious. For some reason an extraordinarily large percentage of the population is gay. You come on by tomorrow and I'll prove it."

Chapter Twenty-four

By the time Andi arrived home from HiHo her mother and grandmother were already preparing dinner. Rather than going into the kitchen, she scurried upstairs and took a shower. She knew she should have gone to help them, but guilt was eating at her. She needed time alone. Guilt was becoming an everyday emotion for her. She felt guilty for not being able to hang on to a productive job and for not trying harder to find another one. She was thirty-four. Why didn't she have a home mortgage like most individuals her age did? She felt guilty for living with her parents, failing her grandmother and not being able to maintain a committed relationship.

After toweling herself dry, she pulled out her favorite sweats. They were ancient and washed to baby softness. She ran a comb through her short dark hair and went downstairs to help with dinner.

As soon as she walked into the kitchen, she saw her mother's disapproving glance at the way she was dressed. "We weren't sure whether you'd be home for dinner or not," Leticia said.

"I should have left a note," Andi apologized. "I didn't plan on being gone so long. Don't ever wait for me or change your plans. I can always fix myself a sandwich or salad."

"There's plenty of food and we won't eat until your father arrives anyway," Sarah replied.

Andi glanced between the two women. She could feel an unusual tension buzzing between them.

"What can I do to help?" Andi asked.

"Nothing." Leticia turned her attention back to the pans on the stove.

"You may set the table," Sarah suggested. "I feel like eating in the dining room tonight."

Andi grabbed the plates and headed to the dining room to set the table. Normally, they ate in the kitchen. The dining room was usually reserved for Sundays, holidays or special meals. Tonight, Andi suspected her grandmother was using it as a way to express her dominance. Afraid to upset the delicate balance hanging between her mother and grandmother, Andi walked softly back to the kitchen. She was shocked to hear them speaking Spanish.

Andi's great-grandmother had been Mexican and all of her children grew up speaking English and Spanish. Sarah had in turn raised her children to be bilingual, but it stopped there. Neither Andi nor her brother Richard spoke Spanish.

The only time Andi's mother spoke Spanish was when she was saying something she didn't want Andi or Richard to understand.

Andi stood unobserved in the kitchen door. "What's going on?" she asked.

Startled, her mother flinched, almost upsetting one of the pans on the stove. "Why are you sneaking around?" she demanded.

Another trickle of guilt began to gnaw at Andi's conscience. Had her mother found out about her trips to HiHo and the reason for them?

"She wasn't sneaking," Sarah said. "We were so busy yelling at each other we didn't hear her."

"Why are you and Mom yelling at each other?" Andi asked.

"Apparently, it's a mother's privilege," Leticia snapped. "Or maybe it's just my mother."

Andi stepped farther into the kitchen. "Look, does this have something to do with me?"

Her grandmother shot Andi a warning glance.

"No," Leticia said. "It has nothing to do with you, and I don't want to discuss this any further. Finish setting the table and get changed for dinner. Your father will be home early tonight."

She wished she had the courage to tell her mother that she didn't want to change her clothes, but it was her mother's table. After setting the table, she went to change her clothes. As she started into her room, her grandmother caught her in the hallway.

"What's going on?" Andi asked in a whisper.

Her grandmother pushed her into her room and closed the door before speaking. "Iggy Acosta called today and left a message for me. He tried to call your cell phone, but it wasn't on or something, so he found my number and called here. He wants you to call him as soon as you can. I didn't have time to return his call before your mother came in."

Andi slapped her forehead. "I'm sorry. I was in HiHo all day and my phone doesn't always work down there. So does Mom know what we're doing?"

Sarah shook her head. "I arrived home just minutes before your mother. I checked the phone messages as I always do and erased his. I thought I had everything taken care of, but I forgot about the Caller ID. Leti saw his name on the call log."

"I'm really beginning to hate technology," Andi grumbled. "What did she do?"

"She asked me why he was calling here, and I told her he was calling me and it was none of her business." She ended the sentence with a firm nod of her head, and quickly moved on. "Why were you back in HiHo today?"

The front door opened.

"That's your father. We'll talk after dinner." Her grandmother turned and went down the hallway toward the kitchen.

Andi took the coward's way out and stayed in her room. Knowing her father would change clothes before eating, she grabbed the cell phone and called Ignacio Acosta's home number. He answered on the third ring. Andi quietly explained to him that she would like to see him as soon as possible and they made an appointment for the following day at noon. She hung up the phone, confident that she could keep her appointment with him and still make it to Rhonda's Saturday afternoon barbecue, if she chose to go. A quick glance at the clock warned her she was running short on time. After changing her clothes, she took a deep breath and prayed dinner would go smoothly. She opened the door and squealed in fright. Her father was about to knock. "You scared me," she stammered.

Frowning, her father apologized. "Why are you so jumpy?" he asked as he extended a handful of papers to her. "You received some more faxes from the realtor."

Andi leaned against the door and sighed.

"What's going on?" he asked.

Andi took the faxes. She didn't want to lie to him. "Has your Spanish improved?" she asked.

His shoulders fell. "Oh, no. Don't tell me they're bickering again." He glanced toward the kitchen. "How bad?"

"Mom's speaking Spanish and Grandmother had me set the dining room table."

He groaned. "I don't suppose you and I could sneak out and hide at McDonald's."

Andi chuckled and gave her father a quick hug. "I love you, Dad."

He smiled and extended his arm. "May I escort you to dinner, Ms. Kane?"

She linked her arm through his. "You most certainly can, Mr. Kane, and after dinner you may help me sort through these faxes and find a house."

"Traitor. Leaving me here alone and unprotected."

They were laughing when they arrived at the dining room.

Andrew Kane pretended not to notice the strain between his wife and mother-in-law. He complimented them both on the wonderful dinner and kept a steady, comfortable flow of conversation going throughout the meal.

Afterward, Andi cleared the table and put the dishes into the dishwasher. When she went into the living room, she found them all studying the sheets from Linda Ramos. *Looks like getting me out of here is one thing we can all work on together*, she thought as she sat on the sofa near her father.

By the time she went to her room, they had ruled out seven of the eighteen possibilities. She would split up the remaining possibilities, view some of them tomorrow and finish the remainder on Sunday.

She changed back into her sweats and checked her e-mail. Christen Enterprises had responded. She quickly opened the e-mail to discover they no longer had a vacancy. They would, however, be happy to keep her résumé on file for future consideration. She contemplated sending her résumé out again but decided to wait a few more days. Her grandmother was probably waiting for her. She went to the window and saw that her grandmother's light was on. She could see the flickering light coming from the television.

As she walked down the hallway, she debated whether to tell Sarah about Gary Wayne Mabry. If Mr. Doleski was wrong, it would only get her grandmother's hopes up. She had a sudden thought. *What if he was telling the truth?* For the first time it hit her—the horrible realization that her great-grandfather might have been unjustly accused and imprisoned. That another man had continued to live a long and productive life, while Sean Gray's had been cut drastically short. She stopped long enough to regain her composure. She wouldn't tell her grandmother about Clyde Doleski's claim yet. She would do some more checking. Maybe Ignacio Acosta would be able to add something of value tomorrow.

140

Chapter Twenty-five

The following morning, Andi was up before anyone else was stirring. After showering and carefully arranging her hair, she spent some time choosing a long-sleeve white shirt, dark slacks and black boots. She grabbed a jacket to take with her. According to the local weatherman, the warm front was supposed to hold for a couple more days, but the air would grow cooler as soon as the sun went down. She left a note on the table saying she would be looking at houses and that she was going to visit a friend and wouldn't be home for dinner.

The day started out badly almost immediately. In her haste to get out of the house, she hadn't taken time to pinpoint the address of each house on the map, and to make matters worse, she'd forgotten her map. With a general idea of where a couple of the houses were located, she went to see them first. They were both on the northeast side of town. The first one was nice but much too large for her. While looking for the second one, she got hopelessly lost. After twenty-five minutes of weaving back and forth through neighborhoods, she stopped at a convenience store for coffee and directions.

By the time she made her way back to Loop 410, it was almost time to head for HiHo. She abandoned her house-hunting expedition and headed south. She had driven the route so many times during the past week she no longer had to concentrate on the directions.

As she drove, she tried not to think about whether Janice Reed would show up for the barbecue or not. Or what would happen if she did? Andi felt she needed to apologize to Janice, but the slim possibility that Clyde Doleski was right held her back.

She was ten minutes early for her appointment with Ignacio Acosta but decided to go ahead and stop. He lived in a large, well-maintained older stone home. A white picket fence encircled the generous front yard. Andi opened the gate and made her way up a sidewalk lined on both sides with carefully trimmed salvia bushes. Several rocking chairs sat peacefully on the front porch that spread across the width of the house. As she knocked on the door, she noticed a plaque proudly proclaiming that the house was on the National Register of Historic Homes.

A tall, slightly bent man with a shock of blue-gray hair opened the door. He was dressed in a white Western shirt and navy blue dress Wranglers. His highly buffed cowboy boots cast a sparkling shine.

"*Hola*, Senorita Kane. Please come in." He held the door open for her. Arthritis knotted the joints of his hands, leaving them like the roots of an ancient cypress tree.

He led the way slowly through the house to a glass-enclosed room at the back. Sunshine poured through the windows. The room was empty except for several comfortable chairs and a long coffee table.

"Please sit down. I've made a pot of fresh coffee. Will you join me?"

"Yes. Please. Can I help you with it?"

"No. No. Sit." He excused himself and carefully made his way back into the main part of the house. Andi used the time to study the backyard that held a rock garden with a bubbling fountain in the center. Several tall pecan trees provided a haven for the squirrels that were chattering and running playfully along the top of the back fence. She watched the squirrels' impressive acrobatic display until he returned with the coffee.

"You look like your grandmother," he said as he poured coffee into her cup.

"Thank you. Mr. Acosta, I don't mean to be rude, but I'd like to ask you some questions about my great-grandfather."

He chuckled. "You young people are always in such a hurry. My children and grandchildren are the same way." He shrugged. "I'm an old man. Too old sometimes. I'll be ninety-four in a few months. Maybe when I was your age, I was in a hurry also. But please, ask your questions."

"I'm trying to prove my great-grandfather's innocence. Is there anything about the day George Zucker was murdered that you can remember that might help?"

Clutching the cup in both hands, he sipped his coffee and stared out toward the fountain. "I've blamed myself for Sean's trouble for many years. If I hadn't asked him to stop and get something for the pain in my leg . . . I was working as a roofer then. I fell off a house and broke my leg in three places," he explained.

"Mr. Acosta, do you think Sean Gray killed George Zucker?"

"No. Never in one million years would I believe such a thing. Sean was one of the most honest men I've ever known. Let me tell you a story. Just weeks before George Zucker died, your father and I stopped by his store on our way home from work. We were working on the same house. I was working on the roof and Sean was building the kitchen cabinets. We made our purchases and left. We were almost home when we stopped by a bar for a beer. When Sean paid for his beer, he noticed that Zucker had given him too much change. Two bills were stuck together. Your great-grandfather walked back to return the money. That's how honest he was."

143

"What do you think happened that afternoon?"

"I've had many years to think about this and I think Sean walked in right after Zucker was killed. Because I was stuck in bed with my broken leg, I wasn't able to talk to Sean until after he was already in prison. I drove over to see him a few times. He told me once that he'd heard a noise that sounded like a door slamming as he came in."

"He heard the shot?"

He shook his head. "I don't know. I always assumed he heard the murderer fleeing out the back door." He rubbed his jaw. "But perhaps it was a shot. Sean knew nothing about guns. I used to tease him about being afraid of them."

"I thought it was odd that whoever it was went to a lot of trouble to rob the store and then left the money. Do you know anyone who would have had a reason to kill Mr. Zucker?" Andi asked.

"No. Times were bad, but I can't imagine who was desperate enough to rob him."

"But if you were desperate enough to rob someone and then kill them, wouldn't you take time to grab the money?" she persisted.

"Maybe. Or maybe I would have gotten scared and ran."

"Mr. Acosta, do you know Gary Wayne Mabry?"

He nodded. "Sure. Everyone around here knows him."

"What was he like as a young man? Say around the time the murder happened?"

"Ah, he was wild. I think he was seeing the Talbot girl then. He did childish, silly things."

"Like what?"

He sipped his coffee. "He got into a lot of fights, and he painted the windows of the school once. He was a small kid, physically, I mean. Maybe because of that he always tried to act tough." He shrugged. "But that was just kid stuff. He grew up and became a fine man."

They drank their coffee in silence.

"Why do you ask about Gary Wayne?" he asked.

She hesitated slightly and then repeated what Clyde Doleski

144

had told her. When she finished, he set his coffee cup down and leaned back. After several long seconds, he looked at her. "Clyde was a prankster. As much as I would like to see Sean's name cleared, I can't believe it was Gary Wayne. He was wild, but he wouldn't kill anyone."

"Do you know anyone else I could talk to who was living here when the murder happened?"

He thought for a second. "No. Everyone has either moved on or died."

"What about the Talbot girl that Gary Wayne was dating?"

He shook his head. "Her family moved away soon after the shooting. Her father went to Detroit to work with his brother or something. I don't remember ever hearing anything else about her."

Andi felt the brick wall between her and the answers needed to clear Sean Gray's name growing taller.

She thanked him for his time and the coffee and rose to leave.

"How is your grandmother?" he asked as he walked through the house with her.

"She's as feisty and stubborn as ever."

"Good. That'll keep her vital," he said and laughed.

As they walked through the living room, Andi spied a display case hanging on the wall. It contained a folded American flag and several military metals. "I'd forgotten you left and joined the Army," she said, pointing to the case.

"One of the best things I ever did," he answered. "I met my wife, Ana, while I was stationed in Hawaii. She gave me five wonderful children, three girls and two boys. They in turn have given me many grandchildren, and kept me going after my Ana died." He picked a photo frame up from a table. "This is my family."

Andi took the photo. It was a group shot. The love and pride of the magnificent family seemed on the verge of bursting out from the photo. "You have a lovely family, sir."

"Are you married?" he asked as she handed the photo back to him.

"No."

"Well, don't worry. I was almost thirty before I met Ana. You still have lots of time."

Andi didn't want to tell him that thirty had already passed her by. She had the fleeting thought that perhaps love had as well.

Chapter Twenty-six

Andi followed the directions Rhonda had given her the previous day. She turned onto a gravel road that had a texture very similar to an old-fashioned washboard. She carefully braked the car to a slow crawl and prayed it wouldn't shake into a dozen pieces.

Easing around a long curve, she caught a glimpse of a log home nestled in the center of a thick grove of oak trees. As she slowly continued around the curve, she blinked in surprise. There must have been twenty-five to thirty cars and trucks already parked along the sides of the driveway. She pulled in and parked her car. As she stepped out, a topless Jeep Wrangler filled with young women whipped in beside her. She felt old and decrepit as they hopped out over the sides of the Jeep. Her knees ached just thinking about the impact of hitting the ground.

She inched closer to the cars to allow the group to swarm past her. As they swept by, she looked up and briefly met the eyes of one of the women. She watched in astonishment as the woman did a double take and smiled. As the group moved away, the woman kept glancing back over her shoulder.

Despite herself, Andi felt her step gain a little more bounce. Maybe she could still vault over the side of an open vehicle.

As her imagination was about to run away with her, she heard her name being called. Looking around she saw Rhonda waving at her. Andi made her way across the yard.

"You made it," Rhonda called with genuine pleasure.

"I wasn't sure my poor little Honda was going to survive that horrible road," she teased.

"Isn't that pitiful?" a voice called out behind her. "You would think the editor of the only newspaper in town could whip out some scathing article and get the road to her house paved."

Andi looked around to find the speaker. She recognized her as the tall, sturdy woman in the photo on Rhonda's desk, Carol.

"You're the county clerk," Rhonda parried. "You have a lot more clout than I do."

"And don't you forget it," Carol said as she gave Rhonda a hug.

Rhonda quickly made the introductions.

"Would you like a drink?" Carol asked. "There's beer, sodas, wine, tea and water."

"I think I'll stick to water for a while," Andi said.

"Carol, where's the ice cream maker?" a short frizzy-haired woman yelled from the porch.

"Show Andi where everything is, while I go see what they're up to," Carol instructed Rhonda as she set off toward the house.

They pushed through several groups of men and women before they reached a table holding a rainbow of brightly colored ice chests.

"Are all these people gay?" Andi asked as Rhonda twisted the top off a bottle of water and handed it to her.

"Every last one of them, and there's a lot more coming."

Andi shook her head in amazement. "Why do so many live in HiHo?"

Rhonda shrugged. "I've been trying to figure that one out ever since Carol and I moved here. I mean there's the obvious part. It's

148

a beautiful little town. Quiet. Everyone's motto is pretty much 'live and let live.' But I don't know if that attitude started before or after we moved here."

The young women from the Jeep made their way toward the table laden with ice chests. The one who had been staring at Andi earlier smiled and gave a small nod as she walked by.

"That was quick," Rhonda teased.

"What?" Andi tried to act as if she hadn't noticed anything.

Rhonda laughed. "Just a word of warning. She moves fast— arriving and leaving. If you know what I mean."

"I'm not looking," Andi said. "I'm seriously considering giving up women and starting a stamp collection."

"That's sure to break several hearts."

Andi whirled to find Janice Reed standing behind her.

Rhonda looked toward the house and waved. "If you two will excuse me, I'm being summoned to the house." She sped away before Andi could grab her.

"For a woman who makes her living with words, she's not very subtle," Janice said as she took Andi's elbow and steered her toward a long bench beneath one of the oak trees.

"I'm sorry about yesterday," Andi said as she sat down.

Janice shook her head. "I'm the one who should be apologizing. I get a little overly protective with my grandfather. I overreacted."

"No. I should have kept quiet until I could prove or disprove Clyde Doleski's claim."

"You'd have to know my grandfather to understand that he's totally incapable of killing anyone."

Andi turned to her. "My grandmother says the same thing about her father."

Janice glanced away. "Sorry. I didn't mean that to sound so cavalier."

"We seem to spend a lot of time saying we're sorry," Andi pointed out.

"We've already started over once. What do you think we should do now?" Janice asked.

Andi's heart rate accelerated. She was no longer certain they

149

were still talking about George Zucker's murder. "Do you have any suggestions?"

Janice leaned closer. "Perhaps . . ."

"Hello, Janice. I see you always manage to find the prettiest woman around."

Andi glanced up to find the young woman from the Jeep.

"Hello," the woman said, directing her attention to Andi. "My name is Bea."

"That's with a capital *B*," Janice said as she nodded to Andi. "Maybe we can talk later, but in case I miss you, I wanted to let you know that I sent those items you asked me for. You should have them before ten Monday morning."

Before Andi could say anything, Janice gave a curt nod to Bea and left.

"Oh, my. Did I interrupt something?" Bea asked.

Andi looked at the young woman she had considered so attractive earlier and suddenly she saw a less sophisticated image of Trish. Bea possessed the same cocksure smile as Trish and she was slowly closing the distance between them.

Andi stood. "Actually, you did. If you'll excuse me, I think I'd like to finish the conversation I was having before you interrupted." She walked away without looking back.

Ten minutes later, she still hadn't located Janice. Tired of wading through the milling crowd, she found an empty seat under a tree and sat.

"You've certainly got everyone buzzing," Rhonda said as she dropped down beside her.

"A new face always draws attention," Andi said, wondering where Janice had gone.

"It's not your face. It was your verbal smacking of Bea Shriver."

Andi blushed. "I'm sorry if I offended your friend."

Rhonda snorted. "She's not exactly a friend. She's sort of like a parasite. Once she attaches herself to you, she's impossible to shake loose. My only regret is I wasn't there to see it."

"It really didn't amount to much."

150

"That's not what I heard. The rumormongers are saying she spied you on the way in and was pretty sure she would be leaving with you."

Andi shook her head. "I'm too old for those games. I gave up one-night stands a long time ago." She kept scanning the crowd, hoping to spot Janice.

"She left," Rhonda said softly.

Andi turned to her. "Am I that obvious?"

Rhonda smiled and patted Andi's knee. "Come on inside. I want to introduce you to some people."

Andi allowed herself to be led back into the house. She caught several women glancing her way as she walked by. As they passed by one group, she heard a woman say, "It's about time someone gave Bea a dose of reality."

Rhonda quickly guided Andi around the group and rushed her into the house.

Andi was introduced to a dozen or more men and women. She tried to remember all the names, but they quickly began to run together.

She stayed a while longer before saying her good-byes and using the excuse of the long drive back to San Antonio as a reason for leaving.

On a whim, she drove by the district attorney's office, hoping that Janice might be in her office, but the parking lot was empty. As she drove away she couldn't help wondering what Janice would have said if Bea had not interrupted them.

Chapter Twenty-seven

Andi thought about Janice during the entire trip from HiHo. She mentally kicked herself for not walking away from Bea immediately. When Andi arrived home, a stack of mail was waiting for her on the entryway table. She flipped through it, stopping to rip open an envelope bearing her former employer's payroll address. Her severance check was enclosed. She smiled as she read the high five-figure amount. The severance payment combined would allow her to purchase a house outright. She found her grandmother sitting in the living room reading.

"You look comfortable," Andi said, leaning over to kiss her grandmother's cheek. "Where are Mom and Dad?"

"They went out to dinner," Sarah replied. "I didn't go because I wanted to talk to you alone."

"What's up?"

"I wanted to know if you learned anything new from Iggy."

Andi sat on the sofa and leaned her head back. "No. I'm sorry, but he didn't really know anything more than what you'd already told me. However, the DA is sending copies of the police report and the trial transcript."

"What good will they do?" Sarah asked.

Andi sighed and closed her eyes. "I don't know. I asked for them because they seem to be the only tangible thing left from the case." She sat up. "I don't know where else to look."

Sarah carefully folded the paper. "I should've never asked you to do this. Too much time has passed since the murder. I should have listened to the private investigators I hired. Let it go, *mija*."

Andi stood and gave her grandmother a hug. "If there's nothing more in those files, I may have to." She returned to her room and began to gather her laundry. As she was emptying her pockets, she found the card Janice had given her. Turning it over she saw a number marked as a cell phone and another for her home phone. Without taking time to think about what she was doing, she grabbed the phone and dialed Janice's cell phone. Janice answered on the third ring.

"I was hoping you would call," Janice said without preamble.

"And I'm hoping you knew it was me when you answered the phone."

"Caller ID is a wonderful thing," Janice replied.

"Why did you leave the party? I went to look for you and Rhonda told me you had already left."

"I assumed . . ." Janice hesitated.

"Well, don't make assumptions about me the next time."

"Does that mean I get a second chance?" Janice asked.

"Maybe."

"I thought we might be able to get together and finish our conversation."

Andi groaned. "I'm already back in San Antonio."

"Good, because I'm in San Antonio also."

Andi's heart gave a small leap. "What are you doing here?"

"I come up every few weeks and spend the weekend with a friend. It's kind of my secret getaway. I was going to call you tomorrow to see if we could get together for lunch, but if you aren't busy, maybe we could make it dinner tonight."

Andi glanced at her watch. It was almost seven. "Where can I meet you?"

"Do you like Mexican food?"

Andi laughed. "I love Mexican food, but it has to be good."

"Meet me at Lupita's. It's on the corner of Thorton and Beacon. Do you know where that is?"

"I can be there in twenty minutes," Andi said, already reaching for her car keys. She was practically skipping down the hallway.

Her grandmother looked up from her paper. "What put you in such a good mood?" she asked with a smile.

Andi couldn't stop the grin that spread across her own face. "I'm going to have dinner with a friend."

"Must be a very good friend," her grandmother teased. "Are you coming home tonight?"

"Grandmother," Andi said. "I can't believe you asked that."

"Andi, please. I'm an old woman. I'm a firm believer that we have to find happiness wherever we can. Life's too short to be tip-toeing around. Who is this woman who's put that beautiful smile back on your face."

Andi shook her head. "Janice Reed. She's the district attorney from HiHo. We're just getting together for dinner to discuss things."

Sarah shook her head and went back to her paper. "Make sure you call if you plan on discussing things all night. You know what a worrywart your mother is."

"I will," Andi promised as she raced out the door.

Lupita's was a small restaurant tucked away in a strip mall. Andi had eaten there many times and knew the food was excellent. Janice was already seated at a table when Andi arrived.

"I was beginning to wonder if you'd changed your mind," Janice said as Andi sat down.

"No. I forgot about the construction on Loop four-ten. They've closed an entire section and detoured traffic off to the access road. I finally gave up trying to follow the detour and cut through side streets."

An awkward silence fell between them.

"I'm glad you called," Janice said at last. "Can we try and clear up a couple of things?"

"I'd like that," Andi admitted.

Janice breathed a sigh of relief. "Good. First of all, I want to apologize again for my behavior yesterday. There was absolutely no excuse for me exploding like that."

"I'm sure I must have shocked you."

Janice nodded. "I'm a little protective of my grandfather. He's the only family I have." She paused. "That's not completely true. My aunts are still living and I have some cousins, but I don't really know them. We've never been close. You see my parents died when I was young and Granddad raised me. He was divorced, but he didn't hesitate. It couldn't have been easy for him, but he never made me feel as though I was a burden." She looked at Andi. "He really is a good, decent man. I can't even imagine him killing someone."

Andi nodded.

"But that brings us back to your great-grandfather. I'm sure your grandmother defends him as strongly as I defend Granddad."

"She truly believes he's innocent," Andi said. "All she wants to do is clear his name. She's not looking for vengeance or any type of restitution."

The waiter brought a basket of chips and a bowl of salsa. He seemed to know Janice and spoke to her in Spanish. She answered in Spanish. They ordered frozen margaritas before he left.

"It took me almost six hours to find those records," Janice said as he walked away.

"Thank you for looking."

"Don't thank me yet. I glanced through them this morning, and evidence-wise, there's nothing in them that would help your great-

155

grandfather. However, if the trial were being convened today rather than sixty-five years ago, I sincerely doubt he would have gone to prison."

The waiter reappeared with their margaritas.

Andi waited impatiently until he left. "Why?" she demanded when he left.

Janice sipped her drink. "There are a couple of things. First of all, there's the missing weapon. If I had been the defense attorney, I would've pounded that point into the jury's head with every other sentence, but strangely enough, your great-grandfather's attorney, Bernard Snell, barely mentioned it. Another thing was the judge, Raymond Wheeler. He was George Zucker's wife's brother-in-law."

Andi tried to put the relationship in order. "His wife's brother-in-law."

Janice waved it off. "Wheeler should have removed himself from the case. Again, I don't know why Snell didn't jump on that."

"Could it have been classism or racism?"

Janice frowned. "Racism?"

"My great-grandfather was Irish and he married a Mexican. The newspaper articles about the murder and the trial were pretty vicious. In one of the articles, the area of town they lived in was referred to as Little Bean Town."

Janice grimaced. "I've read some of the things that R. L. Weiss wrote. The man was poison. His son David wasn't much better. But to answer your question, it's possible that was part of the problem, but I suspect it also had to do with getting the case closed as quickly as possible."

"What do you mean?"

"We've become desensitized to crime. When was the last time someone was shot and killed here in San Antonio?"

Andi shrugged. "I don't know."

"Last night. You're so used to hearing about crime that you no longer really dwell on it, unless it affects you personally or someone you know. You may hear it on the news or see it in the paper, but more than likely, you shake your head and maybe have a kind thought for the victim's family, but that's it. During that period, in a town as small as HiHo, it was different. Even now, violent crimes are so rare that when one occurs, everyone in town is talking about it. I would imagine it was even worse back then. It's probable that since he was caught in the store with the money in his hands, everyone automatically assumed his guilt, and a short trial resulted as a means of keeping the town calm. The mayor and council members would certainly be pushing for a quick resolve. I suspect Sean Gray became a greater victim of politics rather than classism or racism."

Andi rubbed her forehead. "I doubt that's going to make my grandmother feel any better."

"No. It'll probably make things worse for her. Andi, if I thought reopening the case would solve anything I would, but I don't have anything to go on."

"Except Clyde Doleski's statement," Andi said, staring at her.

Janice held her gaze for a second before looking away. "Do you honestly think he's telling the truth?"

Andi shrugged. "What color was your grandfather's hair?"

"Red, but it still doesn't prove that Doleski actually saw him. He could still be trying to get even with Granddad for something."

"If he's such a great guy, why would anyone be trying to get even with him?"

Janice's face reddened. She was about to retort when the waiter arrived with their food.

Andi stared down at her fajitas, her appetite gone. "Maybe I should go," she said, pushing the plate back.

"This is going to always be sitting there between us, isn't it?"

Andi nodded. "Probably."

Janice leaned back in her chair. "I wish I could make this right. I want to get to know you better."

"I think I would have liked that, but the timing is all wrong." Andi stood.

"What can I do to make things right between us?" Janice asked.

"Find out the truth." Walking away from the table was one of the hardest things Andi had ever done.

Chapter Twenty-eight

Andi spent the rest of the evening and the following morning trying to stay busy. She cleaned her room, the living room and the kitchen. When she finished those, she started on her laundry. By noon on Sunday, she'd run out of things to do. She grabbed her map and the handful of spec sheets and headed out the door. By three o'clock, she'd driven past each of the houses and found something wrong with all of them.

She put the sheets aside and promised she would look at the houses again later during the week. Hopefully by then, she would have shaken the cloud of discontent that clung to her. Returning home, she told her mother she wasn't feeling well. After taking two aspirins, she crawled into bed and fell asleep. She slept straight through until morning.

By the time she got up and showered, everyone else had already left. She made herself a good breakfast and settled down to read the paper and eat. She'd just sat down when the doorbell rang. As she walked to the door, she glanced out the window and saw a delivery van. She realized it must be the package from Janice. After signing for the delivery, she took the express envelope to the kitchen and tore it open. While eating her breakfast, she read the meager police records and trial transcript. Janice was right. There was nothing in the reports that she didn't already know.

Disgusted, she took her dirty dishes and put them in the dishwasher. Gathering the papers, she carried them to her room and dumped them on her bed. She tried checking her e-mail, but it kept bumping her off. She finally gave up. Unable to sit still, she grabbed her jacket and car keys. There didn't seem to be anywhere for her to go. She drove aimlessly around town until she saw a movie theater and stopped. After studying the movie lineup, she purchased a ticket for a movie that was about to begin. She tried to concentrate on the story line, but she kept thinking of Janice, and George Zucker's murder. When the closing credits began to roll, she realized she had no idea what the movie had been about. She walked back to her car and sat. Why should she and Janice let a murder that happened sixty-five years ago stand between them? She had tried her best to prove her great-grandfather's innocence. Wasn't that enough? How could she be certain he wasn't guilty? Who was Clyde Doleski anyway? Why should she believe anything he told her? Tired of the endless questions, she started home.

She parked her car on the street. Her father was already home. Maybe they could all do something together . . . anything that would distract her thoughts from Janice. The minute she walked into the house she knew something was wrong. Her parents and grandmother were sitting in the living room. They weren't reading or talking. They were just sitting there staring at her.

"What's wrong?" she asked, walking farther into the room. As she stepped around the sofa, she saw the files Janice had sent her lying on the coffee table. She stared at the folders and suddenly all of the anger of the last two weeks began to burn inside her. "Why are these out here?" she demanded.

"What do you think you're doing?" her mother demanded.

"Why are these out here?" Andi asked again. Her body began to shake.

"I found them when I took your mail to your room," Leticia said.

"You mean you found them when you were snooping in my room," Andi snapped. "You had no right to go through my stuff."

"Andi," her father cautioned. "Don't speak to your mother in that tone."

Andi grabbed the folders from the table.

"I want those out of my house now," her mother said. "And you're to stop whatever you're trying to do with them this instant."

Andi turned toward her. "Mom, in case you haven't noticed, I'm no longer a child to be told what I can and can't do."

"As long as you are in my house—"

Andi held up a hand to stop her. "Don't bother saying it. I'll be out as soon as I can pack." She turned to leave the room.

"Andi, wait," her father called.

She didn't stop, even when she heard her grandmother coming down the hall behind her. Her mother was demanding to know where everyone was going. Andi didn't bother to gather anything but a few of her clothes and her camera equipment. Her grandmother kept trying to talk to her, but Andi didn't listen. She grabbed the bags, her keys and phone. She started to take her computer, but the damn thing never worked anyway, so she left it.

Her father attempted to speak to her as she left, but Andi shook her head and continued walking. She threw her things in the backseat and drove off. Her cell phone started ringing a short time later. Andi turned it off and headed across town to find a hotel room. She found a Quality Inn and registered for the night. Tomorrow she would worry about a permanent arrangement, but right now all she wanted to do was forget about everything and everyone.

Safely locked away in her room, Andi found tears began to replace her anger. She'd never walked away from her parents. She considered calling them but knew they would try to talk her into coming home. She eventually cried herself to sleep.

The banging of the cleaning staff's cart woke her the following morning. Her head hurt from crying and her eyes were swollen. She took a long, hot shower before she called her father at his office.

"Where are you?" he asked when he heard her voice. "Are you all right?"

"I'm fine. I'm sorry I walked out last night, but I'm just . . ." She couldn't find the words to explain the last two weeks of her life. "Dad, I feel like such a failure. Nothing I do is right."

"Honey, you're not a failure."

"I don't have a job, and what's worse, I'm not sure I even want to get one. I can't maintain a relationship. I've let Grandma down and nothing I'll ever do will be good enough to please Mom."

"Whew. Let's take those one at a time," he said. "First of all, your mother loves you more than you'll ever know. She was up all night worrying about you, and she's very proud of you and always has been."

"Why?" Andi demanded. "What have I ever done to make her proud?"

"Andi, you're acting like a child now. If you want to have a serious conversation, I'm willing to listen. I don't intend to be a party to your wallowing in self-pity. Now, do you honestly not know that your mother loves you and how proud of you she is?"

Andi sat down on the bed. "How can she be proud of me?"

"You're intelligent, responsible, caring, and most of the time, you're level-headed. What's going on with your not wanting to work?"

She tried to think of a way to tell him what she was feeling. "I don't know, Dad. I'm tired of the politics. Of constantly wondering if the next budget cuts are going to hit me or if I'll have to tell one of the people working for me that they no longer have a job. And all the while the CEOs just keep getting richer."

He gave a small dry chuckle. "That's life. That's part of living in the corporate world. If you don't want that, why don't you think about doing something different?"

"I don't know anything different. What would I do?"

"Pursue your photography, become a travel agent, wash dishes. Who cares? Do whatever makes you happy. Andi, life is too short to be miserable. You can't spend your life making excuses for not doing what makes you happy. Now, how did you disappoint your grandmother?"

"She asked me to help her clear her father's name and I couldn't."

"Why couldn't you?"

"Because too much time has passed. I tried talking to people, but there was no way I could prove what they were telling me. The police report and the trial records didn't tell me anything. I ran out of places to look."

"What I'm hearing is, you tried everything you could. Can you think of anything else to look into?"

"No," she admitted.

"Then you didn't fail her. Sometimes we have to admit that there are limits to what we can accomplish. As for your relationships, I probably shouldn't say this, but I believe you made the right choice in leaving Trish. I never felt she was right for you."

"Why didn't you say something before?"

He sighed. "What could I have said?"

She knew he was right. "Thanks."

"Will you call your mother now?"

Andi hesitated. "Dad, I need some time. I'm going to start looking for an apartment today."

"What about the house?"

"I think I was looking for a house to make myself feel better. I thought owning a home might make me feel more successful, more grounded. I need to be alone and take care of myself for a while."

"What should I tell your mother?"

"Tell her and Grandmother that I love them and I'll see them soon. I just need a few days."

"We all love you. Call if you need anything," he said before he hung up.

Andi called Linda Ramos and left a message that she was no longer in the market for a house. She checked out of the motel and drove to the nearest McDonald's where she bought a cup of coffee and a newspaper. After circling the ads for apartment complexes that sounded promising, she began the process of finding her new home. She found what she was looking for on the third stop. The newly built complex was a little farther out on the northwest side than she would have preferred, but they had long and short lease options. The manager told her she could move in as soon as her credit check cleared. Andi filled out the application. With nothing to do but wait, she drove to HiHo.

Chapter Twenty-nine

When Andi walked into the office of the *HiHo News*, everything was pretty much the same as her previous visits. Rhonda was working at her desk and Kenny was in the back squealing out a country song.

Rhonda took one look at Andi and stood. "Kenny," she yelled. "I'm going to lunch, watch the front."

"It's only ten o'clock," he yelled.

"I'm a growing girl. I need nourishment."

"Gotcha covered," he called, then continued singing along with the radio.

Rhonda grabbed a light jacket and pulled it on over a navy blue polo with the words HIHO NEWS stitched over the breast pocket. As she pushed her way through the gate, she murmured to Andi, "I have a fantasy that he'll get laryngitis and not be able to sing above a whisper for an entire week."

Andi tried to laugh, but it stuck in her throat.

Neither of them spoke until they were in Rhonda's car and driving. "There's a Sonic at the edge of town. We can grab a burger and have a private conversation. The local ears are too big to try having one in any of the restaurants in town."

They rode the rest of the way in silence.

After placing their order, Rhonda turned to Andi. "What's going on? You look like crap."

Andi slowly told her about dinner with Janice, the fiasco that erupted after she returned home and her abrupt move.

"When will you be able to move into your apartment?" Rhonda asked.

"He said my application would be processed in two or three days."

"You can stay with us until you're able to move in."

"No, Rhonda. I wasn't hinting for a place . . ."

She dismissed Andi's protests. "If you have obligations that require you stay in San Antonio, I understand, but otherwise, why not enjoy a few days of clean country air? Carol and I are at work all day. You'd have the place to yourself. And as you already know, we have plenty of room."

The thought of spending another night in a cold, impersonal motel room didn't appeal to her. "Are you sure Carol won't mind?"

"Of course not. We love company."

Their food arrived. When they were alone again, Rhonda asked, "What are you going to do about Janice?"

"There's nothing I can do."

Rhonda stared out the windshield and thoughtfully munched on a tater tot. "I don't want to meddle, but I know Janice is as upset as you are. You two need to talk."

"It won't do any good."

Rhonda shrugged. "At least think about it."

Andi nodded.

"Enough of my meddling. How's the job search going?"

"I'm thinking about maybe looking into a different field."

"Really? What do you have in mind?"

"Freelance photography."

"That's a tough field to break into." She eyed Andi. "Have you ever sold anything?"

"No. Photography has always been a hobby for me."

"If you're interested, I might be able to use some of your shots occasionally. Kenny is the paper's pseudo photographer. He does okay, but it would be nice to be able to print better quality photos. Occasionally one of our articles from a local event is picked up by one of the larger papers. If we can use your photos, your work might attract the attention of one these papers. It'll take you a while to get a pipeline established, but once you do, you can make a decent living." Rhonda stopped eating suddenly and turned to Andi. "Would you be interested in maybe working as a sort of apprentice with a portrait photographer?"

"I've never really worked with portraits. The lighting and equipment was too expensive for casual use."

Rhonda started digging though a stack of paper and catalogs tucked between the seats. She pulled a cell phone from beneath the jumbled mess. "This could be your lucky day." She punched in a series of numbers. "Kenny, look on my desk in the blue folder marked Classifieds." She hesitated. "Yeah, that's it. There's a worksheet from Norten's Photography. What's the phone number on it?" She flipped the visor down and grabbed a small pencil and notebook from a pocket. "Got it. Thanks, Kenny." She held the number out to Andi. "He called yesterday. He needs someone who's dependable and, as he said, 'can count to ten without using their fingers.' If you're interested, I'm sure you'd have an excellent chance at the job."

Andi took the paper and stared at it. What harm could there be in just going to check it out? She glanced down at her sweater and jeans. "I'll need to go back to my parents' to get some more of my clothes."

"If you're going to get the clothes just for Nolan Norten, forget it. He's an old hippie. His only compromise to conformity was to cut his hair and shave. He once told me he only did that because he scared the kids so badly he could never get them to stop crying."

"Yuck. Are you sure he's someone I want to work with?"

"He's not much to look at, but the man is brilliant with a camera. Go talk to him."

Located three blocks over from the courthouse, Norten's Photography occupied a narrow two-story red brick building. The name of the shop was etched in elaborate italic script across the massive front window. A small bell tinkled when she pushed the door open.

"I'll be right with you," a man's deep voice boomed from the back. A moment later, a tall, bearlike man sporting a barely sub-dued Afro emerged.

Even with a counter separating them, Andi's first instinct was to run. The sheer size of him intimidated her.

"Can I help you?"

She quickly regained her composure. "Rhonda Younger from the *HiHo News* mentioned you had a job vacancy."

He chuckled. "You're not from around here, are you?"

"No. I'm from San Antonio, but I have transportation and I can—"

He waved her protests away. "I only meant that everyone in HiHo knows who Rhonda is. A local wouldn't have mentioned the paper."

"Oh." Andi took a deep breath, wondering why she had come here to begin with.

"Any past experience in photography?" He came out from behind the counter.

Andi tried not to stare at his bare feet. "I took a few courses in college and I guess I could classify myself as a fairly decent amateur photographer. My main interest is nature photography. I don't really have much experience with portraits."

"Are you willing to learn?"

"Yes. Definitely."

"How are your math and organizational skills?"

Andi relaxed. She was now in an element she could shine in. "I'm a Certified PMP. I worked eight years as—"

He held up his hand to stop her. "I don't know anything about a certified whatever. All I need is someone who can handle the office. Starting pay is eight dollars an hour and you're welcome to use the darkroom equipment in your spare time for your own personal use if you want. If you're interested in learning more about photography, I'll teach you whatever I know. I do a lot of school shoots, class pictures and such. I have to go to the schools to do them and I'd need you to act as an assistant then. You'll have to learn to help set up the equipment and such. I also do a lot of restoration work. I can teach you how to do that if you're interested. If you work out, your salary will increase after the first year. If you're still around after the fifth year and you're any good with a camera, we'll talk about making you a partner." He extended his hand. "That's all I can offer."

Andi studied his enormous hand. There had been no mention of a contract or security checks or multiple interviews. She felt a small sense of relief start to creep up her spine. She shook his hand. "When do I start?"

He shrugged. "Now's fine with me."

"What time do you start working?"

"The shop opens at nine, but I get here around eight-thirty."

"I'll see you tomorrow at eight-thirty," Andi promised.

He nodded. "Good."

She started to leave.

"Tell Rhonda Younger from the *HiHo News* that Nolan Norten from Norten's Photography says thanks." He smiled and with a wave disappeared into the back.

Chapter Thirty

Andi was all smiles when she returned to the newspaper office.

"That's better," Rhonda said as Andi made her way to the back of the shop. "I guess the interview went well."

"I start tomorrow morning."

Rhonda slapped her desk. "All right." She wiggled her eyebrows. "Does that mean HiHo is getting a new citizen?"

Andi stopped, confused. "No. I just applied for an apartment in San Antonio." Suddenly it hit her that she'd just agreed to take a job that paid eight dollars an hour and she would be traveling over forty miles one way. She groaned. "I didn't think this through very well."

"You have too many other things to think about. You need to get yourself settled. If you want to look around some more, all you have to do is call the apartment manager and cancel the agreement. You didn't sign a contract did you?"

"No. He wanted to wait until he had the results of my credit check."

"So call him and cancel the application."

Andi rolled her eyes. "Now I know why HiHo has such a high gay population. Do you always recruit so actively?"

"Nope, I want you nearby so that when either you or Janice finally come to your senses the other will be close."

Tears stung Andi's eyes.

"I'm sorry," Rhonda said, grabbing a tissue and handing it to her. "I was joking. I didn't mean to upset you."

"It's not you. I'm just exhausted."

Rhonda pulled a key ring from her pocket and deftly removed one. "This is the key to the house. Go on out and rest."

"Why are you being so nice to me?" Andi asked. "I mean, you don't even really know me."

Leaning back in the chair, Rhonda ran a hand through her short hair. For the first time Andi noticed the numerous strands of gray. "When I originally moved to HiHo, I couldn't let go of the big city paper mentality that had been hammered into me. I was working sixteen- and eighteen-hour days trying to turn the paper into a replica of what I'd known before. My relationship with Carol was on the verge of disintegrating because I was never home. I was physically and mentally exhausted. Then someone helped me to see and understand that there's more to life than work and making money. I suspect you're in a similar situation. You're constantly searching for some elusive thing that's always just out of your reach. You think you can only achieve it by struggling, when in reality all you have to do is relax and learn to enjoy what you have." She let the chair swing upright as she jumped up. "Enough Younger philosophy. Carol and I will be home around six. You can use the spare bedroom. It's all the way down at the end of the hallway, on the right. It has its own bath, so if you want to hunker down and ignore us, you can. Or if you feel like joining us for dinner, we usually eat around seven. Nothing fancy, but we're both pretty good cooks." She patted her solid waistline.

Andi stood and on impulse gave Rhonda a hug. "Thanks. I won't forget this."

"Scat. I have work to do. I have news-hungry subscribers sitting on the edge of their chairs anxiously awaiting the next scintillating issue of the *HiHo News*. Can you find your way to the house?"

Andi nodded and left. As she stepped out of the doorway, Maudie Anderson popped off a bench located in front of the newspaper. Her poodle, Ellie, stood patiently beside her.

"I thought that was you," Maudie chirped. "Ellie and I just picked up the new Sears catalog. Do you want to go over to the Blue Moon and look at it with me?" She waved the catalog.

She was on the verge of declining, but the look of hopeful anticipation on Maudie's face stopped her. "I've already eaten lunch, but I suppose I could use a cup of coffee. I can only stay a little while though. I have errands to run."

"Me too," Maudie said. "Come on, Ellie. Let's see if we can find you a new coat for Christmas."

It was almost two hours later before Andi made it to Rhonda and Carol's house. She used her cell phone to call her father and tell him about her new job.

"I know it's not much," she said after she had filled him in on all the particulars, "but I think I'll enjoy working there. I feel like it's what I need now."

"That's a long drive to make every day. Are you going to move to HiHo?"

"I'm not sure yet. I still have time to opt out of the application for the apartment. I know it would upset Mom if I moved down here."

He was silent for a moment. "Andi, the fact that your mother was unhappy in HiHo doesn't mean you have to be. Your mother will understand that you're doing what you have to do. You have to learn to do what you think is best for yourself and stop worrying about other people. If you're happy, those around you will sense it and be happy for you."

"I'm going to be staying with friends for a few days, but I'll come for my things as soon as I decide what I'm going to do."

"Don't worry about that. Your stuff isn't in the way. You can take as long as you need. I wish you'd call, or better yet, come and see your mom and grandmother."

Andi wasn't so sure her mother would be as understanding as her dad had been. She ended the call quickly to avoid having to make a promise to call her mother.

She walked around the spacious yard. A wide variety of birds provided a symphony as she explored the small wooded area behind the house. She found herself wishing she had a place like this that she could retreat to on those days when the world became too hectic. She walked deeper into the woods until she came upon a small clearing. After a quick perusal of the area for fire ants, she sat down in the middle of it. She let the sun seep into her, warming her muscles and bones until she felt as if she were made of putty. Several deep breaths cleared away the last of the knots that had kept her stomach clenched for the past several days. She slowly began to let go of the anger that had been consuming her. She forgave Trish for attempting to throw away her things. She released herself from any responsibility for the phone company's laying her off. She allowed herself to realize that her grandmother asked for help, not miracles. She'd tried her best to clear Sean Gray's name. She allowed herself to accept the fact that she would never be perfect and, in truth, her mother had never asked perfection from either of her children. Andi's own distorted sense of failure was at the root of her problem, and she'd unjustly tried to place the blame on her mother. Finally, she let go of the anger she felt toward herself for never measuring up to what she thought people expected of her.

When she emerged from the woods, she knew what it meant to be reborn. She felt brand new and full of hope. She looked forward to going to work the next day. After the warmth and brilliance of the sun, the house seemed cool and dark. She grabbed her cell phone and went to the enclosed back porch. She called the apartment complex and told the manager she had changed her mind. He wasn't happy, but there was nothing he could do about it. As she set the phone down, she saw a copy of last week's *HiHo News* lying on the table. She picked it up and flipped to the Classifieds. There were three real estate agents listed. Two were men. She chose the woman.

A short time later, she was following the directions the agent had given her. She turned onto a gravel road just north of town and soon spotted the Baker Realty sign. Dana Clark, the realtor, had warned her that the spacious old farmhouse was in need of work but assured her it was all cosmetic.

Dana was on the porch waiting when Andi drove up.

"I'm glad to see you didn't get lost."

"You gave really good directions." Andi was eager to see the inside of the house.

"You were at Rhonda and Carol's barbecue last Saturday, weren't you?"

Andi looked at her closer and nodded, embarrassed that she didn't remember Dana.

Clearly sensing her discomfort, Dana smiled. "I got there late. We never met, but I heard about how you set Bea back on her heels."

"I really didn't do anything," Andi protested.

"I believe that was the point. I don't think anyone has ever turned Bea down."

"Why not?"

"I don't know. There's just something there when you first meet her. Apparently, you're not easily swayed by shallow charm."

Andi remembered how easily she had fallen under Trish's spell. "Maybe it's like chickenpox. Once you've been exposed, you become immune."

Dana studied her for a moment before dangling a key. "Ready to see the house?"

The door opened into a large living room. Several windows filled the room with light, but the wide front porch would prevent the hot August sun from pouring in. Straight ahead was an ample dining room, to the left was a hallway, and to the right a bedroom with its own bath. They walked through the dining room and into an enormous kitchen. Tall oak cabinets with glass pane doors set Andi's heart to singing. The back porch was enclosed with screen. Returning to the living room, Andi followed Dana down the hallway to three additional bedrooms. The first bedroom had a set of double doors with glass inserts that opened out onto a small side porch. Andi immediately envisioned the room as a library. The second bedroom was smaller, but still of ample size. The master bedroom was huge and had a doorway that led to yet another porch. The house needed lots of paint, some landscaping, new carpeting, window coverings and a host of little things that would keep Andi occupied for a long time, but the roof and foundation were sound.

"The house sits on five acres of land, three of which are wooded," Dana informed her.

"What's the asking price?" Andi asked and held her breath.

"It's a wonderful place, but as you see it needs some fixing up," Dana hedged.

"How much?" Andi asked.

"He wants eighty-five thousand."

"Let's start the paperwork," Andi said ignoring the shocked look on Dana's face.

Dana recovered quickly and shook Andi's hand. "I think you're going to love living in HiHo. The water out here isn't great, but if you install a water softener you won't have any problems. You're less than five miles from town, so your homeowner's insurance won't be too outrageous." She continued talking about insurance, but Andi wasn't listening.

She was busy deciding wall colors and whether the floor in the dining room should be tile or hardwood.

Chapter Thirty-one

It was after five by the time Andi completed the paperwork for submitting a bid on the farmhouse. She decided not to mention the house to anyone until she found out whether her bid had been accepted or not.

Neither Carol nor Rhonda was home when Andi returned. She tried watching television, but she couldn't sit still. She wandered into Rhonda's library and perused the titles. Most of the books dealt with history. As she trailed her fingertips along the spines, one of the titles caught her attention. It was a history of the Mabry family. Andi removed the book and sat down in a rocking chair. The title page told her that the book had been self-published by Marianne Mabry Suttler in 1959. The book had been published before Janice was born. Andi lost interest. She idly flipped through the pages. The center of the book held several pages of black-and-white photos. Andi leafed through them until she found Gary Wayne Mabry. Turning on the table lamp, she studied the photo closer. The caption read "Gary Wayne Mabry, son of Edward Wayne Mabry and Mary Elizabeth White Mabry." He appeared to be in his mid-twenties and was a small man with delicate features. His tiny hands were clasped in front of him and his head seemed to jut forward in defiance. Because it was a black-and-white photo, she wasn't able to distinguish the color of his hair. His eyes were his most arresting feature. They appeared almost translucent. She stared at the image. *Was he capable of murder?* she wondered. She stared until the print began to waver. She flipped the page over and revealed a photo of a matching pair of pistols. The caption told her the .45 caliber Colt pistols had been given to Clayton Mabry when he retired from the bench in 1904. She was about to close the book when she noticed the last sentence of the caption: PHOTOGRAPH COURTESY OF THE TEXAS STATE HISTORICAL COMMISSION. Why had the author gone to the state historical commission when she could have taken a photo of the weapons herself?

She stared at the picture. A .45 caliber pistol had been used to shoot George Zucker. *What had become of the bullet that killed him?* she wondered. *Would it have been kept as evidence?*

A thin phone book sat beneath the phone on Rhonda's desk. Andi quickly found the number to the DA's office and dialed. She was both relieved and surprised when Janice answered her own phone.

"Hi," Andi said. When there wasn't an immediate response, she quickly added, "It's me, Andi."

"Yes, I know. What can I do for you?"

Stop being so cold, Andi wanted to scream, but she knew her next question would drive the wedge even deeper between them.

"One of your ancestors, Judge Clayton Mabry, was given a set of matching pistols in nineteen-oh-four. Where are they?"

"What?"

"Marianne Mabry Suttler published a family history and in it there's a photo of the pistols. She got it from the Texas State Historical Commission. Why didn't she take a photo of the pistols herself?"

176

Janice exhaled noisily. "One of the pistols was stolen years ago."

"When?"

"How should I know? What difference does it make anyway?"

"I need to know."

Andi heard a loud scraping noise, followed by the sound of Janice pacing.

"I honestly don't know," Janice said. "I seem to remember hearing it was discovered missing when Aunt Marianne was working on the book. But the pistols had been stored away in the attic for years."

"Why were they in the attic? I would think these would be fairly valuable."

"I have no idea. This happened before I was born. What's the big deal with these pistols?"

"The pistols were forty-five-caliber Colts," Andi said.

"So?" Janice hesitated. "Oh. You think my grandfather killed George Zucker with that pistol. He was sixteen then. His father owned one of the largest ranches around. They weren't hurting for money. Why would he rob a store?"

"I don't know," Andi admitted.

"What is it with you? Why are you so damn determined to accuse my grandfather of murder?"

Andi rubbed her forehead. It always came back to the fact that Gary Wayne Mabry was Janice's grandfather. "I don't know. Things keep popping up. Maybe I'm angry that my great-grandfather was convicted on so little evidence."

"He was found with a dead man and a bag full of money," Janice snapped. "Let's not forget that."

An uneasy silence fell between them.

"We can't seem to get around this issue," Andi said.

"It's starting to feel like we're beating a dead horse." When Andi didn't reply, Janice changed the subject. "I hear you're going to be working for Nolan Norten."

"How did you hear that?"

Janice chuckled. "You have a lot to learn about living in a small town. Everybody knows your business ten minutes before you do."

Andi wondered if Janice had heard about her placing a bid on the house. "Does it bother you that I'll be working here?"

"No. You have a right to work wherever you want. I was kind of surprised you'd take such a low-paying job."

"It's not so bad," Andi argued. "Besides, it'll give me an opportunity to improve my own photographic skills."

"I didn't even know you liked photography."

"I guess there's a lot we don't know about each other."

"Was there anything else you needed to know about my family or our belongings?"

The comment hurt, but Andi did have another question. "What happened to the bullet that killed George Zucker? Would it have been considered evidence?"

"I'm not sure if they kept it or not. Since the gun was never found, there was nothing to compare the bullet to. They may have simply pitched it after the conviction. Or it could have simply gotten lost over the years."

Andi was disappointed.

"How long will you be staying with Rhonda and Carol?"

"Dang, you weren't joking about everyone knowing your business. How did you know I was staying with them?"

"The sheriff drove past their place and saw a strange car parked in the driveway. He ran the plates and your name popped up. By the way, you need to get your registration updated. You're still showing a Dallas address."

Andi's mouth fell open. "Why did he go to you with the information?"

Janice laughed. "He didn't. My receptionist, Betty, eats lunch with the dispatcher at the sheriff's office. Need I say more?"

"My gosh. This is scary. I'll be too paranoid to go anywhere."

"As long as you aren't doing something you shouldn't, who cares where you are?"

Andi wasn't certain she agreed with that but let it slide. "Do you think we could have dinner some night?"

"Why? You know what'll happen. You'll accuse my grandfather of murder and I'll defend him. There's no future in that."

She wished she could counter the accusation but knew Janice was probably right. She tried to think of something else to say to keep her on the phone, but nothing came to mind. "I guess I'll see you around town."

"Without a doubt. Oh, and you'll love the Carpenter place. Good luck with your bid."

Before Andi could respond, Janice disconnected. "The first thing I'm getting is some heavy drapery," she muttered as she hung up.

Rhonda arrived home a few minutes later. Andi was reading a county history that had been published for the county's sesquicentennial anniversary celebration.

"Cramming to get acquainted with your new community?"

Andi studied Rhonda's smiling face and realized she had already heard about her house-hunting expedition. "I cannot believe how quickly news travels. These people are faster than a wire service."

"You'll get used to it after a couple of years. It bugged the heck out of me for a while, but I eventually found myself doing the same thing."

"Well, if you know so much, are they going to accept my bid?"

"Probably. The Carpenters only had one son and he lives somewhere in Montana. He's been trying to sell the place for a couple of years."

Andi's stomach gave a queasy turn. "Oh, no. What's wrong with it?"

"Nothing as far as I know. He started out asking too much and refused to come down on his price. He apparently didn't remember how low land prices are around here. He finally got the message a few weeks ago and lowered the price. But because it's been on the market so long, people were afraid to buy it, thinking there must be something drastically wrong with it." She headed toward the kitchen and Andi followed. "So you see," she said as she pulled a package of hamburger meat from the freezer, "sometimes the gossipmongers do you a favor."

"You really think he'll accept the bid?"

"I can't say with a hundred percent certainty, but if I were you, I'd start thinking about what color I was going to paint the house."

Andi couldn't stop herself from dancing a little jig. "I can't believe this day. I started out jobless in a motel room and in less than ten hours I've gotten a job and put a bid in on a house."

"That's the way it goes sometimes." Rhonda turned to face her. "Or maybe something deep inside was trying to draw you back to HiHo."

Andi rolled her eyes. "You should give up the newspaper business and start writing science fiction."

"No, thanks. Real life is much scarier. How are you at chopping onions?"

Andi couldn't keep from humming as she began to chop. It looked as though she was finally going to get settled.

After dinner, the three women sat in the living room talking about Andi's new job and the probability of her buying a house in HiHo. When the conversation slowed, Carol asked how Andi's investigation into George Zucker's murder was progressing.

Andi didn't ask how Carol knew. By now she would've been surprised had Carol not known about it. "I guess it's at a dead end. I don't know who else to talk to. There's no evidence to reexamine." She told them about the pair of .45s that had been given to Clayton Mabry, and how one had supposedly been stolen.

Carol frowned. "You think that was the gun used as the murder weapon?"

Andi shrugged. "I don't know what I think. Clyde Doleski was so convincing. I guess I'm having trouble letting go of his story."

"That reminds me," Rhonda said. "He was telling the truth about being a screenwriter, but he wrote under the name of Clyde Doles. That's why I didn't find him the other day when you were in the shop. I had to do some major cross-referencing to tie the two names together."

"I wish I could find an old city map of HiHo," Andi said.

"Why?" Carol asked.

"I'd like to look at one and get the layout of the streets and alleys in my mind. It's hard to drive around town now and try to picture how it looked sixty-five years ago."

"I may have something." Rhonda disappeared into her office.

"I swear that woman collects old document like some women do shoes."

"It could be worse," Rhonda said as she came back with a large flat box. "I could be out collecting the hearts of all those cute young women."

Carol rolled her eyes but smiled. "In your dreams."

Rhonda put the box on the floor and opened it. Inside were several maps of different types and areas. It took her almost ten minutes to finally find one that depicted the HiHo Township. "This is dated nineteen forty-five, but I doubt if much changed during those years." She spread the map out on the coffee table and the three of them huddled over it. The name of the owner of each piece of property was carefully written inside each block.

"Here's the restaurant, so this square would have been the mercantile," Rhonda said as she tapped the map. She moved her finger over two squares to the right. "Here's the barbershop. It shows Doleski as the owner. I'm guessing that's Clyde's grandfather."

Andi studied the map closely. "Let's say Clyde actually saw the killer run past the window. Whoever shot Zucker ran out the back door, slipped through the fence and headed east past the barbershop. If the streets were the same in nineteen thirty-nine, he had two choices. He either had to duck into one of these other buildings or else continue running through the alley until he reached the edge of town." Andi counted the buildings to the end of the street. There were only eight beyond the barbershop.

Carol reached over and began to trace where Andi had stopped. "From there," Carol said, "he either came back out to Main Street or he would have continued on down this road."

181

"That's the old Holstetter place," Rhonda said, tapping the next block. "But it looks like it's owned by Gary Wayne Mabry by 'forty-five."

Andi felt a chill run down her spine. There was something in the back of her memory. Something her grandmother had told her. "The well," she murmured. "They had the best water in the area until it collapsed."

Carol looked at her, puzzled.

"It's something my grandmother told me," Andi explained.

Rhonda was still staring at the map. "Do you know where this road leads?" she asked softly.

Carol glanced down. "Oh, shit."

Andi stared at the square Rhonda was pointing to. The road ran directly to the Mabry place.

Chapter Thirty-two

The clock beside the bed read two forty-eight. Andi didn't know if it was the strange bed, the excitement of starting a new job or the fact that she was fairly certain she knew where the weapon that killed George Zucker was. She turned onto her side and tried to decide what to do. If she found the gun and it matched the photo in the Mabry family history book, she could clear her great-grandfather's name, but Gary Wayne Mabry would probably be charged with murder.

If he killed George Zucker he should be punished, she reasoned. *But then, he wouldn't be the only one punished. Janice would suffer as well.*

Andi turned over onto her back. *My mother and grandmother suffered for years and Sean Gray died in prison for a crime he didn't commit.*

Was there any justice to be found in prosecuting Gary Wayne Mabry at this late date? Was it merely vengeance? By all accounts, he was a frail old man who was partially paralyzed.

Tired of tossing and turning, Andi got out of bed, stood by the window and stared out into the cold night. A security lamp cast a wide stretch of illumination across the backyard. Beyond the reach of the light it was pitch black. Andi strained her eyes trying to penetrate the ebony curtain, trying to understand what it held.

She watched a bat swoop in to prey on the bugs being hypnotically drawn to the warmth and false security of the light. *Why were the insects so compelled to fling themselves into certain disaster?* she wondered.

If she forgot about the past, she might have a chance in getting to know Janice better. But if she exposed Gary Wayne as the real killer, the possibility of a relationship was doomed.

She sat by the window and stared into the night until the sun slowly crept over the horizon. As the first rosy rays peaked over the trees it occurred to her that she didn't have the right to decide Gary Wayne Mabry's fate. Her responsibility lay in finding out the truth. It hurt to know that within a few short hours she would completely destroy any possibility of ever having a relationship with Janice Reed.

She and Rhonda left for the newspaper office a little after seven that morning. Rhonda helped her search through the archived copies of the *HiHo News*. By seven-thirty, Andi held the last piece of information she needed to confirm her suspicions.

She sat in her car in the parking lot at the district attorney's office waiting. She knew Janice would be the first to arrive. As soon as Janice pulled in, Andi got out of the car and waited for her. Even from a distance, she could see the dark circles beneath Janice's eyes.

"I need to talk to you," Andi said.

Janice merely nodded before slowly heading toward the building. They didn't speak until they were both seated in Janice's office.

"I think I know where the gun is," Andi said without preamble.

Janice flinched. "Where?"

"In the well on the old Holstetter place. I checked the archives of the newspaper this morning. George Zucker was shot on May fourth, nineteen thirty-nine. The Holstetters' well collapsed that night. They tried to clear it out, but it collapsed again before they could finish. Your grandfather bought the property when he turned twenty-one. He never lived there or did anything with it. I think he bought it to ensure no one else did anything with it."

Janice stared out the window for several long seconds before she spoke. "He's dying, Andi. What good will it do to bring this out? He's already suffering."

"Who are you protecting? Him or yourself?" Andi didn't ask the question to be mean or hateful. She needed to know who Janice was protecting. She expected Janice to lash out.

Instead, Janice stood, walked slowly to her office door and opened it. "I think you should leave."

Andi stood to leave. As she reached Janice, she stopped and gazed into the light blue eyes that were now frozen in pain. Andi leaned forward and kissed her.

Janice's hands grabbed Andi's head and pulled her closer as their kiss deepened. Just as suddenly, Janice pushed her away and turned back to her desk, but not before Andi saw the tears streaming down her face.

Andi arrived at the photo shop as Nolan was opening the door. He glanced at her, clearly surprised. "You don't have to be here until nine," he said as they went inside.

She tucked her hands into her jacket pockets. "I thought I'd come in early and spend the time just looking around and getting acquainted with things."

He gave a small nod. "Come on back and I'll show you around." He gave her a brief tour of the shop and then showed her to a desk in a small alcove at the back of the building. "I didn't set up the filing or the billing system. I had one of the business career kids from the high school come over and do it for me. It took me forever to figure it out after she left." He scratched his head. "I still don't really know how to use it. I keep changing things to make it work for whatever I'm doing. You can arrange it any way you want, but make sure you explain it to me if you decide not to stay." He turned away. "I'm going to be working in the darkroom this morning. I don't have an appointment until two this afternoon. If you need to talk to me, use the intercom." He pointed to a small white box on the desk. "You know not to open the door of the darkroom when I'm in there, don't you?"

Andi nodded. "Yes. I know it would ruin the film."

With a final grunt he headed to the darkroom.

Andi spent the rest of the day arranging the office files and trying to decipher the strange billing system.

After work Andi walked to the newspaper office and found Rhonda sitting at her desk, staring into space.

"Are you okay?" Andi asked as she pulled a chair over.

"Yeah. I'm bummed out about this whole mess. All day long I've been thinking about how horrible it must have been for your great-grandfather to go to prison knowing he was innocent. And then I think about how this is going to tear Janice up. It's going to affect the entire town. Gary Wayne Mabry is an icon here."

Andi leaned back. "I should've never started this."

"I agree and disagree. From a friend's point of view, I don't want Janice to suffer, but from a moral point of view, an innocent man has a right to have his name cleared, and the guilty should pay for their crimes."

"He's dying. Who's really going to suffer in all of this? Not him. At least not for very long." Andi's words sounded harsher than she meant them to.

"What are you going to do?" Rhonda asked. "If anyone else gets wind of this, the story will spread like wildfire and someone will start screaming for an investigation."

186

"I'm going to talk to my mom and my grandmother tonight. They have a right to know what's going on. I talked to Janice this morning and told her what I suspect happened."

"You know, as the DA, all of this will fall on her office if you decide to pursue it further."

"I know. It's not going to matter anyway. If Gary Wayne dropped that pistol into the Holstetters' well, he isn't going to give anyone permission to dig, and I doubt there's enough evidence to get a court order."

"The problem always comes back to motive. Why would Gary Wayne rob Zucker?" Rhonda asked, shaking her head.

"I've got to get going. If I don't make it back tonight, don't worry. I'll stay with my parents if it gets too late."

"Good luck," Rhonda called as Andi walked away.

Chapter Thirty-three

Andi parked her car in front of her parents' house and walked slowly up the driveway. She took her time searching for the correct key. Locating it, she hesitated. It suddenly seemed wrong to just stroll in and upset everyone. What if she was wrong and the gun wasn't at the bottom of the well? Or worse: What if the gun had been stolen and her bungling ended up convincing everyone that Gary Wayne Mabry was guilty, but he really wasn't? Of course, she could get everything all stirred up, yet nothing concrete could be found and her family would have to endure the entire process all over again.

Terrified at all the pain her probing was causing, she turned to leave, and as she did, the door swung open.

"Andi," her dad said and smiled. "I thought I heard a car. Why didn't you come on in?"

"I . . . I dropped my keys and couldn't find the right one."

He glanced at her key ring and nodded slightly. "Come on in. Your mother and grandmother would love to see you."

Andi followed him inside to the kitchen where the two women were working side by side. She noticed the spark of joy in their eyes as they looked up and saw her. Her mother stepped forward and hugged her. Andi clung to her, praying she wouldn't hurt her mother more than she already had. She hugged her grandmother and tried not to notice how fragile she felt.

"We just finished dinner. Let me fix you a plate," her mother said as she began uncovering dishes.

"No, thanks. I ate before I left," Andi lied. She knew she would never be able to swallow anything without choking on it.

"Are you sure? You've lost weight."

Andi smiled. "Mom, I've not lost weight and it wouldn't hurt if I did lose some."

"Nonsense," her grandmother scolded. "I don't understand young women now. Why does everyone have to be a beanpole?"

Her father handed her a cup of coffee. "I know you won't refuse this," he said. "The weather is getting cooler."

Andi sat at the kitchen table and watched as her parents and grandmother worked together cleaning the kitchen. She wondered if telling them what she had discovered was a mistake.

One by one, they joined her at the table as if they knew she was here to discuss something important. Several major family decisions had been made at this table. She had come out to them at this table.

Her father refilled his coffee cup and was the last to sit down. Without prompting, they all fell silent and looked at her, waiting.

"I may have found something," she began. "But I don't know what to do with the information." She was afraid her mother might leave the table.

Instead, Leticia took a deep breath and looked Andi in the eye. "Tell us what we can do to help."

Andi felt the weight begin to lift from her shoulders. As she told them Clyde Doleski's story, and her suspicions about the Holstetters' well, and the missing Colt .45 belonging to Clayton Mabry, the weight continued to lighten.

When she finished her story, she turned to her grandmother. "I don't know if it's enough, but it's all I could find."

Sarah reached over and patted Andi's hand. "I'm the one who should be apologizing. I never should've asked you to start this. I should've realized it would only cause pain."

Her father leaned forward. "You said that Janice Reed is still the DA?"

Andi glanced down and nodded.

"What's she like?" he asked.

"She's well-respected by everyone I've talked to. She seems honest, but she loves her grandfather. He raised her after her parents died in a car crash. She seems like a decent person. She has a great sense of humor and she's—" Andi stopped, realizing she was going a little overboard on the description. She had been on the verge of telling them how cute Janice was. She glanced up to find them all gazing at her expectantly.

Her parents exchanged glances and a silent agreement must have passed between them, because it was Andi's mother who asked, "Andrea, is there something else you'd like to tell us about Janice?"

Andi's hands slipped to her lap. She struggled to find a way to talk herself out of the corner she had backed herself into. She looked at each of them in turn and finally admitted the truth. "I really like her. I think maybe—" Andi took a deep breath and met her parents' gaze. "I really like her."

There was only a slight pause before her mother went to get the cheesecake, while her father made another pot of coffee, and Andi and her grandmother collected plates and silverware. It was going to be a long night.

As they ate, Andi told them about her new job and the bid she placed on the old Carpenter place.

"That used to be a beautiful home," Sarah said. "I remember when Aida and Jeff Carpenter were married and lived there. They only had the one son. Aida and I worked at the grain elevator together, until we both got married. Thomas and I had dinner with them a few times. We sort of lost touch with them after we moved to San Antonio." She pushed her cup back. "They were good people."

Her mother chuckled. "Well, that son of theirs wasn't so good. He used to try to pay the girls a dime to show him their underwear."

Andrew tilted his head and tickled Leticia's hand. "Were you one of those girls?"

Leticia playfully slapped his hand away and turned serious again. "We need to make a decision on what to do about this situation."

Andrew leaned back. "I think that should be decided between you three. My only input will be to remind Andi that if she has decided to live in HiHo, she might want to think of the repercussions that could accompany destroying Gary Wayne Mabry's image."

"Mom, what do you think?" Leticia asked.

Sarah was silent for a long while. "I want to see my father's name cleared. I'm not interested in revenge. But I don't want Andi to suffer for something that happened before she was even born." She took a deep, shaky breath. "I think it's best to let it alone." Tears shone in her eyes as she turned to Andi. "I don't think Papa would've wanted you to sacrifice your chance for happiness. He's gone and there's nothing anyone can do to bring him back." She placed her hand over Andi's. She tried to sound as though it didn't matter, but Andi could hear the disappointment in her grandmother's voice.

"Mom?" Andi prompted.

Leticia stared at the table. "My first response, as you well remember, was horror. I have painful memories of growing up in HiHo, but during the last few days I've begun to realize I also have some wonderful ones. I would like to see Grandpa's name cleared, but I can't be sure my motives are strictly unselfish ones. I've asked myself how proving his innocence would benefit him, and it all comes back to his name. I believe he has the right to have his name

191

cleared." She turned to Andrew. "Is there any way we could clear Grandpa's name but not prosecute Gary Wayne Mabry even if we can prove he's the murderer?"

Andrew shook his head. "It's not up to us to prosecute him or not. It's up to the DA."

They fell silent.

"Then let it go," Leticia said. "That young woman shouldn't have to go through that. She's not responsible for his actions."

"Let God be his judge," her grandmother said softly. With those words, it was settled.

"Will you spend the night?" Leticia asked.

"No. I have to work tomorrow. I think it would be easier to drive back tonight rather than early tomorrow."

They were walking her to the door when the phone rang. Her father said good-bye and raced to get it.

Andi was hugging her mother when her dad came in holding the phone up. "Andi, you have a call."

She frowned but took it from him.

"If you're interested," Janice began, "I'll be excavating the Holstetters' well tomorrow morning. Granddad signed a release. The digging will start at eight."

"Thanks," Andi replied as the line went dead.

Her dad took the phone from her hand. "What's wrong?"

She stared at him. "That was Janice. She's excavating the well tomorrow morning at eight."

Chapter Thirty-four

After Janice's phone call, it was decided that Andi would spend the night with her parents, and then she and her grandmother would go to HiHo together the following morning to watch the excavation.

Andi called Rhonda to let her know she wouldn't be returning to HiHo that evening and to bring them up-to-date on what was going on. "Rhonda, would you call Janice and make sure she's all right?" Andi asked. "I don't think she'll want to talk to me."

"I'll check on her," Rhonda promised. "How are you doing?"

"I'm afraid they won't find anything, but I'm also scared they will."

"Try to sleep. You have no control over what they find or don't find tomorrow."

Hanging up with Rhonda, Andi called directory assistance for Nolan Norten's home number. She told him something had come up and she needed to take care of some personal business. She was embarrassed to have to ask for time off on her second day, but he took it in stride and told her to come in when she could.

Andi went to bed and finally fell into an exhausted slumber.

The following morning the sun was barely peeking over the horizon when Andi and her grandmother headed toward HiHo. Even with their early start, they got caught up in the morning traffic snarl as they headed across town. By the time they arrived at the Holstetter place, a backhoe was already at work. Lengths of yellow tape enclosed the area around the backhoe. A police officer stood off to the side carefully watching the work. He started toward the car when Andi pulled up.

Janice and a heavyset man wearing a suit stood just outside the tape. She stepped forward and spoke to the policeman. He nodded and went back to his post.

Andi started toward Janice but stopped when Janice shook her head and turned away. Andi and her grandmother went back to stand by the car and watch.

The backhoe would remove a section of dirt and dump it to the rear. Two men with rakes then smoothed the dirt out and a third man walked over it swinging a metal detector.

After watching the first few repetitions of this with no results, Andi's anxiety began to lessen. She noticed the cool morning air for the first time. "Let's sit in the car and watch," she said as she turned to her grandmother.

After getting in the car, her grandmother produced a thermos and handed a cup of hot coffee to her.

"You aren't having any?" Andi asked.

Sarah gave a short shake of her head. "I'm too nervous."

The minutes slipped into hours. By ten, the warmth of the car, coupled with the muffled rumble of the backhoe and the lack of sleep from the two previous nights, were beginning to wear Andi's resistance down. She considered having another cup of coffee, hoping it would wake her up, but she didn't have the energy. Her lids drooped.

A shout startled Andi awake. Sarah threw the car door open and was running toward the excavation before Andi could get out of the car. Andi ran and caught up with her just as Sarah reached the edge of the tape.

The police officer had something in his gloved hand. He took it to Janice.

"It's a gun," Andi whispered to her grandmother.

Sarah leaned against her. "I always knew he was innocent," she said. "I'm cold. I'll wait in the car." She walked away.

Andi wanted to see the gun closer. She went to stand beside Janice, who was looking at the rusted relic. Even with the dirt and rust, Andi could still see the ivory pistol grip. It looked exactly like the guns in the photo. She wondered if the murderer had left fingerprints on the weapon, and if so whether the rust and grime would allow them to be retrieved.

Janice handed the artifact back to the police officer and told him to treat it as evidence before turning to Andi with tears in her eyes. "Are you happy now?" She and the man in the suit walked away.

Andi stumbled back to the car. She had never felt so lousy in her life.

After driving Sarah home, Andi decided to go to work. She needed to find something to keep her busy. A few calls came in to schedule a shooting with Nolan, but she noticed that a lot of his business was from people coming in wanting to have old photos restored. Just before closing time, a woman arrived with three old black-and-white photos she wanted touched up and enlarged. Andi was filling out the ticket when the woman said, "Can you believe it?"

"What's that?" Andi asked, more from politeness than interest. She was so tired she could barely hold her head up.

"Haven't you heard? Janice Reed resigned."

Andi looked up from the ticket. "What?"

"That was exactly my reaction," the woman exclaimed. "She's the best district attorney we've ever had and now she's gone and resigned."

Andi handed the woman her receipt and carefully tucked the photos into an envelope. "We'll call you when your photos are ready," she said automatically.

"I wonder what that was all about," Nolan said as he came out from the back.

Andi couldn't answer. She kept staring at the door, wondering how much larger this was going to get before it ground to a halt.

"You'll get used to the gossip," Nolan said, misinterpreting her silence. "After a while, you'll find yourself joining in. Guess it's human nature."

"I suppose," Andi murmured.

"Let's get out of here before Maudie and Ellie come by to tell us all the latest news," he said. "I love the old girl, but if she gets to talking, it'll take an hour to get her out the door."

"Thanks for letting me have the time this morning," she said as they began turning off lights.

"I figure eventually I'll be one of the first people to know why you were out there while they were digging up the Old Holstetter place."

She looked over to find him grinning at her.

"There's no secrets in HiHo," he reminded her.

After leaving work, Andi walked over to the newspaper office. Rhonda and Shawna were at their desks working, and as usual, Kenny was in the back singing.

"The paper's due out tomorrow night and with Janice's resignation statement, we're having to make some changes," Rhonda explained as she stared at the computer screen.

"How is she?" Andi asked.

Rhonda took a deep breath and slowly let it out. "She's not doing so well. How are you?"

"I feel like crap."

"I know what you mean. This is the first issue of the paper that I've hated working on. Are you staying at the house tonight or going back into San Antonio?"

"I thought I'd stay here, if that's all right. I know I've put you and Carol in the middle of all this."

"Go on to the house and rest. Carol could probably use some company. Tell her I'll call her if I'm going to be later than ten."

"Is there anything I can do to help you here?" Andi asked.

Rhonda shook her head but called out loudly, "You could steal Kenny's radio. That would be a big help."

Shawna giggled and Kenny began to sing louder as Andi made her escape. As she stepped out the door, she held her breath, hoping Maudie wouldn't be lying in wait. She slowly relaxed as she safely made her way to her car and drove toward Rhonda and Carol's. She turned off Main Street and rolled down her window, hoping the crisp night air would revive her. Somewhere in the distance, she heard a siren. Looking in her rearview mirror, she saw an ambulance blur through town. As she left the city limits and picked up speed, the cold wind forced her to roll her window up, but as soon as she did, the car felt too warm. She partially opened her sunroof and let the cold night air gradually fill the car. Her skin felt bruised, and a headache was beginning to build at the base of her neck. As she eased onto the gravel road leading to Rhonda and Carol's, she slowed down to lessen the impact of the bumpy road. She gritted her teeth as headlights appeared ahead of her. She wasn't used to driving on such a narrow road, and so far she'd been lucky enough not to meet another car. She eased over to the side and practically stopped as the approaching vehicle grew nearer. It too moved over and without slowing flew past.

"Asshole," Andi shouted, as an enormous blinding cloud of dust bellowed out in its wake.

She intended to wait for the dust to clear but noticed in her rearview mirror that the car that had just passed was backing up. She suddenly remembered her sunroof was open. Had the driver heard her cursing him?

"Oh crap, I don't need this." She maneuvered her car back to the center of the road and took off. Her heart crawled into her throat as the vehicle turned around and followed her. Andi sped up as much as she dared and prayed Carol would be home. The car was gaining on her. Andi took a chance and accelerated. The headlights dropped back but continued to follow her.

As she reached the house, she whipped into the driveway and screamed as the car careened sideways. She fought the steering wheel until she regained control. The headlights behind her drew closer. Andi's limbs grew weak at the sight of the empty driveway. She had been depending on Carol's being home. Suddenly it hit her that she didn't have to remain on the driveway. There was an open field on either side. She would drive back to the newspaper office. She knew Rhonda would still be there. She tried to judge where the best point to make her move would be. She didn't want to give the other driver time to cut her off. She took her foot off the accelerator and forced herself to let the other car draw closer. As it did so, she swung her car sharply to the right and stomped the gas pedal.

Dirt and grass flew everywhere as Andi tore past her pursuer. As she roared toward the road, she realized the other vehicle had stopped and was flashing its lights on and off. She looked back through the haze of dust and saw someone getting out of the car. She slowed down and finally stopped. Was it a trick? The person moved to the front of the car and began waving her back.

Andi shifted into reverse and slowly eased toward the house. As she drew closer, she recognized the waving figure that was now running to meet her. It was Carol. Releasing a loud shaky breath, she stopped and waited. "You scared the crap out of me," she said as Carol crawled into the passenger seat.

"Let's go," Carol yelled.

Confused, Andi put the car in gear. "Where are we going?"

"The hospital. Rhonda called. She heard over the scanner that the police and an ambulance have been dispatched to the Mabry place."

"What happened?"

"She didn't know, but the dispatcher said shots had been fired."

Andi tore out of the driveway. "My God, you don't think she confronted him and he . . ." She couldn't finish the thought. It was too horrible to comprehend.

"He wouldn't hurt her," Carol said.

Andi never noticed the bumps in the gravel road as she raced back into town. All the way in, Andi kept repeating in her mind, *He wouldn't shoot his granddaughter. He wouldn't shoot his granddaughter.*

Chapter Thirty-five

The hospital was on the far northeast side in an area the locals called New Town. Andi screeched into the nearest parking slot before they raced to the front entrance. Rhonda was waiting for them beyond the second set of electronic doors.

"What happened?" Andi asked. "Is Janice okay?"

Rhonda held up her hand to stop the questions. "I don't know much. So far, no one's talking. I saw Janice and one of the deputies walking down the hallway when I came in. They're in the emergency room. I tried to go back there, but a nurse ran me out."

"Did she look hurt?" Andi asked.

"No. As far as I could tell she looked fine. A little shook up maybe, but like I said, she was walking."

"What do we do now?" Carol asked.

"Wait until someone comes out," Rhonda said.

They stood in the hallway outside the emergency room. Andi paced the short distance between the emergency room and the nurses' desk, torn between leaving and staying. She was certain Janice wouldn't want to see her when she came out. She tried to make herself leave, but she couldn't until she was certain Janice was unharmed.

Almost an hour later, Janice and the deputy came out of the emergency room. Andi was halfway around her circuit when the doors opened. She turned and saw Janice hugging Rhonda and Carol. She slowly inched her way closer. Janice's back was to Andi. She stopped several feet away, but was still close enough to hear.

"What happened?" Andi heard Rhonda ask.

"It's a long story," Janice said. "I'd rather not get into it here." She hesitated. "Is she still staying with you?"

Andi felt sick; she knew Janice was talking about her.

Rhonda made a slight nod toward Andi.

Janice stopped talking but didn't turn around.

Andi realized she wasn't wanted there. As she left the hospital, the headache that had been threatening hit full force. She drove back to Carol and Rhonda's, took two aspirins and climbed into bed. Through the pounding haze of pain, she set the alarm and slept.

When the alarm went off, she continued to press the snooze button until she barely had time to shower and get to work. No one was stirring when she slipped out of the house. She spent the morning finishing the filing and setting up an electronic calendar on the computer to track Nolan's appointments. Each time the door opened or the phone rang she held her breath, hoping it would be someone who would tell her what had happened the previous night. After lunch she placed calls to individuals whose photos were ready to be picked up, and afterward gave the small office a thorough cleaning. *Where were all the gossips when you needed one?* she wondered as she scrubbed a window sill. Whenever thoughts of Janice threatened to overwhelm her, she picked up the pace of her work. When the office was clean, she directed her attention to the front. She was polishing the counter when Nolan came out of the darkroom.

"Do you always work this hard?" he asked.

Andi pushed a stray lock of hair away from her face with her wrist. She was tempted to ask him if he knew what had happened the night before, but she didn't have the nerve. "I like to stay busy," she said. "It makes the time go by faster."

"Why are you in such a hurry?" He turned and headed down the hall. "You need to slow down and enjoy life."

Dana Clark called midafternoon to let her know her bid had been accepted on the Carpenter homestead. While Dana explained that she would arrange for the title search, a survey and the inspection of the house, Andi was trying to think of a way to casually bring up Janice's name.

"I know you're eager to get started working on it," Dana said.

"I'm more eager to get back into a place of my own. Don't get me wrong," she added quickly, "Carol and Rhonda are great."

"I understand. When I first moved here I spent three weeks with my sister and her husband. I love 'em to pieces, but I was never so happy to get out of a house in my life. And God love 'em, I know they were just as happy to have me leave." She laughed. "I'll see what I can do to get things moving. It usually takes about a three weeks, but since we're not having to worry about dealing with a financial institution, we can probably cut that time in half. I'm going to try my best to have everything completed within the next ten days."

"I really appreciate that, Dana. I can't thank you enough for all you've done."

"You remember that when you start scraping off those multiple layers of wallpaper."

Still with no news of Janice, Andi hung up and started organizing the supply cabinets.

After work, she made her way to the newspaper office. Surely Rhonda would tell her what was going on. When she walked in, Shawna was talking on the phone. She paused in her conversation long enough to tell Andi that Rhonda had left and wouldn't be back.

Andi drove to Carol and Rhonda's, expecting them to be there, but the house was empty. Physically and mentally exhausted, she went to her room and curled up on the bed. Before drifting off to sleep, she made a pact with herself to remove Janice Reed from her life.

A light knocking woke her. The room was dark with only a sliver of light showing beneath the closed door. There was another light knock. Andi stumbled to the door and opened it. The sudden glare of light made her squint.

"Are you okay?" Rhonda asked.

Andi nodded. She wanted to ask about Janice but wouldn't allow herself to do so. She had made the decision to get Janice out of her life and she intended to stick with it.

"We're about to have dinner. Why don't you join us?"

Andi started to decline. She didn't want to listen to them talking about Janice, but the fragrant smells floating from the kitchen reminded her she hadn't eaten all day. With a nod, she followed Rhonda back to the kitchen.

Rhonda and Carol kept up an easy steady flow of chatter during the meal, leaving Andi to concentrate on her new resolution of forgetting Janice.

"I heard your bid was accepted on the house," Carol said.

Andi nodded. "Dana called me this afternoon." She wondered if Janice had heard about the house.

"You don't seem very excited," Rhonda pointed out.

"There's still a lot to do before it's actually mine. Dana thinks she can have everything completed in ten days."

"You won't be able to live out there for quiet a while," Rhonda pointed out.

"Why not? It shouldn't take long to have the utilities turned on."

"You're going to live there while you're working on it?" Carol asked.

"Sure."

Carol and Rhonda looked at each other but didn't say anything. Andi began clearing the table. She washed the dishes while they put things away. After the kitchen was clean, they moved to the living room and sat down. Andi longed to retreat to the solitude of her room, but didn't want to be rude.

They sat in silence for a while before Rhonda asked, "Did you hear what happened last night?"

Andi's heart pounded and a fine sheen of sweat dampened her collar and back. She tried to be nonchalant. "No. What happened?"

Rhonda started the story. "After the gun was recovered from the well, Janice went home and asked her grandfather what had happened to the set of pistols given to Clayton Mabry. At first he told her they were packed away in the attic somewhere. So she crawled up there and started tearing the place apart until she found the case with the one Colt .45 still inside. She brought the case with the other gun down and set it on a little side table next to where he was sitting. She opened the lid and asked him where the other pistol was. He kept staring at the case and telling her to take it back to the attic. She asked him again where the other gun was. He told her it had been stolen years ago. Janice asked him when the theft had occurred but he couldn't remember. She told him she was going to call the sheriff's office and have them look through the old files and find the police report. When she picked up the phone to call, he became very agitated and demanded that she take the case back to the attic."

Rhonda took a deep breath before rushing on with her story. "When Janice started asking him questions about George Zucker and Sean Gray, he began crying. Then without warning he reached over with his good hand, slapped the case off the table and sent it flying across the floor. It turns out the gun was loaded, and apparently sixty-five-year-old ammunition isn't very stable. The gun went off and hit the window Janice was standing beside." She leaned forward in her chair. "At this point, it gets a little confusing. Janice thought someone had shot through the window and she hit the floor. Somewhere during all this, a piece of glass from the broken window cut an ugly gash in her arm. He saw the blood and kind of lost it. I guess he thought the bullet hit her. Anyway, he got extremely agitated and started screaming, 'I didn't mean to shoot him,' over and over. She couldn't calm him down. She got scared that he would have another stroke and called an ambulance."

Andi held her breath. "You mean he confessed to killing George Zucker?"

Rhonda nodded. "After Janice called the ambulance, she called the sheriff, the assistant DA and Gary Wayne's attorney and informed them what happened. When the ambulance arrived, one of the paramedics saw the blood all over Janice's clothes and the gun on the floor and he called dispatch and told them they had a gunshot victim, and that's the call I heard over the scanner."

"That's what happens when gossip gets out of control," Carol said, shaking her head.

"Is Janice all right?" Andi asked.

"Physically, yes. She's got a few stitches in her arm, but it's nothing serious. She's pretty messed up about her grandfather though. She's blaming herself," Rhonda said.

Andi knew she should be jumping with joy that she had cleared her great-grandfather's name, but there was no joy in the victory. "What about Gary Wayne?" she asked.

Rhonda sighed. "He's in the hospital. They think he may have suffered a light stroke. He's conscious, but he won't talk to anyone except Janice."

A silence settled over the group.

Andi finally stood. "I guess I should go call my grandmother and let her know what's happened." She excused herself and went to her room. It took her a few minutes to actually place the call. When she did, her mother answered.

"Andrea, how are you?"

"I'm fine. Are Dad and Grandmother there with you?"

"Yes. We're playing cards. Honey, is something wrong? You don't sound like yourself."

"Listen, Mom, I have some news. It's kind of complicated. You may want to put me on the speakerphone." When everyone was able to hear, Andi repeated the story Rhonda had told her.

"Oh, that poor girl," her mother said when Andi finished her story. "What she must be going through. Andrea, you help her all you can."

Andi flinched. "She doesn't want to see me."

"When are you coming home?" her grandmother asked.

"I don't work weekends. I'll drive back tomorrow afternoon after the shop closes."

"Are you okay?" her father asked.

"I'm fine, Dad," she lied. "I'll see you tomorrow night."

She hung up the phone, crawled into bed and cried herself to sleep.

Chapter Thirty-six

Before leaving for work that Friday morning, Andi informed Carol and Rhonda she would be spending the weekend at her parents' and wouldn't be back to HiHo until late Sunday afternoon. After packing her meager belongings into the car, she left for work early in order to have time to drive out to the Carpenter homestead. A sense of pride filled her when she turned into the driveway. *Her* driveway. Even though the papers hadn't yet been signed, Andi knew in her heart that this would be her future home. As she stepped from her car she made a vow that once she moved in, she'd never move from this house. Grabbing her jacket from the backseat, she walked slowly around the house. Birdsong poured from the wooded area in the back. She walked toward the woods and froze in awe when she spied a chubby, long-eared rabbit huddled beneath a clump of brush. The distance between her and the rabbit was so short she could see the frantic quivering of its nose. They continued to stare at each other for several seconds before the rabbit burst out from its hiding place and bounded away.

The sun began to peek from the morning clouds. Andi closed her eyes and inhaled deeply. She felt at peace here. For a few precious moments she refused to let any of the dreadful events of the last few days intrude on her solitude. She held on to the feeling for as long as she could before returning to the front porch and sitting on the steps. The wood of the steps and porch was worn smooth in several places. She ran a hand lightly over one of the areas beside her. How many people had walked across or sat on this very spot? Had they been happy or sad? What had become of them? Had her own grandparents stood at this very spot when they visited the Carpenters? Time slipped quickly by and before she was ready she was forced to drive back into town to work.

Shortly after she arrived, Nolan emerged from the back and handed her a key.

"There might be times when I won't be able to get here on time, and you'll have to open," he said.

She took the key, flattered that he trusted her enough to give it to her.

He quickly took the wind out of her sails by adding, "Of course, there will be other days when I'm just feeling the urge to grab my camera and head out somewhere, and you'll have to close the shop. That's how I'm feeling today."

She glanced up to find him smiling.

"In other words, you're abandoning me?" she replied.

"Precisely. It's going to be a beautiful weekend. I have no appointments today and the great beyond is calling me forth."

Andi chuckled. "Are you sure you weren't a drama major?"

He grabbed his car keys from the counter. "Actually, I'm a med-school dropout."

"Really?"

"I made it all the way through, up to my residency."

"What happened?"

"I discovered I didn't like being around sick people." He headed out the door, leaving Andi to wonder if he was serious or simply joking around.

A slow steady stream of customers kept Andi partially occupied. During the gaps she began reading through a stack of photography magazines she had found when cleaning out the supply cabinet. She was deeply engrossed in an article explaining digital resolution when her mother called.

"Mom. What's up?"

"We received a call from Mr. Leal. He's the acting district attorney in HiHo and wants to meet with us this afternoon. I told him we could be there at five-thirty. Will that work for you?"

"Yes. I get off at five. What did he want?"

"He wouldn't say. Why don't we meet you somewhere and we'll all go in together?"

Andi gave her directions to the photography shop. "How's Grandmother holding up?"

"I thought she would be happier, but I think she's regretting ever getting any of this started."

"What about you?" Andi asked.

Her mother hesitated. "It's difficult. On one hand I keep remembering the days after that horrible article was released and the murder was hauled back to the front page of the newspaper. That's when the taunting and cruel remarks from the other kids began." She stopped and cleared her throat. "I have to remind myself that it was that adversity that drove me to succeed. Without that article, I might never have won the scholarship to Princeton, or met your father, or had you and Richard. As cruel as it sounds, I owe some of the best parts of my life to my grandfather's imprisonment. Living with that knowledge can be burdensome."

Andi had never heard her mother speak so openly about her emotions. She remained silent and let her continue.

"At the same time, I know I overcompensated in areas. After we moved from HiHo, I made myself a promise that I would never do or say anything that would give anyone cause to laugh at me again. I pushed myself to achieve the best education possible so I could construct my perfect world, which included a career that was not only successful but above reproach as well, along with the ideal husband, a house in the right neighborhood, and the right clothes. Falling in love with Andrew fit into my plans. Don't misunderstand me. I fell in love with him before he decided to go to law school. But I have to admit, his decision to go to law school reinforced my belief that he was the perfect choice. Then you and Richard were born, and I set about trying to mold you into the ideal children. Thank goodness your father kept me balanced. There were times when I would be going off the deep end. Like the time I enrolled you in ballet."

Andi cringed at the memory. She had hated everything about the class. For Andi, the final break came when the first recital was announced. It was one thing to prance around in a tutu in front of a dozen other seven-year-old girls wearing the same ridiculous outfit, but there was no way she was going to get on a stage with people staring at her wearing that silly getup. On the day of the performance, Andi locked herself in her room and refused to budge. Her father was called from the office. She could still remember how he sat on one side of the door and she on the other talking for a long time. He talked to her about responsibility and about not letting other people down when they were depending on you. She ranted about the stupid costume and how she was scared the audience would laugh at her. In the end, he convinced her to go to the recital and do her best. He made her a promise that if she would do the recital, she could quit ballet afterward.

Andi went to the recital and, to her amazement, no one laughed. On the way home, she told her parents she wanted to stop going to ballet. Years later, she realized the request was more to test her father's commitment to sticking to his end of the bargain than it was to be rid of ballet. He stuck to his agreement, and she never went back.

"Am I upsetting you?" her mother asked.

"No. I wish we could have had this conversation years ago. I've always felt like I let you down at everything I did."

"No, honey. I've always been so proud of both of my children.

You are so strong and independent. There were times when I envied you."

"Why?" Andi asked, amazed.

Her mother paused. "A good example would be what you've done in the last few days."

"I've screwed up a lot of people's lives. How can that be enviable?"

"All you've done is bring to light a dark secret that's been hiding in the shadows for sixty-five years." When Andi didn't respond, Leticia continued, "When I accidentally discovered what you were doing—and it *was* an accident. I wasn't snooping." She rushed on before Andi could reply. "My reaction was purely selfish. I didn't want anything from that period of my life to taint my current one. I had nightmares that the faculty and students from the university would hear about it and laugh at me. I was angry with a man who died more than ten years before I was born. Rather than being concerned with what all of this would do to Mom or you, I was worried about my own precious image. I'm so sorry, baby."

Andi heard the tears in her mother's voice.

"Mom, it's all right. We'll make it through this. We've made it through worse, and I think we're still doing fairly well."

Leticia sniffed. "Perhaps it's time we stopped blaming ourselves for something we had no control over."

"I love you, Mom."

"I love you, too, Andrea."

"Since we've had this great heart-to-heart, do you think you could possibly start calling me Andi?"

"Oh, Lord, no. That was your father's idea. You will remain Andrea to me until the day I die."

211

Chapter Thirty-seven

Andi, along with her parents and grandmother, arrived at the district attorney's office shortly before the scheduled time. Betty, the receptionist, informed them it would be a few minutes yet.

As they waited, Andi could almost feel Betty's curiosity as she cast inquiring glances their way. The phone lines in HiHo would be buzzing tonight. Andi almost felt sorry for her. It must be difficult to want to know something so badly and not be able to ask. Picking up a magazine, Andi tried to convince herself that she wasn't thinking about where Janice was at that very moment or what she was doing. What would she do now that she had resigned from the DA's office? Would she move away? A stab of fear hit her so strongly she gasped, drawing the attention of the others in the room. They were all staring at her. "Sorry." She struggled for an excuse. She meekly held up the magazine. "The price of this car shocked me."

"Isn't that the truth?" Betty had been handed the excuse she needed to begin a conversation. "Why just the other day I was telling my husband, Harvey, that we need—"

"You all can come on back now."

Andi turned to find the heavyset man who had been at the excavation site with Janice.

"Betty," he said, "you can go on home and have yourself a good weekend. Lock the door when you leave, please."

Andi imagined she could hear Betty's frustrated cry. Her opportunity for a juicy night of gossip had been ruined.

"If you folks will follow me to the conference room, I'll delay the introductions until after we're seated."

They followed him down the hallway, with Andi bringing up the rear. As they passed Janice's office door, Andi was hit by a wave of memories. Knowing it would never be repeated, she had deliberately kept at bay the memory of the kiss they shared. As she stood before the doorway, the full impact of it came back. She leaned her head against the wall for a brief moment to steady herself. When she glanced up, her grandmother was watching her.

"We're right in here," the heavyset man called back to them.

Andi walked into a room where several people were already seated. She noticed the small wizened man in a wheelchair, Gary Wayne Mabry, but her gaze was drawn to his right, where Janice sat. Her eyes looked bruised and swollen, as though she had not slept in several hours, but to Andi she had never looked more beautiful.

"If everyone will find themselves a seat, I'll get on with the introductions," the heavyset man said.

Andi and her family sat together on one side of the long conference table. At each seat around the table was a pad of paper, a pen and a glass of water. It reminded Andi of the numerous staff meetings she had sat through. As soon as they were seated, he began the introductions.

"My name is Percy Leal. I'm the assistant . . . um, sorry . . . the acting district attorney until we can get this matter settled. Standing to my right with the videocam is Ms. Marie Morano. She will be recording today's meeting."

213

A middle-aged woman peeked from behind an expensive-looking recorder perched on a sturdy tripod and nodded.

Leal continued, "The distinguished gentleman to her right is Mr. Roy Thompson. He's a weapons expert specializing in small arms and is here today to help with any technical questions that might arise. Mr. Thompson is from Dallas, Texas. Next to him is Mr. David Rankins, the attorney representing the gentleman next to him."

Did he pause or was it my imagination? Andi wondered.

"Mr. Gary Wayne Mabry."

Andi studied the three men he had introduced. Thompson was of medium height but possessed the heavy muscles of a bodybuilder. The attorney was pasty white, as though he never stepped out into the sunlight. Mabry was a small man, just as Mr. Acosta had said. It was likely that in growing up he had been the target of more than one schoolyard bully. *He was big enough to pull the trigger that killed a man*, she reminded herself.

Leal's voice cut into her thoughts. "Also with Mr. Mabry is his granddaughter, Ms. Janice Reed." Leal glanced at a sheet of paper in front of him and turned to Andi. "And you would be Ms. Andrea Kane?"

"Yes." Andi was about to introduce the rest of her family, but Leal surprised her as he continued.

"With Ms. Kane today are her grandmother, Mrs. Sarah Gray Mimms, and her parents, Mr. Andrew Kane and Mrs. Leticia Mimms Kane." He exhaled gently and looked at everyone around the table. "Do I have all of the introductions correct?"

There was a murmur of agreement.

"Good. Then let's get down to the matter at hand. First, on behalf of the district attorney's office and the entire judicial community of HiHo, I wish to offer an apology to the entire family of Mr. Sean Patrick Gray. No matter how hard we try, there are a few unfortunate occasions when justice is by far too blind. Mrs. Mimms, I cannot pretend to imagine the pain and suffering this grievous error has caused you and your family. I will offer no excuses or try to lessen the horrendous injustice your family has suffered. Please accept my humble apology."

Sarah nodded slightly.

Leal began to speak again. "With that said, I would like to try and clarify why we're here today. This morning at eight a.m., this office filed murder charges against Mr. Gary Wayne Mabry for the May fourth, nineteen thirty-nine, murder of Mr. George Zucker." He pulled a large white handkerchief from his pocket and wiped his face.

It took Andi a moment to realize he had tears in his eyes. These proceedings were hurting everyone involved.

Regaining control, Leal pushed the handkerchief into his jacket pocket. "Mr. Mabry was the victim of a paralyzing stroke and as such, has difficulty speaking. In an effort to ensure his statement is fully comprehensible for everyone, he asked that it be previously recorded and read by his granddaughter, Ms. Reed, who will now read it for everyone here."

Andi wanted to disappear. She didn't want to sit in this room filled with so much pain and misery that it seemed to seep from the walls.

Janice flipped over the paper lying in front of her. Without looking at anyone in the room, she began to read. "I, Gary Wayne Mabry, do hereby swear that I've made the following statement at my own request and without coercion or threat. In light of my limited capacity to speak, I hereby authorize my granddaughter, Janice Reed, to read this statement on my behalf."

Janice glanced up and met Sarah's eyes for the briefest moment before continuing. "On the afternoon of May fourth, nineteen thirty-nine, I was with a young woman whom I will not name. She had nothing to do with events that followed except to have the misfortune to be with me, and since she died ten years ago, nothing can be gained by involving her. As adolescent boys are prone to do, I had spent the afternoon falsely bragging about the cigarettes and beer that I bought on a regular basis at Zucker's store. The young lady challenged my boast and I felt I had no choice but to follow through, even though I knew he would never sell me these items.

"We arrived at George Zucker's mercantile at approximately five-fifteen that same afternoon. When we entered, Mr. Zucker was putting money into a paper bag. I can only assume he was preparing to close for the day. Attempting to continue the charade, I requested a package of cigarettes and a carton of beer. Mr. Zucker laughed at me and told me he would sell me a chocolate bar and a Coca-Cola, but since he knew my father disapproved of cigarettes, and I was underage, he refused to sell me the items I'd requested. The young woman became irritated and called me a baby. In a foolish attempt to salvage my pride and regain the respect of the young woman with me, I removed a Colt .45 that I had recently started carrying around. I had stolen the weapon from the safe in my father's study. He never locked it. In fact, the lock may have been broken."

Janice stopped long enough to take a sip of water. She kept her gaze firmly on the paper in front of her, careful to avoid everyone's gaze.

"Upon seeing the weapon, Mr. Zucker again laughed at me and told me to take my toys and go home. I tried to frighten him by moving closer and waving the pistol in his face as I had seen the gangsters in the movies do. Without warning, Mr. Zucker grabbed the pistol with one hand and struck me across the face with the bag of money he was still holding. I stepped back to avoid him and he let go of the pistol. Somehow during the process of falling, I must have pulled the trigger, because the gun went off and Mr. Zucker fell across the counter. I stood and saw what I had done. I was horrified. I didn't know what to do. And then we heard the bell over the door. Someone was coming in. Without thinking, we ran out the back. We slipped through a hole in the fence separating Zucker's from the restaurant next door and ran down the alley. When we reached the end of the alley, I ran toward home and the young woman I was with did likewise. As I ran by the Holstetter place, I threw the gun into their well before going on home. I stayed in my room, terrified that one of the Holstetters would draw a bucket of water and pull the gun up with it.

"I waited until I was sure everyone was asleep before I slipped out of the house. Then I went to the barn and hitched up one of Dad's mules. I had helped him wrestle stumps out dozens of times and knew how to hook the trace chains up in such a way as to pull the old well's housing down. The wood and mortar were in much worse shape than I thought. It toppled over almost as soon as the mule began to pull. I pushed as much of the debris as I could down into the well and hurried back home. I hadn't anticipated that they would try to clear the well out, but that was exactly what they were doing when I walked past their place the next day.

"I went back again that night, but this time I knew how weak the mortar holding the old stones was. I took a long pry-bar and used it to dislodge the stones around the lip of the well. I didn't have to remove many before the others gave way and collapsed on their own.

"I knew eventually Dad would notice the missing gun, so a few days later while everyone was gone, I tore a screen off the window in Dad's office, pulled out a few drawers and scattered some papers around. I meant to take the other gun and the case and toss them in the river, but as I was taking it out, I couldn't. I knew how much the set meant to him, so I grabbed a pillowcase off my parents' bed and stuffed in a handful of things from around the house that could be easily replaced. Then I put the case with the pistol by the window, hoping everyone would think the burglar had accidentally dropped it as he crawled out the window.

"I have no excuse for what I did except to say I was young and stupid. I offer my sincerest apology to Sean Gray's family."

Janice turned the paper over, fixed her gaze on an invisible spot on the table in front of her and said, "End of statement."

Chapter Thirty-eight

No one in the room moved. Only the soft whirl of the video camera could be heard when Janice finished reading her grandfather's statement.

Dazed, Andi stared at Gary Wayne Mabry. How had he lived with himself all these years? Knowing he was the cause of an innocent man going to prison. The awful waste of it all made Andi's blood boil. Sean Gray had gone to prison because a sixteen-year-old boy wanted to show off in front of his girlfriend.

Percy Leal cleared his throat softly. "Mr. Rankins, I believe you wanted to say something on behalf of your client."

The lawyer undid the button on his coat and leaned forward. "My client acknowledges that he was wrong in not stepping forward and accepting the responsibility for his actions of May fourth, nineteen thirty-nine, but I wish to remind everyone that he was only a child himself."

Andi rubbed her forehead, wondering where all this was leading. This whole thing almost sounded like a trial. A sick feeling began to erupt in the pit of her stomach. She stared at Janice, praying that what she was thinking wasn't about to happen, but Janice continued to stare at the tabletop directly in front of her. Andi turned her attention back to Rankins.

"In the years since then, Mr. Mabry has been an outstanding citizen in this community. He is responsible for many of the youth and elderly facilities that we have. He has donated untold hours of his time to charitable functions that are far too numerous to mention here. When the hospital was ready to pull out of HiHo, he persuaded the members not only to stay but also to expand their health care services, an arrangement that benefited both the hospital and the community. He is personally responsible for the establishment of a scholarship fund that has sent dozens of our finest young people to college. The South Texas Scholastic Scholarship is a crowning glory to what this man—"

Leticia and Sarah gasped at almost the same instant. It took a moment for Andi to realize what had happened. The South Texas Scholastic Scholarship was the scholarship that put her mother through Princeton. Andi glanced at Rankins, who was smiling slightly. He had done his research well. He knew the reaction that mentioning the scholarship would cause. Andi had never hated anyone as much as she hated David Rankins at that moment. She turned to see if Janice was enjoying her family's discomfort as much as her grandfather's lawyer did. She found Janice looking from Rankins to her grandfather.

Gary Wayne Mabry had not moved since the meeting began. He was still staring straight ahead. Andi wondered if he even knew what was going on.

"Shall we take a break?" Rankins asked.

"No," Andi said before anyone could speak. "By all means, Mr. Rankins. Please continue, because I for one am eager to see exactly where this is headed."

Andi's anger seemed to send a light current of uncertainty around the table. Sarah reached over and placed a hand gently on

Andi's arm. It felt more like support than a rebuke. Rankins continued to list the wonderful things his client had accomplished during his lifetime, and this time when Andi looked at Janice, she thought she saw the slightest shake of Janice's head.

"In short," Rankins said, "the town of HiHo and even several young people beyond our own township would have suffered greatly had Gary Wayne Mabry not been here. He is now gravely ill and knows his days are numbered. He is confined to this wheelchair and will never walk again. It's with these considerations that we are offering the following proposal. To subject Mr. Mabry to the rigors of a trial would serve no purpose. He is fully aware that he will probably die before a trial and the sentencing even occur. We are offering that Mr. Gray's record be expunged and that Mr. Mabry be confined to his home for the duration of his life. We see no reason to sully the heroic deeds of his honorable work."

Andi saw red. "His heroic deeds. He killed a man and let another man pay for his crime. Tell me, Mr. Rankins, where is the honor in that?"

Rankins leaned back and buttoned his coat. "Ms. Kane, I believe it is your grandmother who should be making these decisions. After all, neither you nor your mother were even born when this happened."

Sarah patted Andi's arm. "Perhaps he's right, Andi. You young people have been pulled into something that neither of you knew anything about until recently." She turned to Rankins. "Sir, you're right in regards to Gary Wayne going to jail. It would serve no useful purpose."

Rankins looked at Andi and smiled.

Andi bit her tongue and fought to hold back tears of anger. Her grandmother was going to give in.

"However," Sarah continued, "I want my father's name publicly cleared."

The smile disappeared from Rankins's face. Andi glanced at Janice, who was once again staring at the table. Nothing in her expression gave away her feelings.

"As I said, we will certainly remove the conviction from his records," Rankins said.

"I want Gary Wayne's statement printed in both the *HiHo News* and the *San Antonio Express News*," Sarah said.

"Mrs. Mimms, you don't seem to understand what this would do to the reputation of a good man."

Sarah stood up. "Mr. Rankins, my father was a good man. He might have been poor, and he probably wouldn't have been able to do all the things you mentioned." She turned address Gary Wayne. "Did you ever stop to think about what you did to his reputation? My father was a proud man. All he had was his family and his reputation and you took both of those things away from him because you were a coward. My father died without ever having held his only son. Do you remember how you felt the first time you held your son, Gary Wayne? Did you have the honor of walking your daughters down the aisle? Were you there when their first child was born? Because of your need to impress a girl, my father and his children and grandchildren were denied all those things."

If he heard her, he didn't or couldn't respond.

Sarah turned to Percy Leal. "My family and I have no desire to put Gary Wayne's family through the hardships that a trial would cause. We'll leave his punishment up to God, but I want my father's name publicly cleared."

Without waiting for an answer, Sarah turned and walked from the room. Andi and her parents followed. No one spoke until they stood beside their cars. Andi had a fleeting thought that this was what the term *shell-shocked* meant.

Several seconds went by before Leticia put her arm around Sarah's shoulder and hugged her. "Grandpa would have been proud of you. I know I am."

Sarah tilted her head up to gaze at Leticia. "I didn't embarrass you?"

Leticia shook her head. "You never embarrass me, Mom."

"So you'll go with me to the Market Center even if I'm wearing my red sweatpants?"

Leticia hugged her tighter. "Yes. Even in your red sweatpants. I may even get myself a pair."

Andrew interrupted their teasing. "Andi, I think she's here to talk to you."

Janice was standing a discreet distance away from them. "I'm sorry to interrupt," she said, "but I wanted to talk to all of you." She moved closer and Andi could see she was struggling. "I wanted you to know that I tried to stop Rankins. What he said was offensive and callous." She seemed to realize that they might be taking her apology incorrectly. "Don't think that I don't love my grandfather, because I do and I always will, but what he did was horribly wrong. He may have been young, but his carefully planned coverup of the crime was not carried out in a childish manner. He knew right from wrong." She turned to Sarah. "Mrs. Mimms, I am so sorry for all the pain my family has caused yours. If there was some way I could make it right, I swear to you I would."

Sarah approached Janice. "Maybe you could answer something for me."

"I'll certainly try."

"Why did you resign?"

Clearly flustered, Janice wrapped her arms around her body. "I couldn't prosecute my grandfather, and when I became DA I swore an oath that I would uphold the law. When I made that promise, I meant it, but after I knew grandfather was guilty, I realized I couldn't keep that promise. If I'm not capable of prosecuting everyone equally, then I shouldn't be in the job."

"I respect your sense of honor, and I'm sorry you got caught up in this."

Janice shook her head. "I'll be fine."

Sarah startled everyone when she hugged Janice. "You come to see me and I'll make you the best *chiles rellenos* you've ever tasted."

Janice blushed. "I'd like that."

Sarah turned and took her daughter and son-in-law by the arm. "Walk with me. I want to look around and see how the town has changed since I left."

Andi pushed a small pebble around with the toe of her shoe.

"Are you all right?" Janice asked.

Andi gave a dry laugh. Maybe it was time for her to tell the truth. "You have no idea how many times I've been asked that in the last few days, but to answer your question, no, I'm not all right. I seem to have these rather strong feelings for a woman who can't or won't return them."

Janice looked away. "There's too much between us."

"What?" Andi demanded. "What's between us? Your grandfather, my great-grandfather. Why don't we dig back a little further, maybe we'll get lucky and discover our ancestors fought each other at Shiloh, or Lexington or a thousand other places? I'm tired of excuses. If you don't like me, just say so."

"I do like you. I like you a lot and that scares me."

"Why?"

Janice wrapped her arms around herself again. "Things I like have a way of disappearing."

"I don't think I'd disappear on you."

"How can you be a hundred percent sure?"

Andi shrugged. "I can't. Nothing's a hundred percent, but I'd certainly like a chance."

Janice stared across the parking lot. "I'll need some time. My grandfather still has to go before the judge. I doubt he'll ever go to trial, but there's still some issues to settle. I don't have a job, and although I think I'll be able to ride out whatever backlash occurs from this, sometimes these small towns surprise you. I may have to move away from HiHo."

Andi didn't want to face that possibility. "Can we at least see each other occasionally? I want to get to know you better."

Janice avoided the question. "I heard your bid was accepted on the old Carpenter place."

Andi nodded. "Do you think it'll ever be known as the old Kane place?"

Janice chuckled. "Probably, but you'll have to live out there forty or fifty years first."

"I think I can handle that."

"About that kiss the other day," Janice began.

"What about it?"

"Do you suppose we could try that again?"

Andi looked at her. "Right now?"

Janice shrugged. "What have we got to lose?"

Andi stepped into her arms and their lips slowly came together. Aside from the heat of passion, Andi felt a deeper, stronger pull. When the kiss broke she gazed into Janice's eyes, "I think I'm falling in love with you."

Janice kissed her again softly. "I'll see you as soon as I can. Don't give up on me just yet."

Chapter Thirty-nine

Andi spent the following week in a spiraling cloud of hope and disappointment. The Thursday edition of the *HiHo News* carried the full text of Gary Wayne Mabry's confession. A condensed version of it appeared in the *San Antonio Express News*. The citizens of HiHo met the news with various reactions; some saw it as the Mabrys finally getting their comeuppance and a few saw it for the tragedy it was. Many of the younger people saw it as old history, something that happened long before they were born, and as long as it didn't preempt their favorite sitcom or require them to pay more taxes, then it was something to perhaps mention as they perused the newspaper article and then be forgotten.

Janice hadn't called and Andi was determined to wait. The day after Thanksgiving, Dana Clark called to tell her the house was hers. They met at the title company the following Monday to complete the paperwork, and at last, Andi had a home of her own.

After arranging to have the utilities turned on, she purchased a wide selection of cleaning supplies and simple tools. Every afternoon after work, she went to the house and cleaned. As soon as all the utilities were on, she moved in a rollaway cot she'd found stored in her parents' garage and began staying in her new house on the weekends, but she still lived at Carol and Rhonda's during the week. When the cleaning was complete, she gradually began to make minor repairs. As her confidence grew, she tackled the larger tasks, like removing several years' worth of wallpaper.

On the Sunday before Christmas she was ripping up layers of old linoleum when her cell phone rang. She answered it and had to walk outside before the reception was clear enough for her to hear. Her landline phone had been connected, but she hadn't yet purchased a telephone. The caller was Rhonda, telling her that Gary Wayne Mabry had died the night before in his sleep.

His funeral was held two days later. The sun warmed the backs of the scores of people who stood outside the church after it had been filled to capacity. The local radio station set up their broadcasting van so the crowd outside would be able to hear the service. Andi had gotten caught in HiHo's first-ever traffic jam. The delay left her at the back of the crowd. She watched with a sense of awe as the entire town of HiHo closed down to attend. She tuned the preacher out and tried to ease her way closer to the door in an attempt to catch a glimpse of Janice. For all her efforts, she ended up trapped against the broadcasting van and its booming speakers.

After the service, the crowd dispersed. The graveside services were closed except to family and friends, and Andi didn't seem to fit into either category. When she was finally able to inch her way out of the gridlock, she drove to her parents' to celebrate the Christmas holidays with her family.

Her brother and his family came in from Houston, but after two days with his two rambunctious kids and seemingly endless hours of football, Andi found herself longing for the peace and quiet of her new house. She kept thinking about Janice, wondering what she was doing. *Was she alone or did she have someone to share Christmas dinner with?* Andi wondered.

Andi made herself stay a respectable time after dinner, but as soon as she could, she pleaded having to work the next day and headed home.

As she drove along the gravel road leading to her house, she kept repeating the phrase *my home* and found she liked it. Turning into the driveway, she tried to visualize what the house would look like come spring. By then it would have a new coat of paint, and hopefully a yard full of flowers.

After changing into her work clothes, she returned to the kitchen and the linoleum she'd been ripping up when Rhonda had called to tell her about Gary Wayne. She found a comfortable pace and worked steadily. As darkness began to settle in, she switched on the lights and kept working. It was nearly ten before she hauled the last of the linoleum out.

She knew she wanted to install hardwood floors, but she wanted to make sure she got exactly the right shade. She liked the color of the hardwood floor in the living room, but it wouldn't go well with the kitchen cabinets. As she stood pondering where she should start next, someone knocked at the front door.

After flipping on the porch light, she looked out the window to see Janice standing on the porch. Andi threw the door open and made herself not fly into her arms.

Janice stayed at the edge of the porch. "I'm having a rough night," she admitted.

Andi opened her arms and Janice walked into them and began to cry. Standing in the open doorway, Andi held her until the sobs eased. "Come inside," she urged.

Janice followed her into the living room.

"I'm sorry I can't offer you a chair," Andi said. "I'm not really living here yet."

"This will do fine," Janice said as she sat on the living room floor.

"I'm sorry about your grandfather. I tried to talk to you at the church, but there were so many people, I couldn't get to you."

"I can't believe he's gone. In some ways, I feel like he was my anchor, and now I don't know what I'll do alone."

Andi sat beside her. "You aren't alone. A lot of those people at the church Tuesday were there for you as well. You have people you can turn to. Just don't push them away."

"Like I did you, you mean?"

"You said you needed time. I'm willing to wait."

Janice gazed around the living room. "This is a magnificent room. When do you think you'll be able to move in?"

"I'm trying to get the kitchen finished. As soon as I get it painted and get the new flooring in, I'll be able to install a stove and refrigerator." She hopped up. "You haven't received the official tour. Come on."

They walked through the house and Andi explained her plans for each room.

"This would be a great house for kids," Janice said as they stood on the screened-in back porch. "Have you ever thought of having kids?"

"I used to, but as I got older and never seemed to settle into the right kind of relationship, I sort of let the idea go."

"What would you consider the right kind of relationship?" Janice brushed a lock of hair from Andi's forehead.

Andi tried to ignore the jolt that shot through her. "Someone I thought I could spend a lifetime with. Someone stable, dependable, who could make me laugh."

"Do you know anyone like that?" Janice had stepped so close Andi could feel the warmth of her body.

"I think I might. I haven't had much of an opportunity to really get to know her."

"Would you like an opportunity?"

Andi nodded. "More than you can possibly imagine."

Janice stepped away. "I have a gift for you in the car, but I need some help bringing it in."

"What is it?" She tried to hide her disappointment at Janice's sudden withdrawal as she followed her back through the house.

"I'll bet you were one of those kids that snooped around looking for their Christmas presents."

"I was not. I have the patience of Job."

Janice looked over her shoulder. "I sincerely doubt that."

"I am too patient. So, what did you bring?"

Janice chuckled but refused to answer her. When they reached the car, Janice opened the back car door and pulled out a box. "Grab the other one," she instructed.

They carried the boxes into the house and set them on the living room floor.

"This is a little something to make your time out here more comfortable," Janice said.

Andi dug into the first box and pulled out a telephone.

"No one can reach you on that blasted cell phone," Janice said.

Also in the box were a small coffeepot, a pound of freshly ground coffee beans, an electric skillet and a radio. The second box contained a large wicker basket with an assortment of wines and goodies.

"Thank you." She hugged Janice. Her intention had been an innocent hug, but as their bodies came together, the desire she had been feeling for so long seemed to explode within her. Andi's hands slipped to the back of Janice's head and pulled her closer. "Please," she whispered as her lips sought the tender valley beneath Janice's ear. When she wasn't stopped, she planted a warm trail of kisses along Janice's cheek until she was kissing the corner of her lips. With slow deliberation, she brushed her lips with feathery softness across Janice's.

"You're teasing me," Janice moaned.

"Do you mind?"

Janice pulled her closer and kissed her with a hunger that left Andi's knees weak.

Andi's fingers ran through Janice's golden red hair as her lips made their way to Janice's neck. She kissed the soft skin at the base of her throat and ran her tongue down the opening of Janice's shirt as she leisurely opened buttons. When she reached the top of Janice's bra, she worked her way across the skin above it, alternately kissing and then sucking it gently between her lips. She let one hand casually brush over Janice's breast and thrilled at her gasp of pleasure. Feeling the stiff nipple pushing against the silky fabric of the bra, Andi caught the nipple gently between her teeth and rubbed it with her tongue.

Janice placed her hands beneath Andi's hip pockets and pulled Andi against her as their pelvises began a slow, sensual grind.

Janice's groans and movements grew more urgent.

Bending at the knees, Andi kissed her way to the waistband of Janice's jeans. With deliberate slowness, she unbuttoned them and lowered the zipper. She eased them off Janice's hips, being careful to leave the black lacy underwear. As the jeans slid down Janice's hips, Andi allowed first her hands and then her mouth to follow. She ran her tongue along the top of Janice's panties.

"You're killing me," Janice muttered.

Andi didn't respond. Without stopping her explorations, she helped Janice out of her jeans. With Janice's legs no longer hampered by the jeans, Andi tapped the inside of Janice's legs, encouraging her to spread them farther. Andi dropped between them and ran her tongue beneath the inner leg band of Janice's panties. She breathed deep, inhaling the heady musk of Janice's passion. She pressed a kiss again the damp fabric and almost came herself when she felt the heat radiating from Janice's swollen lips. Unable to prolong her own pleasure any further, Andi hooked her thumb inside the leg opening and pulled the thin damp material out of her way. She used her hands to open the swollen lips and gain access to the object of her quest. As she sucked the swollen flesh, a low tone began deep in Janice's chest. It erupted into a deep cry of release as Andi continued feasting.

Chapter Forty

Twenty years later

Andi showed the caterer where she wanted the food tables set up before racing into the house to change clothes. She pulled on a pair of white cotton slacks and a canary yellow blouse before running a brush through her hair that now contained more gray than black.

As she hurried down the hallway, she heard car doors slamming and a chorus of voices. Flustered, she glanced at her watch. She was running late. She relaxed slightly when she heard her mother's voice. Now in their seventies, both of her parents were still healthy and active. Coming out of the hallway, she heard her grandmother scolding one of the twins.

"I'm ninety-four. I'm not going to live forever." Her grandmother's hearing was failing, but she still managed to lead a fairly active lifestyle.

"You've still got a lot of good years," Andi said as she entered the simple but warmly decorated living room. It was Andi's favorite room of the house. The light oak floor was buffed to a bright gleam. She and Janice had installed the flooring themselves. They both had suffered from sore knees and backs for a week afterwards, but the result had been worth all the hard work.

"Happy twentieth anniversary," her parents called out as she hugged them and her grandmother.

"Yeah, happy twentieth," a voice yelled from the doorway. Andi turned to find her oldest and dearest friend Becka clinging to Stacy's arm and leaning on a cane.

A chorus of greetings erupted around the room as Rachel raced over in a flurry of energy to hug her aunts Becka and Stacy. "I didn't think you were going to be able to come."

"We almost didn't," Stacy said. "But you know how bullheaded this woman is."

Andi hugged her friends. "How's the knee?" she asked, pointing to Becka's leg.

"It hurts like hell, but it gets me a lot of sympathy," Becka chirped as she squinted at Andi.

"She's decided it's a permanent excuse to whine," Stacy said as she gave Becka's curly gray hair an affectionate pat.

"What does a woman have to do to get a beer around here?" Becka said.

"Everything is out in the backyard," Andi said.

"Well, then, come on, woman," Becka said and motioned for Stacy with her head. "Let's go grab a chair by the beer."

"You don't need to be drinking beer," Stacy scolded as they waved good-bye to Andi and started through the house.

"Why not? Are you afraid it's going to stunt my growth?"

Andi stood smiling and watching the two.

"What can we do to help?" her mother asked.

Andi rubbed her forehead and turned to her parents before pointing toward the backyard. "Dad, if you don't mind going to check on the kegs. They sent a kid out with them and I'm not sure he knows what he's doing. Just make sure he taps them correctly."

Her dad nodded and left.

"Mom, he's not a kid," Rachel said, rolling her eyes in much the same manner as Andi was prone to do.

Andi and Janice had flown to China and adopted Rachel and Ruth when they were five. The twins were now eighteen and the center of their parents' universe. "Go help your grandfather," Andi scolded as she playfully shooed Rachel out the door.

"Where's Ruth?" Leticia asked.

"She's out back somewhere with Janice. They were trying to hang a piñata the last time I saw them."

"I'll go help them," Sarah said as she headed through the house.

"I'd better go keep an eye on her," Leticia said as she too left.

"Grandmother, please don't go climbing up on anything," Andi called out after them. "I have enough to worry about with Ruth and Janice."

Arms grabbed her from behind and a large sloppy kiss was planted on her neck. "What do you have to worry about, woman?"

Andi turned and kissed her lover of twenty years. "You." She brushed her hand across Janice's cheek.

"You never have to worry about me," Janice replied, gazing into her eyes before kissing her.

The kiss lingered and intensified. Andi pulled back enough to break the kiss, but remained in Janice's arms. "We have guests due to arrive at any moment, so don't even start something we don't have time to finish."

"Do you remember our first time in this very room?" Janice asked.

"Yes. As I recall, after that night, every time I came home, I found you on my doorstep."

"Hey. I'm no fool. I know a good thing when I see it."

"Twenty years. Where did the time go?"

"A lot of it went into fixing this house." Janice grimaced. "The last thirteen were pretty much devoted to raising the twins."

Janice had gone into private practice after her grandfather died. The change from prosecutor to defense had been a struggle at first, but she soon became a name that prosecutors dreaded facing.

She seldom lost a case. Occasionally, something would come up that would rekindle the old stories about the murder, but for the most part, no one cared.

Andi had stayed with Norten Photography and eventually became a full partner. Over the years, her own photos had gradually begun to sell on a fairly regular basis.

"Any regrets?" Andi asked.

"No. You and the twins have given me a life most people only dream of. I love being a defense attorney and I love our family. What more could a woman ask for?"

Andi saw movement in the driveway and glanced over Janice's shoulder. "How about a hundred and fifty of our closest friends?"

Janice turned to look down the driveway where Rhonda and Carol's old pickup was making slow progress. "Did you think we'd make it twenty years?"

Andi smiled. "I think we'll be doing this again twenty years from now."